THE PERFECT NEIGHBOUR

An absolutely unputdownable psychological thriller

SUSANNA BEARD

Joffe Books, London
www.joffebooks.com

First published in Great Britain in 2021

This paperback edition was first published in Great Britain in 2022

© Susanna Beard 2021, 2022

This book is a work of fiction. Names, characters, businesses, organisations, places and events are either the product of the author's imagination or are used fictitiously. Any resemblance to actual persons, living or dead, events or locales is entirely coincidental. The spelling used is British English except where fidelity to the author's rendering of accent or dialect supersedes this. The right of Susanna Beard to be identified as author of this work has been asserted in accordance with the Copyright, Designs and Patents Act 1988.

Cover art by Nick Castle

ISBN: 978-1-80405-111-5

For all the lost people, everywhere

CHAPTER ONE

Sofia

The front door slams. The door to my room rattles every time, though it's locked. Locked from the other side, the key taken, as it is every night when I go to bed.

Sir is leaving, which means it must be six in the morning. I hear the crackle of gravel as his car rolls towards the tall gates. A click as they reach their widest, more crunching as the car creeps through, then the soft buzz and creak as they close behind it. You can't see the road from inside the house. Every time I pass the window on the landing I check to see if the gates are open. They never are.

I feel my body tense. In a moment there'll be the sound of a key in my door and Madam will say: "Get up, get to work," or something like that, in her loud, clipped English. I have only a few minutes to visit my tiny toilet, drag a flannel across my face and get dressed before I start work. No breakfast for two hours, and then just the cold leftovers. Soggy buttered toast, no crispness left. If I am lucky, half a banana, already turning brown on the edge where his teeth have ripped a hurried last bite.

I'm used to the routine now. I go down a floor to the cupboard on the landing and pull out the vacuum cleaner, a duster and a can of furniture polish. I step into their room. Here everything is old-fashioned, in traditional, heavy Russian style: big wardrobes and chests with painted designs, an enormous carved wooden bed. The furniture looks old, well-used, perhaps from Madam's family home. I wonder how much it must have cost to transport it all the way across Europe. It must mean a lot to her. Even the drapes are different here, with their complicated floral patterns. The room is a stark contrast to the rest of the house: everywhere else the furnishings are modern, like in the magazines she buys, with mirrored furniture, pale colours and hard edges.

The bed is rumpled, the silk cover pooling on the carpet, the pillows creased. I reach over and smooth the undersheet, pulling at the edges, tucking them in tightly at each side. I throw the duvet and the bedcover back into place and punch the pillows into shape. They sigh gently as I straighten them. From the sofa by the window I gather up huge velvet cushions and arrange them according to size at the bedhead. Madam likes them just so — she gets upset if they are out of order.

And when she is upset, she hits me.

In the bathroom, which is bigger than my entire bedroom, I open the cupboard beneath the sink and pull out cleaning fluid, a cloth and a toilet brush. I set to, my mouth working. If Madam could understand Bulgarian, she might hear her own name among the curses.

When I have finished dusting and polishing and vacuuming, I wave around the perfumed room spray that Madam orders from Harrods. It smells of sweet roses and reminds me of home. I close the door quietly behind me.

* * *

I wait in the hall downstairs. I pretend to dust the pictures, the mirror, the side table with its huge display of fresh flowers.

I am not allowed into the kitchen until Madam leaves it, but I have to do the rooms in the right order.

Madam takes her time; she chatters in Russian on the phone. Pop music plays in the background, so I can't distinguish her words. Though I read Russian well, I have to focus to follow the spoken language, especially at the speed Madam talks. They do not know I speak Russian; it is a small secret among the many I keep, hoping they might be useful one day. I gather them to me and think about them when things are particularly bad.

I move my arm gingerly. I can still feel the bruising where she grabbed me yesterday.

I did not mean to drop the rubbish as I was transferring it from a waste bin to a plastic liner. Though I inspect everything they throw out — I can't risk missing even the smallest of chances to find something useful — I never do it openly. Usually I do it when they are out of the room, so they can't see when I take an empty envelope, a slip of paper, an unwanted staple. This time I was careless — I did not notice Madam slipping back through the door behind me and I was startled, spilling the rubbish all over the floor.

"What are you doing, stupid girl?" Her voice cut through me like a knife. Trembling, I turned to her.

"I'm sorry, Madam, I didn't mean—"

Her nails, painted green and gold, were like dragon's claws, biting into the soft flesh of my upper arm, gripping and tightening until tears came into my eyes. I struggled, helpless to escape her grip.

"Clean it up, now — you are clumsy, lazy girl." She removed her hand, leaving pockets of pain in the flesh of my arm. I couldn't rub it to ease the hurt — she stood over me like an army general, waiting for me to clear up the mess. With shaking fingers, I bent down. She pushed me from behind so I ended up on hands and knees, tears of humiliation pricking at my eyelids. But I refused to cry. That would only please her.

* * *

Recently I have noticed little habits creeping up on me. I would not be like this if I lived a normal life, but they help me. Like the cursing as I clean the bathroom. It is automatic now and I enjoy the freedom of it, the words tumbling over each other in spiteful streams, like vomit.

There are other small wins against my employers. My kidnappers, I should say. They may never realise, but the wins exist — oh yes, they are real. They wait in corners, creeping under their feet and over their heads.

The kitchen is empty now, the remains of breakfast left to be cleared up or eaten, if they are not too spoiled.

There is coffee cooling in the jug, but I am not allowed to heat it up and it tastes too bitter cold. When I first came here, I grabbed what I could, unsure where my next meal would come from, but now I know what to do. I take small amounts, quietly, when Madam is on the exercise bike or watching TV, so she does not hear the click of the fridge door or the bread bin closing. She never offers me food, though she must know I take it from the kitchen. She does not care if I eat or not, as long as I keep quiet, stay out of the way and do my work.

In the kitchen, every day, I am required to mop and wash and wipe and scrub until everything shines. She will check later and it is best to get it right. Punishments are bruises on the arm or slaps to the face.

One day I missed a small stain on a cupboard door. It was tiny, really small — anyone else would have missed it. When she saw it, she flew into a rage, screaming and shouting, drops of slimy saliva landing on my cheek as I cowered before her.

"Stupid, stupid girl!" she yelled in Russian, cursing me in the worst possible way. "You dirty Bulgarian whore, you are no use to me! You are a horrible slimy little worm — I should crush you with one heel of my shoe, it is what you deserve!"

With one hand she gripped my arm, those nails biting hard as always. With the other she took my smallest finger, smiling as she twisted, waiting for the sickening crack and my scream of pain.

The finger still has a bend in it where it should be straight.

I find small ways to hurt them back. I spit on the cloth and wipe the kitchen surfaces. I remove the cobwebs but leave the biggest spiders for Madam to find, laughing into my hand when I hear her scream. I don't do that too often, because I will be punished for not having found and disposed of the creature, but sometimes it is worth it.

The Wi-Fi router often stops working. They told me never to use that socket, so now I always do. Things disappear — small things that can't be blamed on me. Fresh flowers die early, though they have plenty of water and only arrived the day before. The edge of a carpet comes loose, tripping Sir as he climbs the stairs. Once, his newly washed underwear had a strange smell — it spread through the chest of drawers in his bedroom, until everything else smelled too.

* * *

There are other little habits. Before, when I was free, I held my head high, looked people in the eye. Now I have learned to keep my chin low, flicking my eyes to the side, even when I am alone. It has become normal to submit, not to make eye contact. My nails, once strong and long, are bitten down, the tips of my fingers flat and ugly. When I get out I will kick these habits, the cursing, the head-hanging, the nail-biting. But for now they serve a purpose.

I work from early morning to sometime in the evening, often twelve hours or more. I clean every part of the house, every day. I do the washing, however small a pile is in the basket, every day. And dry it, and iron it and put it all away neatly. At the end of each day, they lock me in my room. They also hide me away when other people come over. They are clever. They make no mistakes. I have no days off, no pay, no thanks. I am nobody.

In my room, when it is safe, I look at my collection. A small pile of envelopes, mostly white, with a couple of larger brown ones. Some receipts, printed on one side only: the blank side is what interests me. A single stamp, unfranked, peeled carefully from a crumpled envelope. The last two centimetres of a pencil. I need a better one — one that will last — but I must be patient. A tube of moisturiser and one of hand cream, both thrown out with tiny amounts left at the ends. I will roll them up until the last bead of cream is squeezed out. If I had some scissors I would cut them in half so I could use my fingers to search out every drop. But I haven't found a way yet of stealing scissors or a knife without it being noticed. One day I will, but then I won't be using them to cut tubes of cream in half.

In my collection there is also a tiny sparkly stone that fell out of Madam's evening shoes. I like to pick it up and stare through it at the triangle of window, letting the light dance on its angles. I pretend it's a diamond worth a lot of money. I hope she misses it. An old pair of her tights rescued from the bin might be useful one day; they have a small hole, but it won't show much, and it doesn't matter anyway, no-one will see them. In winter my room is cold and the tights will help keep me warm. I have a couple of toothbrushes, barely used. I have washed them again and again, to remove every last trace of their previous owners. My collection of old toothpaste tubes is quite good, now. I have always looked after my teeth.

I do all right from Madam's rubbish. I have emery boards and cotton buds, one end unused. I have soap and a little shampoo and conditioner for my hair, which is growing long now there is no chance of cutting it. I tie it back with an elastic band. At first, I stole tampons from Madam's bathroom cupboard, making them last as long as I could. Now I am thin, though, I don't need them anymore. I am thankful for this.

One thing I long for is a razor for my underarms and my legs. The hair there has grown into a forest. Though I know it does not matter as there is nobody to see it, I think it is ugly and unhygienic. But there is never a disposable razor in the rubbish. Sir shaves with an electric razor and Madam has a matching lady's one — no good to me.

I also have a box for food. I have to be careful what I take. Sometimes Madam entertains friends, buying cream cakes, tempting packets of biscuits and boxes of chocolates. But she would notice if I opened anything like that, so I get only the regular items, waiting until they are old and neglected, forgotten at the back of a cupboard. I can't keep much in my room anyway, so I live from day to day. But when I manage to steal a corner of chocolate or a slice of cheese, I take them upstairs and look forward to eating them all day.

* * *

Today she wants me to clean the windows on the inside. I hope I can find an open window. I have tried before, of course, but each one has a strong lock. When she opens a window she never forgets to close and lock it afterwards. I have never seen a key except in her hand.

I start at the top. Not my room, of course. My room is excluded from the daily cleaning schedule and it never gets cleaned. Not that she knows anyway.

There are six bedrooms and five bathrooms. The main bedroom has four windows, split into many small squares of glass. The others have one window each, except for the second bedroom, which has two. Each bathroom has one window. This makes fifteen windows on the first floor alone. On the landing is a huge one where the stairs turn down towards the hall, and then there are all the long ones on the ground floor. It's a very big job and she wants it all done today — as well as the normal cleaning, of course. She has people coming tomorrow and she likes to pretend she's a perfect housewife. I know I will be doing this until late tonight.

I can't cheat much because she inspects the windows afterwards, from many angles, checking for finger marks and smudges. Even so, I manage to get away with a flick of the rag in the spare rooms. They are not used much and the windows are still clean from the last time I did them. I have to wait a few moments before I leave these rooms though, so that she thinks I have done a thorough job.

I spray and rub and polish and sweat until my shoulders ache. In one of the guest bedrooms at the back of the house, where the window panes are spotless, I pause to look out at the garden. A wide, striped lawn stretches towards a wooded area at the far end, where the grass is longer and wildflowers grow amid the tall chestnuts and beech trees. Along each side of the lawn are beds of bushes and flowers. A strong wooden fence, mostly covered with ivy, runs around the entire space. There is no gap at the bottom and no gate. The front garden is different from the back because there is a broad stretch of gravel in front of the house and a tall fence to hide the view from passers-by. The borders are there too, and the tall fence, and the massive front gates, of course.

I have tried many times to see what lies beyond the fence, but I can't, however much I stretch my neck. There must be locked gates. I don't imagine my employers would leave much to chance.

As I stare out into the garden with the feeling of helplessness that dogs me every day, Matt, the gardener, walks into view, pushing a wheelbarrow towards the middle of the border on the left. He looks up at me. I step away from the window and withdraw into the shadow, out of sight.

CHAPTER TWO

Beth

The unpacking is taking forever.

Beth sighs, wiping her forehead with the back of her hand. How did everything get so dusty? Already her hands are dry and grey with dirt, her fingernails chipped and ruined, and she's only unpacked three of the boxes for the kitchen. They could have paid for help with the unpacking, but her husband, in his wisdom, decided they would save the money. Beth isn't working, after all, and they're new to the area. He reasoned she wouldn't have much else to do in the first few weeks. She could have argued, but he was right. Though it's not her favourite job, it needs doing and it's important for her to feel useful.

Skirting around the huge pile of packing cases in the centre of the floor, she gathers the scrunched-up paper scattered around the room and sticks it in an empty box, ready for the recycling later. It will take weeks to get rid of all the packaging from this lot, and they only collect fortnightly.

Thank God she had the sense to pack the kettle, the tea and the mugs into a single box and label it properly. She bought a big bottle of milk from the supermarket on the way through the town, so at least she can have a proper cup of tea. Now she needs to find the radio or the TV, so she can listen while she works.

She carries her mug over to the window and stares out at the garden, with its long stretch of lawn and wide flowerbeds. She'd like to get started on that, rather than trudging through this endless unveiling of crockery, kitchen equipment, books and pictures.

Everything seems out of place in their new home. It's not surprising, really, as they've moved from a comfortable Victorian terrace in the London suburbs to an almost-new house on the outskirts of Reading, set on its own in a large, leafy garden. Beth believes that houses have characters, and though she felt from the first — and only — visit that this one was friendly and calm, it's still a stranger, welcoming them politely rather than warmly, not yet comfortable in their presence. Their house in Kingston, by comparison, felt like an old slipper. Solid, familiar, companionable, accommodating their changing needs like an old friend.

There were good reasons for the move. Adam's company moved from London to Reading, and he couldn't face the commute. She doesn't blame him for this — she wouldn't want to do it herself — or for the fact that his job commanded so much more money than hers that she couldn't object. She'd been happy in Kingston, mostly with her job in the bookshop, her group of close friends and all the delights of London close by. Reading, by comparison, seems shabby and tired, a sprawl of untidy buildings shuffling up against tall office boxes, layer upon layer of reflective windows revealing nothing, like sentinels overseeing the rabble. And though the house is outside the main town, in a pleasant area where the straggling remains of the suburbs give way to the green beginnings of agricultural Berkshire, it all feels alien to her.

She turns back to the daunting mountain of boxes, puts down her mug and sets to again.

* * *

By supper time she's created a cavern in the mountain, to her relief. The kitchen looks almost civilised. Most of the empty boxes and packaging materials are cleared away, the crockery and glasses stashed in the cupboards lining the walls, and she's hidden away the pots and pans. There are some tins and packets in the larder cupboard and the frozen food has been transferred to the freezer. Supper's going to be pizza — she's too exhausted to do more. The kids will be delighted.

Both children are home from their third day at the new school. "Mum!" Abigail yells from the top of the stairs. "I don't have enough space for all my stuff in the cupboard! I need another chest of drawers . . . Mum!"

Abigail is twelve years old and changing rapidly from a little girl who loves dancing to a pre-teen experimenting with moods, clumpy boots and makeup. And an admirable, though sometimes bombastic, opinion on everything, particularly equal rights and the environment. Since she arrived here she's spent her time arranging and rearranging her new bedroom, which is quite a bit larger than her previous one. It goes without saying that everything fitted very well in the last house.

"Just leave it for the moment, Abi. I'll have a look later," Beth calls back, tearing the packaging off a frozen pizza. She stares at it for a moment, then takes another out of the freezer: these days, sixteen-year-old Tom eats like a horse, though he's as slender as a ten-year-old. She adds extra cheese, puts them in the oven, then slices tomatoes and cucumber into a bowl. There's garlic bread too — if they're still hungry after that, they'll have to have ice cream. It's all there is. Tomorrow she'll do a big shop, stock up on everything. While she's there she'll check out the local shops, maybe even join the library, if she has time.

Once all the unpacking is done, she's going to start looking for a job. She needs to meet people soon or she'll go out of her mind.

* * *

"How was school today, Tom?" Adam asks, wiping ketchup from his chin. The pizzas are disappearing at an alarming rate, though Beth has only taken a small slice for herself.

Tom, his mouth fully occupied, nods and shrugs. Adam waits.

Tom swallows noisily. "Fine," he says, reaching over for more pizza.

"Informative," Adam says. "I was looking for a little more than that, to reassure me that your new school is providing the excellent education we were hoping for, that you're settling in well, making friends. Learning something, even." He opens his hands, his eyebrows lifted, expectant.

"Yeah, it's okay, Dad." Tom checks the look on his father's face, which hasn't changed. "Chemistry teacher seems pretty cool. He brings his dog into school every day. It's called Higgins. I've made a couple of friends too. We're going to the skate park at the weekend."

Adam glances at Beth, who tries to warn him with a look. "I suppose I'll have to make do with that," he says. "How about you, Abi?"

Abi's response is the opposite of Tom's, turning into a rambling story about every girl she's met, what music each likes and what Abi has already managed to learn about their lives. It's an astonishing amount for three days. Beth watches as a glazed look spreads over Adam's face. She conceals a smile as she clears the table. He still seems to expect coherent answers from both his children. But he only ever gets the information they choose to release: a drip, drip in Tom's case, a torrent in Abi's.

Supper is over in a flash, the teenagers rushing to clear their plates. They leave the room in a flurry of arms and legs, their feet drumming on the stairs.

CHAPTER THREE

Sofia

Alone in my room, I take the tiny pencil and a white envelope from their hiding place. Taking care not to rip the paper, I open the envelope out into an oblong of blank paper, lay it on one of Madam's old magazines for firmness and start to write.

Every week since I found the means to write, I have kept my journal, and the pile of paper is growing large. Some of the entries are very short, some a little longer, when something has happened. The pencil has turned from a long stick of red-and-black striped wood, barely used, to this stub, chipped and splintered like my fingernails. I pick away at the edges of the lead to reveal the next millimetre. I must find another one soon, or maybe a pen. They are like gold dust in this house, my captors being too stupid to write much. Madam spends hours on her laptop, watching rubbish YouTube clips and ordering designer clothes. Sir is barely here. When he is, he spends his time in his office with the door closed or glued to the football on TV.

Writing the journal is a record of my life as a prisoner. I am hoping that one day it will help to send Sir and Madam to prison for the rest of their lives.

I don't know the punishment for kidnapping in this country — I just know these people deserve to be locked up for a very long time. I have been slapped, punched and beaten. Kept here, in a tiny, cold room against my will. I have been treated like an animal. I was just sixteen years old when I was taken. I am eighteen now, and every month that passes is my childhood wasted, my life stopped. Stolen from me, my parents, my sister, my friends.

* * *

In the first days, I was terrified. I did what I was told, too scared to speak or object. I thought if I just waited, kept myself safe, if I behaved well, did what they asked and did not make trouble, then rescuers would come. My parents would worry I had not contacted them when I arrived. The alarm would be raised, leading to a police investigation and my certain release. The British police, I knew, were good people, known for being honest. They would be my saviours. I had visions of high-hatted, handsome young men in uniform storming the house, handcuffing my captors and carrying me out to my waiting family. But as the days turned into weeks and nothing happened — nothing at all — my hopes began to fade. I was confused. I stopped jumping up, holding my breath and listening, my ear glued to the door, whenever the telephone or doorbell rang. Each false alarm just left my hopes crushed.

I began to think the police were not interested in a young Bulgarian girl who had made a terrible mistake. I was just another missing person.

It was all my fault. I was naive and stupid. My parents were not to blame, not at all. They warned me to be careful. I thought I could handle it, but I was overconfident and I didn't believe them. Stupid, stupid.

At first, I spent my evenings slumped on the bed, crying or dozing, unable to move or motivate myself. I could feel myself losing hope, confidence and courage. I carried out my work in a daze, barely bothering to feed myself, imagining that my employers would notice and help me in some way. But Madam's reaction was to shake me when I seemed listless, to yell when the work wasn't done properly or to slap me round the face when she caught me crying.

* * *

Today I cleaned thirty-one windows with the little squares of glass that need wiping all round the edges. I can hardly reach to the top of the large ones, but Madam got a stepladder and made me reach until my arm ached and my head spun with the effort. That was on top of my normal day's work, though when she realised I was still working at nine in the evening and she wanted me out of the way, she let me off the ironing. So, fifteen hours in all.

I am almost too tired to write, and the pencil is getting so small I have to keep this entry short. I wonder how to get hold of another one. Perhaps I can open Sir's desk with a paperclip, the way I saw it done once on TV. It will be hard, but I can be patient. I will try one day when she is on the phone, and if I can't do it I will try the next day, and the next. The other thing I might do is look in the garage, which is attached to the house via a door from the laundry room at the side of the kitchen. It is out of bounds to me, of course. Once, Sir forgot to lock it and I put my head round the door to look. I saw a big cupboard in there, with many drawers. I couldn't go in because I was being called, but now I check the door every day.

This week has been difficult. Apart from bruising my arm, Madam slapped me across the head for not working fast enough. Since Monday there has been barely anything to eat in the fridge. I took handfuls of frozen peas from the freezer and hid them in my pocket until I got back to my room. My pocket was soaked — it was lucky she did not notice. A slice of frozen bread down the front of my trousers did not last long either. I had to put the bits in my other pocket when it defrosted. That was all I had to eat on Tuesday, apart from some dry cereal I found in the cupboard. I drank a lot of milk, though. Now she gets it in big plastic bottles I can take quite a lot. I top it up with water and she doesn't notice.

Matt the gardener is the only other person I have seen for months. I dare not ask him to help. But I am watching and waiting, just in case.

CHAPTER FOUR

Beth

"Mum, can we get a dog? Please?" Tom's voice is muffled as he squats, squashing his football kit into his school bag. She watches and wonders, again, why she bothers to iron anything. Maybe she should change things, now they're in a new house, with a new life. It would be a good time to instigate new habits. It wouldn't be depriving Tom of anything; he'd probably never notice. Abi would, probably, but it's time she learned to iron anyway.

"Mum?"

"Tom, you're late," she says, for the third time in ten minutes. Getting the kids out of the house in the morning has always been a challenge, and even though it's their first week at a new school, they leave it until the last possible moment to leave. "Why are you asking me now? You need to get going."

She takes him by the shoulders, noticing again how much he's grown — all of a sudden, it seems. She turns him around to face the front door, which stands open, Abi having pointedly left it gaping as she departed without waiting for her brother.

He allows himself to be pushed, his feet dragging. "But Mum, will you think about it? You need some company, now you're not working. And I'll walk him, I promise . . ."

"And feed him and train him? Okay, okay, I'll think about it — now go!" Tom grins at her and at last he's gone.

She closes the door with a sigh and leans against it, contemplating her day. There's still so much to be done, and nothing to relieve the tedium of unpacking, unwrapping, sorting and tidying. Perhaps she can go into the town at some point, just to get out for a while.

As she reaches into the first packing box in the living room her thoughts are still with Tom. He has always loved animals, always wanted a pet. As a small boy he persuaded his parents into a series of small animals including a hamster, two gerbils (and their unexpected babies — that was a mistake) and some rather creepy stick insects. Beth and Adam had resisted demands for longer-lived pets like cats and dogs while both were working.

But now, in the new place, where she has no job, no friends and nothing to use up her time except the house and the garden — now might be the time. A dog would certainly get her out walking, discovering the local area and meeting other dog walkers. And she does love dogs. Her parents always had one while she was growing up and she misses the unconditional love, the unbridled joy, the walks. Perhaps she'll talk to Adam later. She can't imagine he'll be against the idea. He loves animals too, and only resisted before because he thought it unfair to the dog to be left for long periods. If he agrees, she can plan it while she finishes the unpacking.

* * *

The doorbell goes, interrupting her thoughts. She has always hated doorbells like this one, chiming out like a Disney version of Big Ben. She'll have to sort that out too. Eventually.

Wiping her hands on her jeans and scraping them through her tousled hair, she goes to the door. A blonde woman in brightly patterned leggings stands on the doorstep, her face almost hidden behind a large bunch of flowers.

"Hi," the woman says with a smile, peering around the foliage. "I thought you might like some flowers to brighten up the unpacking."

"They're beautiful! Thank you so much, how kind of you." Tucking a stray lock of hair behind her ear and wishing she were looking a little more presentable, she smiles back at the woman, opens the door and ushers her in. "It's all a bit of a mess still, but come and have a cuppa. I'm Beth."

"Hi Beth, I'm Karen. Don't worry, I'm on my way to the gym. I'm sure you don't want someone hanging around while you're trying to get sorted. I just wanted to say 'welcome' and let you know we're your neighbours. We live directly opposite, behind the big hedge."

Beth looks over to the other side of the street. A pair of large wooden gates, flanked by a dense hedge on either side, give no clues about the house that lies beyond. Everyone in this street seems to like their privacy, or perhaps their security. She'd noticed when they arrived that almost all the houses had impressive gates, and most of them were closed. Perhaps these people are all wealthy — or maybe Beth and Adam have missed something and it's a hotspot for burglars. Or it could be that they're not wealthy at all, and the gates are just there to impress. All this passes through Beth's mind in an instant.

"It's lovely to meet you," she says, hoping she wasn't being rude. "Why don't you come round in a week or so, when I'm a bit more sorted? It would be good to talk to someone who knows what it's like round here."

Karen looks around forty, well groomed, her body toned. She probably spends a lot of time keeping fit. But her smile is open and the flowers are beautiful.

"Great. Would next Wednesday work? I can't promise I know much, though. We're relatively new ourselves, and everybody seems to keep themselves to themselves. I'm not sure you'll get anyone else dropping by."

"Wednesday it is — does morning work for you? I'll be here anyway."

As she closes the door, burying her face in the sweet fragrance of the flowers, Beth feels for the first time that she might be all right here, after all.

* * *

"I met one of the neighbours earlier."

The September evening is still warm as they sit on the terrace, watching as the birds flit around the flower beds.

"You did?"

"Yes, a nice woman called Karen, from the house opposite. She brought me those flowers in the kitchen."

"Ah — I wondered. That was kind of her. Did she come in?"

"No, she was on her way to the gym. She looks pretty fit. Probably spends all her time there."

"Did she tell you anything about the other neighbours?"

"We only had a brief chat on the doorstep, though she's coming for coffee next week. But she did say most people keep to themselves." She takes a sip of her drink, avoiding the lemon slice nestled between the ice cubes. "I was wondering, do you think, when everything's unpacked and we feel settled, we should invite the neighbours round for a drink? Get to know them a bit?"

"Maybe. This doesn't seem like the kind of street where you bump into people very easily. You could ask Karen what she thinks of the idea when you see her."

"It's very different from Kingston, isn't it?" Beth feels a pang of homesickness for their solid, friendly Victorian terrace, where neighbours dropped in, shared barbecues in the summer and gathered often at the pub. Many of them had become friends, their children growing up together. Impromptu suppers, games nights, children's parties and joint celebrations for all the landmark moments of family life had been shared and enjoyed. All this had changed before they left, but she still misses it. She tries not to think about it.

"It is — quite different," Adam says. He reaches over for her hand. "Are you missing it?"

She shakes her head, surprised to find herself a little teary. "I'm just tired, that's all."

"It's different, but it doesn't have to be in a bad way," Adam says, squeezing her fingers. "You'll feel much better once you get to know some people. Ask Karen where she goes to the gym. Perhaps you can join, do some classes, meet people that way."

"You're right, it's just unfamiliar. I'm sure I'll get into the way of it all soon. Though I'd like to get a job, if only to keep my brain ticking over."

"You don't need to, you know. We don't need the money," he says. Then, seeing the look on her face: "But if you prefer to work, of course, you must."

Beth has never liked the idea of relying on someone else for an income. Since she was a little girl, her independence has always been important to her, and she resisted fiercely giving up work when she had the children. Then she remembers. "Tom wants us to get a dog."

Adam glances at her. "Good idea. But not if you have a job — unless you can find something part-time, or I suppose if you can take a dog to work."

"I know. I was thinking, get the dog first, train it properly, get it used to being out and about and among people. Then see if I can find a friendly place where dogs are welcome. The bookshop in Kingston would have been fine with it."

"True. But don't be pushed into it by Tom. He'll be off out with his friends all the time and not interested in taking on the responsibility."

"That's not what he says. But I know what you mean. Really, though, this is about me wanting one, not just him."

Adam looks around. The garden is fenced on every side, with gates leading to the front garden. He ponders for a moment. "It would be great to have a dog here," he says. "The garden's perfect, and I did notice a park on the way to the station. Look, it's up to you. If you want a dog, let's go for it. But preferably not too big and bouncy. Small is good . . ."

Beth follows his gaze along the tall fences bordering their garden on every side. They look as if they've been put there by someone looking for the highest level of privacy and security. The gardens on either side — and even the houses — are hidden from view. There'll be no chatting over the garden fence here.

Or perhaps, she thinks, remembering the imposing gates facing the street behind her, these people aren't looking for privacy, but for secrecy.

CHAPTER FIVE

Sofia

My cousin Elena and I were always close. When we were little, we all lived in the same village in Bulgaria and both of our families were farmers. We had a tractor, some goats, a pig and a small piece of land for growing vegetables, which we sold at the local markets. Elena and I were born within a couple of months of each other. We grew up together and were like sisters. Every day we met outside her house and walked to school, there and back. We helped our parents, climbed trees, picked wildflowers and played with our dolls. Sometimes my little sister Simona would play with us too. She was three years younger than us, but she loved being with us and cried when she was not allowed because it was her bedtime. Our families were poor, but we didn't know it, and we were happy.

Then, when I was about ten, my uncle and aunt had a bad year with their farm. My uncle was ill and couldn't work for the summer months. There was a terrible drought. My aunt did her best, but the potato crops failed. They had friends in England who were doing well — they'd found jobs and were sending money home. It sounded like a good idea to my uncle, so they left, taking my lovely cousin Elena with them. I was heartbroken.

At first, my only consolation was our letters. In her rounded, childish writing, Elena told me all about her new house in England — with heating on all winter, a roof that didn't leak and a little garden with flowers in the summer. Her English, she said, was getting better: sometimes she would write a sentence or two in English and I would do the same. I was always good at English at school — it was my best subject.

My parents' farm thrived. We started growing sunflowers and tomatoes and sold them at the markets for export to other countries. My mobile phone was not the most up to date, but I was so happy to have it. Elena persuaded her parents to let her have one too, and soon we were texting each other all the time. The letters came less regularly, which I was sad about, but I remember rejoicing whenever I heard the "ping" of a text, knowing it was from her.

When I was sixteen, I decided to get a summer job in England, so that I could see Elena again. I knew from friends that there were farm jobs for summer workers, paying good money, so I bought the newspaper every week and scoured the ads. My parents thought I was too young, but I was determined, begging and pleading with them to let me go, and I worked all my spare time on the farm to show them that I was serious about it.

At last I found the perfect job, fruit-picking on a farm a few miles from Elena's home. The hours were long, but the pay was good, accommodation included. They were looking for young people to go across and help for a few weeks over the summer holidays. I would be able to see Elena and her family at weekends and at the end of the holidays, before I came back. My parents were pleased I'd found paid work and reassured that I would be looked after by my aunt and uncle if anything went wrong.

All I needed was some money for the journey, a long bus trip across Europe. Eventually my poor parents gave in to my constant pleading and agreed to pay for the trip. I was to take their advice and follow their instructions to the letter. Of course I promised I would do everything they asked.

It took for ever to get a passport, but when it arrived I couldn't have been prouder. I was going to England, to see Elena!

* * *

My parents came with me to meet the bus. I was so excited I could barely sit still.

On the way, they went through everything again. Keep your passport with you at all times. Make sure your bag is properly closed; don't leave it for one moment. Text us when you get there. Don't talk to strange men. Eat properly. If you don't like the place or you're not well, go to stay with Elena. They went on and on until I protested, but I know they were worried about me, my first trip away from home.

I know now why they were so anxious.

We found the meeting-place easily, in a small car park in a back street. A small group of other girls was also waiting, bags by their feet, and we greeted each other shyly. When the bus arrived, I remember thinking how small it was, and old — I'd imagined that for such a long journey we would need a big, sleek, modern bus with toilets. But the woman who met us was lovely and friendly, and as she ticked my name off her list she reassured my parents that she would look after me well.

There were tears in my parents' eyes as we hugged goodbye.

It was a long, uncomfortable journey, through many different countries. As soon as we got started, the woman came round everyone to collect passports, so that they could show them at the borders. Water, crisps and sandwiches were passed round, but the supply soon ran out and we became hungry and thirsty. The bus was hot, with no air conditioning, and I remember the smell of sweat and dust as we trundled across the countryside of Europe, only stopping in roadside petrol stations for toilet breaks and to fill our water bottles.

I sat next to a girl called Ivet, who didn't say much, so I spent a lot of time looking out of the window. At first I was thrilled by the changing landscapes, the road signs in unfamiliar languages, the strange towns. But there were parts of the journey when the land was flat and boring, and I dozed uncomfortably, my head knocking against the window as it drooped. It was dark when we finally reached the coast. The journey across the water to England was a blur — we were all so tired that we slept the whole way and saw nothing of our arrival. It can't have taken long, though, because it was still dark when we stumbled off the ferry, bleary-eyed and hungry. The woman hurried us towards an empty car park where a group of vehicles was waiting for us. She ignored our questions, giving orders and marching ahead, rushing us as we struggled to carry our bags.

But I still suspected nothing, even when she split us up. Each girl seemed to be going to a different place. She pointed me to a car, had a quiet word with the driver and handed him my passport. I was confused, but the driver smiled at me, took my bag and put it in the boot.

He opened the back door and gestured for me to get in. "Come, let's go," he said with another smile.

I climbed in.

Inside, he handed me a bottle of Coke, which I drank gratefully. Though I was excited to be in England at last, I soon became very drowsy. My head dropped onto the back of the seat and I fell into a deep sleep.

CHAPTER SIX

Beth

"Tom, can you let Ruff out please? I'm in the middle of baking."

Beth is making pastry. Already she's spilt some on the floor, got margarine in her hair and lost the recipe when the book flipped its pages over as if possessed.

Ruff has been scratching at the door for some minutes now. She doesn't want to spread even more pastry mix around the kitchen, or risk an accident which will need mopping up, so when Tom fails to appear, she grunts with annoyance, rubs her hands together for a moment and stalks to the bottom of the stairs. "Tom! Can you come please? Ruff needs to go out and I'm making pastry!"

A couple of thumps upstairs indicate she's been heard, so she goes back to the kitchen. "Sorry, Ruff. He's coming." She's already talking to the dog as if he's her third child, and it's only two days since they brought him home from the rescue centre.

Ruff was their first choice as soon as they heard his background. Just a few months old, he'd been living on the streets of Reading for several weeks, evading all attempts at capture.

Eventually he'd been cornered behind a garden shed and taken to the rescue centre. When he got there, he was half the weight he should have been, his coat dull and matted, with the first signs of mange on his skinny legs. The centre had taken him in, cured the mange, and fed him up before he was listed as ready for homing.

The staff had started calling him Ruff after his little hoarse bark, and the kids liked the name. It suited him. He had deep black fur, coarse down his back but soft around his face and on his tummy. Under his chin the black faded into a grey beard, giving him a comical look, and his little ears were always pricked, as if he was ready for anything. As for his breed, he seemed a total mixture.

They all fell for him, and he for them.

"Come on, Tom — if he pees or poos on the floor, you'll be clearing it up," she calls, kneading the pastry with one hand.

"Okay, okay." Tom appears at the door. "Do I need to take him out on the lead? It's raining."

"Yes, they said just for a few days, to get him used to it. You heard them. Go on, it's only water. And if he poos, you know what to do."

Grumbling, Tom attaches Ruff's lead and ventures out, hunched against the rain.

* * *

Beth walks through the rain, hood up and head down. It was too much to hope for, to get good weather the first few days of having a dog. Anyway, she'll have to get used to it. Every morning she's going to be out walking, whatever the weather, because the dog needs it and that's what she promised. There may be other walks to discover, but for the moment, while Ruff's new and they're still getting to know each other, the park will be a regular haunt. Tom and Abigail have promised to do a second walk after school and Beth has instigated a rota for them, knowing that if she doesn't, there will be trouble.

She's glad of the need to walk every day — it stops her feeling too housebound. This is another good reason for getting a dog. It might even keep her fit.

Ahead of her, a woman pauses to call her dog, a slim black spaniel racing to collect his ball. On the other side of the park a man walks with two dogs on the lead. Otherwise it's empty — even the swings hang damply, deserted. It's September, the schools are back and it's raining hard — it's not surprising people have stayed home.

As they head back to the house, Ruff stops to sniff and mark, giving Beth the chance to examine the other houses in her street. It's frustrating not to be able to see through the hedges and over the walls, but there are a few whose gates stand open, and one or two who don't bother with that level of security. The houses on this street are all different, as far as she can tell, some of them newly built, like theirs, some with a 1950s look and shady, mature gardens. In general the street seems affluent, the cars in the drives big and shiny. Signs of children litter a few of the gardens: brightly coloured plastic slides, wooden climbing frames, even a deflated paddling pool in one, a leftover from the summer holidays.

As she approaches home, she knows she doesn't belong here yet. The house is still polite and proper with them — it hasn't made up its mind yet whether it likes them or not. The houses closest to theirs seem buttoned-up and impregnable, their front gates solid, with dense hedges or tall fences either side.

As they reach their house, Ruff pauses to sniff at the entrance next door, giving Beth the chance to take a proper look. But the house is completely hidden — there isn't the tiniest gap through which she can sneak a glance. A camera watches over the enormous gates. She takes a hurried step backwards, not wanting to be caught prying. Two entry phones are fixed to the gatepost, one marked *Deliveries*, the other *Visitors*. A large metal post box with a lock is labelled *No circulars, free papers, magazines or leaflets*. It's all very intimidating.

Why would anybody need that kind of security?

As they reach their own front garden, Beth wonders if she should introduce herself to the neighbours, as Karen did. Should she go round with a plate of home-made biscuits like a proper housewife? No, she can't pretend. Maybe she could knock on the door and say hello, just to be friendly . . . But something tells her that won't be well received.

CHAPTER SEVEN

Sofia

Once I realised that my dreams were hurting me, I abandoned any hope of rescue. If I longed for it, I would only be disappointed. It was up to me to get out of this — nobody was going to help me. How could they when they had no idea where I was?

I needed to use what resources I had. I decided that anger was good, it gave me strength. I would not allow these horrible people to win — I was going to escape.

And I would get my revenge.

So now I plan. I bide my time, keep my eyes open and my mouth shut. I do the work, always alert for opportunities. My journal, hidden under the mattress, helps me to keep track of time. I mark the days at the top of each sheet, and I generally write on a Monday. I know this because Sir has a clock on his bedside table that shows the day and the date.

My clothes are all black. Madam bought me two sets of trousers, T-shirts and jumpers when I got here, all in cheap black material. Nothing fits well, especially since I have grown taller, but she won't buy more. Black socks, black shoes. Ugly black underwear. When I get out of here I am never going to wear black again.

Under my clothes on the floor in my room is hidden a small pile of Madam's old magazines, rescued from the trash. In one of them is a set of exercises to make you strong. Now, every evening, I take stolen tins of beans and I exercise my arms, raising them above my shoulders, holding them out from my sides and lifting them over and over until my muscles scream in agony. I strengthen my stomach with fifty or more sit-ups — my goal is a regular one hundred. I hold the plank position until my body trembles with the effort. I dare not run on the spot, in case she hears and stops me exercising, but when I am cleaning the house and she isn't paying attention I run up and down the stairs a few times. Sometimes I even hop up and down the stairs until the sweat drips off my forehead and my legs ache.

I have been doing this for many weeks now, and I can see the effects. My arms look wiry, my shoulders square. My stomach is flat, almost concave, and you can see the muscles at the sides of my belly button. My legs feel hard to the touch when tensed. But I am thin. My body has lost its softness — now I am skin and bone and muscle.

I am tired, though. Sometimes too tired, almost, to move. At the end of the day I drag myself up the stairs to the top floor and it is hard to stick to my fitness plan. I allow myself a day off now and then. I don't want to end up exhausted.

I must eat well to sustain myself — it says so in the magazine. It has guidelines on healthy food, and from these I have learned what I should eat. It is not easy, though.

Finding protein is the biggest challenge. If there is leftover chicken in the fridge I will steal mouthfuls with my fingers. I never take a leg or a wing. I learned that lesson early on. It was in the first few months I was here, when I was still learning Madam's cruel ways. Thinking she was upstairs, I took a chicken leg from the leftovers in the fridge. She caught me right in the middle of eating it.

She said nothing, just stepped forward and slapped me across the face with her open hand. The chicken leg flew across the room, landing in the doorway as I bent double, my hands at my reddening face, a cry escaping from my lips.

"Dirty little thief," she hissed in my ear. The pointed toe of her designer shoe jabbed painfully into my ribs as she stalked from the room. "Clear this up — now."

These days I take the soft chicken flesh from the breast and mould the carcass back into shape so she can't tell. I don't bother to wash the spit off the fingers I've licked clean.

* * *

When I think of my mama, I feel her absence like a broken bone. I broke my arm once, when I was small, falling off our donkey. It hurt so much. I had to go to the hospital and have it covered in plaster. It was in a sling for weeks. I remember that sharp pain, the dull ache that followed.

My mama is pretty and kind, and she looks after us. When I was hurt, she held me close and stroked my hair. She gave me warm drinks with honey, wrapped me in soft blankets and told me stories until I fell asleep. She works hard every day, growing fruit and vegetables, looking after the animals, cleaning and cooking, while Papa helps on the big farm on the other side of the village. We don't have much, but we are happy. We were, that is.

Summer days in Bulgaria are long and very hot. After school, Simona, Elena and I would do our chores, then run up the hill at the back of the village to play in the shade of the woods. Once we built a den from branches and pieces of wood discarded by our neighbour. We loved our den. It was more like a little house, really, and one day Papa came and made us a roof, so that even when it rained, we were dry. When the sun was out, the hills were beautiful, the birds sang. Even the goats seemed happier, butting us with their little heads, searching for food, nibbling our clothes until we ran.

I can hardly believe now that I was so excited to leave my home. When I think about it, I can almost smell the flowers on the breeze, the animals in the yard. Before I left, before I became this new, miserable person, I would complain about the chores I had to do, my homework, our simple life — and I longed to get away. Now I know my life there was wonderful. I should have been the happiest girl alive.

I ache for the sound of my mama in the kitchen making supper, humming a familiar song, calling to the animals. The windows open, the thin curtains lifting slightly as I prepare for bed. My little room, shared with my sister, my comfortable bed with its embroidered cover and cool cotton sheets, washed so many times they were feather-soft on my skin.

I used to think my life was poor and drab, that places like England could give me so much more. Now I know that there, in our little house in Bulgaria, I was rich in so many ways.

Our farm was small, but it provided for us. We had a small field for the goats and the donkey, an enclosure and a little shed for the pig, a greenhouse for the tomatoes. The sunflower field was above the house and was shared with our neighbours. In summer the flowers grew strong and fast and I will never forget how they turned their heads towards the sun, their yellow and brown faces bathed in golden light.

Everyone helped with the harvest. There were celebrations, music and dancing when it was done. Many of the villagers were old, their faces lined and tanned by working outdoors their whole lives. There was so much friendship there — everyone knew each other. We went to school together, worked together, laughed, loved and mourned together.

Here, in my prison, I have nobody.

* * *

"I go out today," Madam says, her harsh Russian accent grating on my nerves. Her heels click like a ticking clock as she walks across the kitchen floor.

She is dressed-up, tall in her heels and a tight blue dress that shows off her figure. Over her arm is the cream coat she favours. It has a designer label and feels as soft as a duck's down. Sometimes, when it is in the wardrobe, I stroke the sleeve and imagine stealing it when I escape. I think of her reaction and smile: she would be so furious.

"Matt is coming in while you do your work. You must do everything, you hear? Not missing any room. Dust, polish, clean all floors. I am checking when coming back. You are lazy girl, I know what you do if I am not here. You hear?"

I nod, head down. *Bitch*. I know this English word from the TV. In my head, I use the worst Bulgarian word I can think of.

Matt is at the kitchen door. He mutters something that I can't hear and Madam nods her head, pointing to his boots. He pulls them off and she waves him into the little sitting room next to the kitchen, where there is a big TV but no cream carpets or sofas for him to muddy. Madam continues to click around the kitchen, gathering her keys, her sunglasses, a handful of tissues, loading them into an enormous leather bag.

I back away, duster in hand, as if to go upstairs.

"I telling Matt to watch you all day," she says to my back as I climb the stairs. "You hear?"

"Yes Madam," I say without turning my head. I listen for the thump of the front door as she leaves.

I do not know much about Matt, but I do not trust him. He is not on my side, I think. He is usually in the garden, cutting the grass, weeding the flower beds, watering the pots and the baskets. Or he is in the large shed at the bottom of the garden, though he does not live there. He arrives on a bicycle and works all day, every day except Sunday, or when it rains. Sometimes he fixes things in the house: a loose door handle, a light bulb that needs replacing, a broken cupboard door. He says very little. I think he is British, about thirty years old. He has longish black hair and a dark shadow of stubble across his chin and his upper lip. His eyes give nothing away, though they sometimes follow me from the garden when I move from room to room.

I climb the stairs slowly to the bedrooms to start my work. My heart is heavy today. Despite my plans to be patient, to wait for my chance, I woke this morning in deep despair. How long must I wait? How can I bear this half-life, this nothing of a life, a moment longer? Why did this happen to me? All those questions that I try not to allow crowd into my head. My stomach churns. This must stop — I must be strong.

But today I feel I need to make something happen. If I don't, nothing will change. Madam looked as if she was going out for the day, as far as I could tell, perhaps into London. She always dresses up when she is going into London. It is my chance to do something. But what should I do?

I drag the vacuum cleaner from the cupboard, making sure the noise is enough for Matt to hear over the sound of the television. I bump it around Sir and Madam's room, bashing into the furniture, moving things around as if I am cleaning underneath. I leave the cleaner on and sit on the edge of the bed, thinking.

I must make something happen.

CHAPTER EIGHT

Beth

At the front gates, feeling slightly ridiculous, Beth presses the buzzer on the entry phone. While she waits, she examines the gates, hoping to find a gap and catch a glimpse of the house. But there are no gaps, not even when she crouches down to examine the bottom of the gate. When the gadget above her gives out a loud crackle, she jumps up, startled and embarrassed. Suddenly aware of the camera with its single eye, she forces a smile onto her face.

"Who is it?" a woman's voice says.

"I'm Beth from next door." She waits, but the contraption is silent. "I'm your new neighbour. I wanted to say hello, if you're not too busy."

"I'm the cleaner. There's nobody home. Try later." The voice is flat, the accent indeterminate.

"Oh, okay. Sorry to disturb—"

The handset is returned to its cradle at the other end with a crash.

". . . you. Don't worry, I won't leave a message, though it's very kind of you to offer," she says to the machine. "Thank you anyway." This isn't wasn't going quite as planned.

So much for getting to know the neighbours. That was the house on the right — there's still the one on the left to try. Maybe another time. A chance encounter would be less embarrassing than turning up unexpectedly. Thank goodness for Karen. At least she has found one friendly person in the street.

* * *

This time Karen arrives with a tray of flapjacks. Today's outfit is a replica of the first, but in different colours. Beth wonders if she spends her whole time at the health club.

"Please, you don't need to bring something every time you come," Beth says. "I've already got some catching up to do."

Karen waves away her comment with a gesture. "Don't be fooled — I didn't make them," she says. "I bought them from the school fete at the weekend, and thought I'd better share them before I was tempted to eat them all myself. Well, who's this then?" Ruff, appearing at the top of the stairs with a bark, runs down to greet her, his paws drumming a beat on each step.

"Our new family member, Ruff. He's a rescue dog. Get down, Ruff! Sorry, he's quite young — not trained yet."

"It's fine," Karen says, leaning down to stroke Ruff's head. "He's sweet. I love dogs. Wish we could have one. My husband's a bit resistant, though I'm working on him."

In the kitchen, Karen settles onto a bar stool and takes the wrapping off the flapjacks. She gazes round the room. "It all looks great. You wouldn't know you've only just moved in."

"You haven't seen the garage," Beth says. "But thanks anyway. You don't realise how much stuff you have until you move house. I've chucked out armfuls."

"I know what you mean. But with kids, you soon start to accumulate again. It's never-ending."

"Tell me about your family." Beth places a coffee mug and a plate in front of Karen and sits down.

"My husband, Fred, works in the City. He's a banker. He works long hours, so I hardly see him in the week. We have two girls — Hannah's fifteen, and Olivia's thirteen. They're both at the high school."

Beth hopes Abigail will get on with the girls: it would be good for her to have a friend nearby, even if they're not at the same school.

"What about the other neighbours?" she asks. "Are there other children in the street?"

"I don't know," Karen says. "They're all a bit — well, I would say stand-offish. I have tried with a couple of them, but some of them are never home, and others don't want to know. I do know our immediate neighbours: on the right of our house as you look from here. They're nice, but I'd say they're more acquaintances than friends. Have you met anyone else yet?"

"I tried the house on the right. But I got the cleaner."

Karen smiles. "That's no surprise. The bigger ones all seem to have staff. I hasten to say, we don't — I'm the staff."

"Me too. It all seems rather different after London. All our neighbours were good friends." She hesitates, aware that this is no longer true. "I suppose in a row of terraced houses it's much easier to get to know each other. But these big gates, the high hedges, they're pretty intimidating."

"Don't worry, I'm sure you'll soon feel at home. It felt the same to me when we moved, but I've settled in now. Listen, why don't you join the local fitness club? That's where I go — it's only a five-minute drive. I've met loads of people there."

Beth hesitates. She hates the gym, and finds most classes intimidating. "Is there a swimming pool? I might be tempted by that."

"There is, but you won't meet many people ploughing up and down with your goggles on." Karen laughs.

"True. Probably best if I pop in one day and check it out, I suppose. When I've finally sorted this lot." She looks wistfully towards the garden. "I've still got to get cracking on the outside before it all goes wild."

"You've got loads of time, haven't you?" Karen says. "No need to rush it. It'll be winter soon anyway. No point doing much until next spring."

That's true, she thinks, with a touch of sadness.

* * *

Once Karen has left, on her way to a yoga class, Beth opens the back door on to the terrace, which is drying out after the rain. With Ruff at her feet, she walks slowly down the path that leads to the bottom of the garden, where a small shed sits lopsidedly in the corner, its window dark with cobwebs. She pulls at the door, which opens after a short struggle, and peers inside. There's not much there — only a few plastic pots and half a bag of compost left by the previous owners. It will be useful storage, once she's sorted out the mess in the garage and found the garden tools.

Closing the door, she turns and surveys the house. It looks different from here, more friendly somehow. Perhaps it's because there's more variety at the back than the front, with the kitchen extending out into the garden, the terrace and the steps leading down to the lawn. Flowerbeds run up each side of the garden, and someone has trained creepers along wires nailed into the wood. She's no gardener, but she recognises some of the plants, their flowers almost over now. Faded petals litter the lawn and parts of the wet earth, the rain having taken its toll. Towards the bottom of the garden is a gnarled apple tree and a couple of small cherry trees. Next door on both sides the trees are taller, more mature: a silver birch, a sycamore, another apple tree, casting shade over sections of her garden. It has potential, this garden, she thinks. Perhaps she'll make an effort with this one. In London, working full-time and with young children, all she had to do was water the pots in their courtyard garden. Here there's the chance to create something beautiful.

Ruff, tail held high like a pennant, is busy investigating the flower beds, his nose already damp, mud sticking to the fur on his paws. She watches him for a moment, smiling at his enthusiasm, his snuffling among the plants. She needs to buy him a ball, some toys to keep him busy.

She looks up towards the houses either side. The one she'd tried to visit is a tall, many-windowed mock-Georgian mansion. All she can see of it is the top storey, where curtains are looped back at each side of the windows. There's no movement, nothing to be gleaned from this point of view.

On the other side is the house with the intimidating gates and the two entry phones. It's similar in style, its many-paned windows forming a repeating pattern across the rear, but at some point an extra level has been added on top. A tiny window sits in the sloping roof, reflecting the grey of the sky. It's probably an attic, or a store room — there can't be much light in there. She wonders again who lives next door, if they have children or maybe a dog. She hasn't heard or seen any signs of life, but then again her head's been buried in the unpacking, her ears tuned to the radio for days.

She resolves to call in soon. It's important to know your neighbours, even if they seem determined to keep everybody out.

CHAPTER NINE

Sofia

I must take my chances while Madam is out, without Matt becoming suspicious.

I try to organise my thoughts. The most important thing is to make progress, find something to help my escape. But I have no idea what is possible. I was not expecting this opportunity, if indeed that is what it is, and I am not prepared. I force myself to think. What is it I need most?

An escape route. A weapon. A pen or a pencil — no, that is not so important. I need to go into forbidden places, take risks, look for any chance, any possibility of escape.

To get out of this house, I need a key, for a window or a door. I have searched everywhere, but they must lock them all away. I need a weapon. Or a phone. But there's no chance of that, not in a million years.

So I need to search. I start the vacuum cleaner and look around the bedroom. Is there anywhere I haven't tried? I pull the vacuum behind me to one of the huge wardrobes and open the door. Rows and rows of Madam's shoes take up the whole of one side, the heels pointing outwards like rows of sharp teeth. Fancy stilettos, sparkling party shoes, leather thigh-high boots — who needs this many shoes? Her clothes, racks of designer dresses and coats and trousers and jackets, occupy the rest of the space. Sir's wardrobe is the same, huge and looming, painted with fading patterns of flowers and leaves. His suits and shirts are sorted by colour, ironed and arranged as he likes them — by me — and his shoes are beautiful, shiny leather.

I must think. I must be cleverer than this. I must not waste time.

I race through the rooms that hold no secrets. Every now and then I stop and listen for Matt, for the rumble of the television. I finish upstairs and carry the vacuum cleaner down the stairs, watching the back of Matt's head in the sitting room.

At the bottom of the stairs, the vacuum clatters onto the tiled floor and his head swivels towards me, those dark brown eyes watching. He nods. I nod back, avert my eyes.

I know the kitchen too well to have much hope of luck there. Over time I have learned the contents of all the drawers, searched the many cupboards, dusted the tops of the units to check for hidden secrets. There is nothing here for me. Moving fast while out of sight, I clear the breakfast things, wipe all the surfaces, mop the floor.

I have my eye — and my mind — on the office. I clean in there as part of my daily chores, but have never dared check the drawers in the desk, the computer, the heavy wood cabinet in the corner. Usually Madam hovers around, checking her phone but also supervising me. She is suspicious when I am in there, which makes me suspicious in turn. It must be where they keep the important things, like the keys. Perhaps that is where I might find something, a piece of luck, an open door. At the very least, a new pencil.

With the vacuum droning on, I place the waste-paper bin in front of the door so that if Matt comes, it will make a noise. It is the best I can do — I don't have much time.

I start with the big cabinet in the corner. Inside there are deep drawers and many shelves with folders and box files in rows, unlabelled. I don't touch them. There is no time to investigate, to look through papers. To be caught would be disastrous. I dare not imagine what punishment Madam would think up for me. One deep drawer is unlocked and my heart gives a lurch of excitement — but it is full of files, labelled at the top: utilities, accounts, legal. They don't interest me.

The cabinet also houses the safe, a square metal box crouching beneath the shelves. Probably it contains Madam's most precious jewels: her over-the-top, glitzy necklaces and bracelets, her glittering prizes for marrying a rich man. It may contain what I need, but there is nothing I can do about it.

Switching the vacuum cleaner off in case Matt starts to wonder at the lack of movement, I turn to the desk, duster in hand, ears pricked for a sound from the hallway. The desk is huge, robust, like Sir himself. I dust with one hand, trying each drawer with the other, taking care not to rattle the handles. Every single drawer is locked, eight in all. The locks, dark yellow metal inlaid into the wood, are solid and strong. I have no hope of breaking them, certainly not without causing damage, even if I had the strength and the tools. I wonder what can be so important, that each drawer contains something so secret that it has to be locked away. Frustrated, I give the desk a push, to see if I can move it, but it is very heavy. I move the chair and crouch down between the two columns of drawers, mirrors of each other. Something has fallen down the back: two things, it looks like. I crawl in to investigate.

"What are you doing?" Matt's voice startles me. I bang my head on the underside of the desk with a painful crack. With one hand, I cradle my head, sparks shooting in my eyes; with the other, I hold a scrunched-up piece of paper, which I wave at him while crawling backwards from beneath the desk.

"I am cleaning," I say, my voice flat, keeping my eyes from his. "Waste paper."

"Okay," he says. I try not to shake as I place the scrunched-up paper into the bin bag. He pauses for a moment as if to say something, then shrugs and leaves.

I breathe out in a rush, closing my eyes with relief. The pen in my left sleeve feels cold on the inside of my arm.

* * *

The washing machine makes a whooshing, sloshing noise behind me as I set up the ironing board. This is what she calls the laundry room, a space twice the size of my bedroom. It holds a washing machine, a tumble dryer, all the cleaning equipment for the downstairs, the iron and the board. There are many cupboards, most of them empty.

I like this room. It overlooks the garden. I gaze out as I iron. I think Matt has a good job. He is outside, among the plants, the trees and the sky. I love to watch the sky as I work. Sometimes a plane passes high above, like a silver dart, free and full of hope. One day I hope I will fly home to my parents.

The ironing is okay. She barely comes into this room. It is almost mine, except for the door to the garage, which is his.

I know the garage is my chance.

I listen intently but there's no sign of movement. Stepping silently to the closed door, I try the handle. It creaks alarmingly but the door opens. I send a quick "thank you" to God and slip through, careful to pull it almost closed behind me.

Inside, it is dark and I wait a moment for my eyes to adjust. I could turn the light on, but I prefer not to. With the daylight from the cracks around the huge automatic doors I can see just enough for my purposes. It is an enormous space, big enough for three cars at least, but there is not much else in here. Though I am sure all the outside doors are locked, I try them anyway.

No luck. I turn and look around. At the back, close to the door I have just come through, is a large motorbike with a black cover over it. Hanging from a row of pegs on the wall next to it are leather jackets, trousers, gloves and helmets, in a row. I think Sir imagines he looks cool when he dresses for a bike ride, but he is just a balding old man on a motorbike.

Along the walls are stacks of cardboard boxes containing vodka and wine. The cupboard I saw before is my best chance.

I am hoping it has something, a treasure, a workman's tool, anything to help me get out of here. I start from the bottom drawer, feeling like a burglar. My father once told me burglars start with the lowest of a set of drawers when they search, because then they don't need to close one drawer before they open the next. If you start from the top, it doesn't work.

I hope there is something here worth stealing.

The drawers are in a mess. If Madam came in here, they would be organised into perfect Russian order. I find car manuals, dusters, dirty old rags, a man's jumper covered in oil stains. I find engine bits, plastic pipes, paintbrushes. Paintbrushes? Perhaps this isn't Sir's domain, after all. This must be used by Matt, or it could be builders, decorators, mechanics brought here to fix the cars. I rummage, my fingers searching into the backs of filthy drawers, desperate to uncover something, anything, that might help me. I don't have much time before Matt wonders where I am.

I'm beginning to lose hope when my fingers finally grasp something hiding under a pile of nuts and bolts in an old cardboard box.

A set of keys.

I close my eyes briefly and breathe. But I don't have time to waste. I stuff them into my sock and carry on searching, my fingers trembling with tension. A couple of rubber bands, a handful of long nails and a screwdriver go into the pocket of my trousers; they are small enough not to show too much under my T-shirt.

I am closing the last drawer when there is a sound from behind me. I spin round, my heart thumping. The door to the utility room is opening. I step away from the cupboard but turn towards it, as if I have only just entered the garage. The light goes on, startling me with its brightness. I feel like a rabbit trapped in headlights.

"Here you are," Matt says.

"The door was open, I was checking..."

He waits. I drop my eyes.

"You were checking...?"

"I thought I heard something. But it was nothing."

His eyes travel around the garage, registering the motorbike, the cupboard. I brush past him into the house, my knees trembling. My new possessions feel like they are burning holes in my clothes, but he doesn't notice.

I am sure he will tell Madam. When he does, she will hit me. I am used to that — but if she finds anything it will be a different matter. If she searches my room and discovers my collection, I could be back where I started. I can't bear the thought of all my precious things, gathered so carefully and over so much time, being taken away from me. Shampoo, toothpaste, paper, pencil, the magazines: these are so important to me now, these simple things. If she removes them, I am not sure I can carry on.

I have been thinking hard in the last days about a new hiding place. Nowhere in the house is completely safe, of course, but there are a few corners she never visits. The laundry room is as good as any place. It is where I work, not her.

I wait for a long while after Matt has gone. I iron two more shirts before I pluck up the courage to hide my new finds. I have kept an old box of washing powder for this purpose, behind the new supplies of powder and conditioner, bleach and stain remover. I pull it out and open up the top. About two inches of powder are left in the bottom. My ears straining for the sound of an approaching step behind me, I bury the keys, the nails and the screwdriver at the bottom and return the battered box to the back of the cupboard. I have to wash my hands afterwards — the powder has stuck to the sweat on my palms. I can't afford to get marks on his shirts.

This is going to be my new hiding place. Anything I don't need up in my room, I will keep here.

* * *

Madam hasn't flown into a rage or hit me. So maybe Matt didn't tell her. Perhaps he didn't think it was so bad, finding me in the garage. I am grateful to him for this small reprieve.

In my room, I lie on my bed, smiling to myself at the thought of my new treasures. Keys! They are old and need cleaning. I am pretty sure they won't help me escape — they are probably out-of-date, or not even for this house — but I will try them on every door and window anyway. If they don't work, I will try not to be upset — keys are useful in other ways. They can be used as weapons, at the very least. The screwdriver too could be a useful weapon.

The pen is the best find of the day. A cheap, throwaway plastic ballpoint, almost full of ink. It is sad, how happy I am to find it. I retrieve my sheaf of unfolded envelopes from under the mattress and start to write.

CHAPTER TEN

Beth

"Ruff? Ruff, where are you?" Beth calls from the kitchen door, standing in her socks on the mat. He's been outside for too long, and she's worried.

Ruff loves the garden. When it's warm he'll spend hours sitting on the terrace watching the birds, sometimes stalking them like a cat, though never quick enough to catch one. Today isn't particularly warm, and while it's not actually raining, everything is sodden. The trees drip like ticking clocks, the grass is squelchy underfoot, the soil in the flowerbeds has turned chocolate brown. Leaving the door open, she collects her boots from the hallway and slips them on. Thinking he might be working his way along the fence, which he likes to do, she walks slowly up one side of the garden, along the top and down the other, peering into the shrubs and clumps of fading flowers as she goes. There's no sign of him.

She calls again. The side gate is firmly closed and the gap beneath is not big enough for even his small skeleton to squeeze through. The other side of the house is divided from the front garden by a fence with a trellis on top, a creeper draped along it. No escape for a dog there.

She hurries back inside, calling his name. Perhaps he came in while her back was turned. But there's no response. This is unusual — usually he follows her around everywhere. If he was here, he would have responded by now.

He must have escaped. The road at the front is not busy, but still, a small dog travels fast and he could get to the main road in moments. She can't bear to think what might happen then. There's a tag on his collar and he's chipped, at least. If someone picks him up, they'll be able to contact her. She fumbles her mobile from her pocket to make sure the sound is on.

He must have found a way out of the garden and into next door's, it's the only answer. This time, she walks in the flowerbeds, along the fence, pushing past dripping bushes, scratching herself on climbing roses. It takes a while and she's soon soaked and dishevelled, her hair pulled into a tangle by hanging foliage. Halfway round the perimeter she finds the spot. At the very bottom of the fence, hidden behind a dense bush, the wood has rotted, just a few inches of weakness in a panel, leaving a puppy-sized hole.

* * *

"Hello?" She glues her ear to the speaker as a van passes on the street behind her, its engine roaring. This is the house of the neighbour on the left, the one she hasn't tried yet, and she's pressed the button three times now.

She's about to give up and go home to get the ladder out, in a wild plan to climb the fence, when the intercom buzzes.

"Hello?" It's a woman's voice, deep and slow, and Beth knows instantly that she isn't British.

"Sorry to disturb you, but I live next door and I think my dog has escaped into your garden."

"Excuse me?"

She repeats herself, enunciating the words clearly, trying not to sound impatient.

"Could I come and look for him, please?" she says, summoning the calmest voice she can and hoping the camera definition isn't too good. She probably looks like a bag lady, soaked to the skin, her hair a bird's nest, her wellies filthy. There's no reply and she's about to yell into the intercom when there's a click and the gate glides silently open.

"Oh thank goodness," she says out loud, hurrying up an immaculate front drive. The house ahead of her seems enormous, with huge windows on three levels, an imposing front porch with pale Doric columns and a broad flight of stone steps up to the front door. She's too flustered to take in the rest, but is dimly aware of a garage on one side and manicured borders beyond the gravel.

The front door opens to reveal a young woman, blonde hair piled in an intricate chignon, in full make-up and high heels. She's dressed for a fashion shoot. Or so it seems to Beth, intensely aware of the state of her clothing.

She wipes her hand on her trousers just in case, then holds it out to the woman. She is offered fingers so cool they could be made of porcelain. It's not a handshake, more of a regal touch, and she can't help noticing the nails — long and painted in metallic silver, like tiny mirrors on each finger.

"I'm Beth," she says. "I live next door." There's no sign of any understanding on the woman's face. "I'm so sorry, but I think my puppy has managed to get through the fence into your garden. Have you seen him?" She cranes her neck to see past the door. But the woman guards the space — a tiny movement but made with intent. She doesn't want Beth to see. There's an awkward pause.

"Wait a moment."

The door closes, leaving Beth open-mouthed on the doorstep. She waits a minute or two, then three. She presses the bell to the side of the door and listens. There's no sound from within. This is unreasonable. She only wants to retrieve her dog, not be shown around the house, for God's sake. And the longer it takes, the more chance Ruff will have to find another escape route into another garden — or onto the road.

She runs down the steps and looks up at the windows, to see if she can see anyone. There's no sign of movement, so she goes around the side of the house. Perhaps there's a gate, or maybe she'll be able to see through to the back garden from there. She's about to try the handle on a sturdy wooden gate when the sound of bolts being drawn back startles her, and after more unlocking and rattling of keys, it opens. A young man in muddy boots holds the gate open for her.

"This way," he says, inviting her through with a gesture. He closes the gate carefully behind them.

An immaculate lawn stretches ahead of her, flanked by borders she could only dream of. Though summer is almost over, flowers still bloom in splashes of vibrant colour. Seating areas nestle in the dappled shade of spreading trees. This garden is much bigger than hers, both wider and longer, reaching further into a wooded area at the end, which has been left untended, creating a backdrop for the manicured formal area closer to the house.

It takes a fraction of a second to register all this before she breaks into a run, crossing the enormous terrace leading down to the lawn.

"Ruff! Ruff, come here! Come!"

Ruff could be anywhere. She stops, detecting movement at the end of the garden, beyond a large shed. There she finds herself among columns of huge trees. Beneath them the ground is soft but not overgrown, though she can see that at the very end of the garden there's a tangle of brambles and weeds as high as a man.

From behind her there's a shout. She whirls round to see Ruff running up the lawn towards the man.

"Ruff!" The dog turns and runs right to her, his tail wagging as if nothing has happened. Crouching down, she hugs him to her with relief. "Where have you been? I was so worried about you . . ."

She straightens up, Ruff's wet paws making muddy marks on her crumpled shirt.

The man smiles. "Well done," he says. "Seems like a nice little fellow." He musses the top of Ruff's damp head, turning to lead Beth back up the garden.

"Thank you so much," she says. "Please can you tell your . . . employer?—"

He nods.

"— we'll check the fence for holes, make sure it doesn't happen again."

As he escorts them along the drive to the front entrance, Beth glances sideways, curious to see the woman who answered the entry phone. But there's no wave from a window, no sign of life at all.

* * *

"It was really bizarre," she says. "She let me in, but then ignored me. You'd have thought she would at least have introduced herself!"

Adam, buried in the sports section of the newspaper, shrugs and peers at her over his reading glasses. "Perhaps she's not used to visitors, or perhaps her English isn't any good. Or she could be shy . . ."

"What, dressed like that? I don't think so." The image of the glamorous woman has stayed with her, together with her own bedraggled state at the time.

"You can't tell." Adam shuts and folds the newspaper, leaning forward in his chair. "Anyway, what's important is you got Ruff back. I'll make a temporary barrier for that hole until I have time to do a proper repair. I'd better check for more escape routes, if he's going to be that sort of dog." Ruff lies at his feet as if nothing has happened, fast asleep, his belly rising and falling, his paws twitching gently.

Beth sighs. "I suspect he is. He's a terrier, I suppose they're used to finding small holes in things. I'm so glad he didn't get onto the road. We'll have to use the lead in the garden until it's all fixed and secure, then."

"Afraid so. Get the kids to do it when they can. I'll sort it out at the weekend."

CHAPTER ELEVEN

Sofia

My employers — no, I will not use that word — my keepers, my kidnappers, my tormentors are the worst kind of people. I am not allowed to use their actual names, Keith and Oksana. They insist I use "Sir" and "Madam". At first, I refused to call them anything, but she slapped me every time I forgot. She doesn't miss much, that woman.

Oksana — Madam — has no pity. She treats me like a slave and expects me to behave like one. I am not allowed to talk to her or to ask for anything. I am expected to creep around the house as I work, invisible, the servant. Sometimes, when she is in a really bad mood, she even yells at me for the noise of the vacuum cleaner. She drinks a lot of vodka, all day long. There is a never-ending supply in the house — it is delivered regularly and stored in the garage, the freezer, the fridge. Sometimes she goes back to bed after waking me and stays there until lunchtime. On those days I have to dust and iron and wash until she gets out of bed. I can't use the vacuum cleaner. I am not permitted to do anything that might disturb her.

She is tall and thin, and always smells of expensive perfume. I suppose she is beautiful, with her high Slavic cheekbones and her long slender legs, but she is cold. Her pale eyes have no life in them. She is not very old, under thirty I would say, though it is hard to tell. She certainly has no lines on her face, but I suppose if she did she would have them removed. When she smiles, which is rare — to me, anyway — her lips part to show perfect white teeth, but there is no sign of the smile in her eyes. She goes to the hairdresser every week, having her hair washed and blow-dried into beautiful, thick waves. Every day she puts on a dress and high heels, as if for a photo in a magazine. I must take the utmost care with her precious clothes when washing or ironing. Luckily for me, she sends most of them out to be cleaned. Her makeup is caked on, her eyelashes false and long, her nails like tiger's claws.

I hate her.

She knows this, watching me constantly. It is my own fault. I must make my face neutral if I want her to think I am harmless. Which she must, because escape will be impossible with her watching me all the time.

Sir is British, though I don't know where he is from exactly. His accent is unfamiliar. I can't guess his age, but he is much older than her — older than my father, I think. I feel sick when I think of them in bed together. When I change the sheets I look away and breathe through my mouth. She is with him for his money, for sure. His hair is greying and getting thin, with a bald patch on top. He has cruel eyes, but I don't know what colour they are because I don't look at them long enough to see. He wears a heavy gold chain around his neck, and his watch is huge and shiny.

Sir always leaves the house early, returning after dark. He travels a lot and is often away. This is a relief to me, because I dread meeting him on the landing or in the bedroom, in his pyjamas. I avoid him as much as possible — he scares me with his deep voice, his heavy tread around the house.

Sometimes I wonder what business he is in, to have so much money, but there are no clues in the house. Madam's jewels are real, or she wouldn't put them in the safe. His cars are new and smart, his suits beautiful, soft fabric. He has a boat — I don't know where, but there is a picture of it in the study: it is enormous, white with many windows. He and Madam pose on the deck, uniformed staff behind them. He also has racehorses — there are pictures of them too. Madam seems to spend what she likes. Her purse is always bulging with credit cards.

* * *

Sometimes I try to work out where I am. It will be important for when I escape. I believe I am in England, but I might be in Wales, I suppose, or Scotland. I believe I was drugged, so anything is possible, but I prefer to think this is England. It gives me a grain of hope, thinking I might not be too far from my aunt and uncle and my dear cousin Elena. I can't remember the name of their town — it is a difficult name, hard to pronounce. I didn't memorise it, but their address was on my mobile and written down on a piece of paper in my bag.

But I haven't seen my bag since I was taken.

That first morning I woke in a room that was empty except for the pile of dirty blankets on the floor where I lay. I was dreaming of home, of the animals and the woods and Elena, so when realisation came to me, the shock was terrible. My head was thumping, my mouth dry. I had no idea of the time. The last thing I remembered was drinking the bottle of Coke in the back of the car, still thinking I was on my way to work on a farm.

I started up from the floor and stumbled to the door, my bare feet cold on rough concrete — but it was locked shut. Through iron bars, a small window looked out into a well between walls — a square space with a patch of sky at the top. I could see nothing in any of the other windows: no movement, no drapes, no sign of life. All that view told me was that I was on the bottom level of a tall, office-like building. I ran back to the door, pulling and pushing and rattling the handle.

With my fists I hammered on the painted wood, crying and screaming, "Let me out! Let me out!" until the silence told me I was alone.

Many hours went by before someone came, or it certainly felt like it. They had taken my watch along with my bag, my case, my shoes. I was helpless.

The only other thing in that room was a bucket. When I realised what it was for, I knew I was truly a prisoner and I wasn't going to get out, even to visit the bathroom.

I was barely sixteen and I was terrified.

I sat in the corner on the cold floor, hugged my knees to my chest and trembled, imagining all the terrible things that might happen to me. At home I knew of girls disappearing, taken from their families by criminal gangs, forced to work as prostitutes from a very young age. I never imagined it would happen to me, though.

In that cold, empty place my imagination crossed a line, and by the time the door opened and the driver came in, I had destroyed myself. Unable to speak through my sobs, I couldn't plead with him or question him. I could barely hold myself up as he dragged me out of the building into a car park and shoved me into the back of a van. He said nothing as he tied my hands behind my back. I curled into a ball and wept as the engine started up.

I was in no state to look around me, to take mental notes as I was dragged out of the building, or to think too much about the journey. My only memories are the stench of diesel, the hum of traffic, the shaking of the van when it drew up at junctions. There seemed to be a lot of hold-ups at first, so we must have been in heavy traffic, but then the van went faster and I wasn't aware of anything but the drone of the engine for what seemed like a very long time.

Now, with all the hours I have in my room to think about what happened, to plan my escape and my revenge, I chide myself for not keeping my head. If I had been clever, I would have tried to remember everything about that building, noted details in the few seconds between the exit and the van. I might even have managed to get the registration number. I could have counted the minutes to our destination, or banged on the walls of the van when it stopped to catch someone's attention. But I didn't. I don't even know if it would have done any good, though I suppose it might one day help the police to find my captors.

So to add to my troubles, I have no idea where I am.

CHAPTER TWELVE

Beth

Ruff is easy-going, friendly to other dogs and to humans. In the park the same people walk every day, and soon Beth feels able to stop and chat with the regulars. So far she hasn't met anyone from her street, though, apart from Karen. Both next-door houses remain silent, the only sign of life a periodic crunching of tyres on the gravel drive to the left of theirs, signalling the coming and going of cars. To the right, she concludes the owners must be away, it's always so resolutely quiet.

"I think we should invite the neighbours for drinks," she says again at supper. "At least we know Karen and her husband would come, and I can probably rustle up a couple of people from the park. Otherwise, I can't see how we're ever going to get to know anyone. What do you think?"

Tom helps himself to a second huge helping of pasta and piles in with his fork.

"Do you want to get to know them, Mum?" he says, his voice muffled by a mouthful. "They might be awful and you'll regret ever asking them round."

"They could be the opposite, though, and end up our best friends." Abigail, always the optimist, gives Tom a look.

"Mum needs to get to know people, she's here on her own all day until we get home."

"She has Ruff," Tom says.

"And he's a great conversationalist." Abigail's voice drips with sarcasm.

Beth reaches for the salad bowl, depositing a pile of greenery onto her plate. "Why would they be awful, Tom? Karen from over the road is really friendly — she brought me those beautiful flowers. And her girls seem lovely. We could invite them too, Abi. You can get to know them a bit."

"Yeah, okay," Abigail says. She's beginning to settle into a group of friends at school, but none of them live close by. She would like to have friends within walking distance.

"I don't know, Mum," Tom says. "I'm not being suspicious but all the houses seem so . . . private. It doesn't seem like a friendly street."

"I think that's more to do with the distance between the houses," Adam says. "It's not like living in a terrace, certainly, but that doesn't mean the people are different."

"But they are, though, aren't they, Mum?" Tom says. "Next door weren't very helpful when Ruff escaped, and you've had no luck at all on the other side."

"Exactly why I want to invite them round for drinks," Beth says. "It's an excuse to make contact, and once you've met people and they've been in your home, they're more likely to reciprocate. Or we might find some real friends, you never know. I'd like to know more about the area and what's going on too. You only get to know things like that by talking to people."

"You miss the bookshop, don't you, Mum?" Abigail says.

"Yes, I do. But anyway it's important to get on with the neighbours. In the old days it was all about supporting each other, especially in streets where the houses were terraced. The women were always in and out of each other's houses, and the men would get together for a chin-wag at the local."

"In the Olden Days," Abigail says, grinning. "When men were men, and women were cooks and maids . . ."

"Enough. You know what I mean," Beth says, smiling back. "Anyway, what do you think, Adam? We could do a lunchtime thing, say on a Sunday, just drinks and nibbles. It's worth a try, isn't it?"

Adam stands up, stretches and starts to clear the plates. "Come on kids, help please. I think it's a good idea, Beth; it's certainly worth a try. Let's keep it informal, just a drink or two and a chat."

* * *

At the stationer's she buys some proper invitations. Nothing too fancy. Simple, modern and to the point.

But now they've made a decision and fixed a date, she's beginning to worry about it. It's hard to know how many to expect, especially as she doesn't know how many people are in each house. Perhaps she'll restrict it to the few houses near their own, and hope to get a few acceptances. To know even a handful of people would help her feel more at home.

Now that the unpacking is done, the house mostly organised, she's beginning to feel restless. Whatever Adam says — and she's grateful for his support, that he's not pushing her to find a job — being at home every day doesn't suit her. This is the longest period in her whole life that she hasn't had a job of some sort and she feels shapeless, uncertain of where she fits, both in the house and in the community.

With the invitations waiting to be filled out, she realises she doesn't even know their neighbours' names. She'll just have to fill in the date and time and hope people will introduce themselves. And how is she going to deliver them? In London she would have walked right up to the front door and posted the invitation, or rung on the bell for a spontaneous chat. Here, the anonymous boxes at the gates reveal nothing of their owners, and it's pretty unlikely she'll bump into anyone on a street like this.

Still, they've decided to go ahead and she's going to do her best to get people there and make them welcome. It occurs to her that — again, with the exception of Karen — none of them have bothered to make her feel welcome, but she banishes that thought. If they're not outwardly friendly, there's no reason why she shouldn't be. There's nothing to lose by trying.

* * *

The cards are delivered. Four weeks to go before the party. As she walks back home, Beth wonders if anyone will come apart from Karen and her family (she checked the date with her in advance so that at least they would be guaranteed). Well, it's done now, and if it is just the two families, they'll have a good time and get to know each other properly.

She must talk to the kids about making guests feel comfortable. Adam, in his straightforward way, can be very direct, a bit too direct for some people, while the teenagers . . . well, they're teenagers, though she hopes they've been brought up well enough to be polite and friendly. It doesn't always work that way, though, and she needs this to be a success.

She hopes she hasn't made the wrong decision.

As for her immediate neighbours, she would love to know more about the model-like Russian woman. It will be a surprise if she comes to the party — and if she does, what will the conversation be like? It could all be rather awkward.

The other day, on the way back from a walk with Ruff, she spotted the husband returning from work, his Aston Martin purring as the gates swung smoothly open. Though she waved, he either didn't see or he chose to ignore her. She suspects the latter.

CHAPTER THIRTEEN

Beth

The wine has been cooling in the fridge overnight, together with a shelf full of beers. There's champagne too: Adam decided they should offer the real stuff — not because he's a snob, but because he prefers it. On the worktop are rows of glasses and soft drinks in ice buckets. Vases of fresh flowers scent the room. Tom and Abigail have been making the canapés, and as usual, Tom eats rather more than he prepares. Eventually Adam intervenes and bans him from taking another mouthful until the guests have had a chance to taste them.

Beth opens up the doors to the garden, where a weak sun warms the air. Adam has tidied up outside and a new set of stripes smartens up the lawn.

Ruff potters about between the house and the garden, aware that something's about to happen. He's not tall enough to reach the food, jumping up at their legs instead with imploring eyes. Beth hopes their guests like dogs. If they have to shut him in the utility room he'll probably howl the place down.

Karen is first to arrive with her husband Fred and their two girls. They've brought with them the only other people they know in the street, their closest neighbours, an older couple called Jenny and Jerry. They've brought gifts: potted plants and more champagne, and at once Beth feels better. This already feels like a crowd, and even if nobody else turns up, it will be enough.

A mother and son from the house at the end of the road soon join them and Beth relaxes, topping up drinks while the children, including Karen's daughters, hand round the food. She's beginning to think nobody else will come when the doorbell rings.

"I'll go," she calls to Adam.

"No, I'm there already," he says, putting his drink down.

The conversation is already loud enough to drown the low-level music they put on before people arrived. Jenny from across the road is telling Beth about their children, both grown and living abroad, one in Spain, the other in California, and Beth has to crane her neck towards her to hear her soft voice. She's about to offer her a top-up when Adam appears at her shoulder.

"Let me introduce you," he says, and steps aside. "This is my wife, Beth. Beth, this is our neighbour, Oksana."

* * *

Today she's dressed entirely in red, her slender body encased in a long-sleeved red sheath that reaches to her mid-calf. On her feet are shoes that Beth could only dream of — red, and high, and expensive-looking. Her lipstick and her nails are the same shade exactly, her handbag too. It's a tiny, exquisite circle of leather, probably only big enough for a lipstick and a tissue. Against the colour of her dress, her hair is a waterfall of gold on her back.

She smiles and says something to Adam as she enters the room. There's a tangible shift in the atmosphere as Oksana makes her entrance, the conversation fading just a fraction as people stare a little too long before turning back to each other. Even Adam seems a little fazed by her, Beth realises, as she takes the porcelain hand again.

"Oksana, how good to meet you properly," she says. Oksana smiles, revealing snow-white teeth, not a hint of recognition in her eyes.

"We met briefly, before . . . when my dog got into your garden?"

"Ah yes." Her voice is deep and melodic. "I remember now. It is good you found him." She speaks English with a strong accent, each consonant given a strange emphasis.

Beth wonders if she does remember, given what she looked like last time they met. She can hardly blame her if she doesn't.

"I was worried, yes. I'm so sorry about that. But we've fixed the hole in the fence now, so it shouldn't be a problem again. What would you like to drink? Adam, could you . . .? Please, come and meet some people. Do you know Karen at all, and Fred? They live opposite us, you as well . . ." Beth's starting to babble, as she does when she feels uncomfortable.

"Oh my God," she says in Adam's ear as she opens the fridge to retrieve more wine. "She came. I'd have lost a bet on that one."

"Indeed. No sign of the husband, though. I'll ask her in a minute if he's going to join her."

"Yes, find out whatever you can."

She watches the room for a moment. Oksana has caused a bit of a stir, the young people staring at her in fascination, the men drawn to her as if to a magnet. Karen catches Beth's eye, raises an eyebrow.

The party has got a lot more interesting.

* * *

"I think that went rather well," Beth says, easing onto the sofa next to Karen. All the guests have gone except Karen and Fred, and the children have disappeared upstairs.

"It did. You're a ground-breaker in the street," Fred says. "Nobody has invited us to anything, or come round to say hello, in the whole time we've been here."

"The ground-breaker was Karen," Beth says. "If she hadn't come round and introduced herself, I'd have been too scared to invite people. Imagine if nobody had come."

"Never mind the ground-breaker," says Karen. "The star turn is what I'm interested in. Oksana herself — that was a coup, wasn't it?"

"I was so surprised she came, especially on her own," Beth says. "Though she did seem to enjoy the attention. I thought she was quite scary, actually, when I first met her. She certainly wasn't friendly. Ice-cold, in fact. Did anyone talk to her properly? I was busy with the drinks and everything, but I would have loved to find out more about her."

"We tried," Karen says, glancing at Fred, who smiles and fingers his drink. "Fred was cosying up to her — he was smitten." She grins at him as he shakes his head.

"Really not my type — as you well know," he says. "She seems charming, but rather . . . haughty. We didn't get to know much about her. Only that she comes from a tiny Russian village in the middle of nowhere — she did say, but I didn't recognise the name."

"Her husband?"

"He's called Keith. He's British, but she didn't tell us much more than that. I get the impression he's always travelling. No children, apparently. From what I can tell, he's a lot older than her. I did find out they have racehorses, though I don't think she has much to do with them. She didn't seem terribly impressed."

"They're obviously loaded," Adam says. "I see him sometimes driving in or out. Sometimes he's picked up by a chauffeur-driven Bentley, sometimes he drives himself. In the Aston Martin, of course."

"Any idea what he does?" Beth says.

"Drug dealer, definitely," Fred says. Then, seeing Beth's face, "I'm joking, of course. I have no idea. Only that it seems to pay, whatever it is."

"Don't tell me you're jealous," Karen says. "Gorgeous young wife, top-of-the range luxury cars, pots of money. You have everything you need!"

Fred laughs. "Very funny. Okay — I'll go with the gorgeous young wife, but the rest is arguable."

"You never know with people like that, though," Adam says. "Sometimes it's just a front, and then you find out it's all borrowed, and they've gone bankrupt, or worse."

"Worse being what, for instance?" Beth is intrigued.

"Arrested for some kind of criminal activity — fraud, or drugs, or any number of other illegal stuff. It happens more than you think," Adam says. "I'm not being melodramatic, but it's not unusual in the City, where there's so much money. We could easily be living among criminals. How would we know?"

Though it's said lightly, it strikes Beth that he could be right. How would they know?

CHAPTER FOURTEEN

Sofia

I hug myself, gazing at the keys. How will I try them out, where should I start? Which one will give me my first step towards freedom? Even once I am out of the house, I will still be trapped behind those high fences. I will have to get over them somehow, find something to stand on . . .

But this is stupid. I am stupid. I must not be too hopeful, must not get ahead of myself.

The keys are probably old, perhaps not even from this house. Some workman could have left them behind, forgotten where he put them. There are five, a couple of them quite small, as if they would fit a padlock or a suitcase — or a window. One long brass-coloured key. The rest seem to be the usual sort, like the ones Madam has for all the exterior doors to the house. Tomorrow, or the next day, if Matt hasn't told on me, I will put them in my sock and try some of them out. Sir is home — I should wait for him to go away, but I can't. I will have to be extra careful, and patient.

It will take a few days to try each one in all the locks. There are so many locks! For a moment, despair settles around me. If I am caught, she will hurt me — she won't care if she kills me. Why should she? Nobody knows I am here, not even the neighbours. And if she does not kill me, she will surely search everywhere and take all my precious things. And then she will make my life even worse.

But I shake off the fear, replace it with dogged determination. I have to get out of here, so I will have to take risks. I have no choice. If I don't, I will die of neglect — if not my body, then my soul.

If none of the keys fit — oh please God, just one is all I need — I will try not to be disappointed. It will be hard, but I must prepare myself. If I allow myself disappointment, then depression and despair will follow. Then the answer will be . . . but I am not going to think about that.

If none of the keys fit, I will still have a weapon. Multiple small weapons, if you like. The keys can still help me, even if they don't fit the locks.

* * *

Today is the fourth day I have carried a single key around for the whole day, waiting for my chances. At first I put them all in my sock, where they were safe, but it was too dangerous to have them all on the same keyring: when I took them out, they made a jangling noise, and it was only because she was chattering on the phone that I got away with it. She has ears like a bat's. A Russian bat, ugly and mean, fluttering about my head. She hears everything.

So I took them to my room and removed each key, one by one, from the circle of metal, and returned all but one to the box the next day. It is safer to try them one by one. When I have exhausted all the possibilities for each key, I make a scratch on it to show I have tried it, so I don't get muddled.

Now I grasp one of the smallest keys tightly in the palm of my hand as I try another room. I've already tried the windows in the laundry, the downstairs toilet, their bedroom and bathroom. I don't think the little keys are for the windows — they don't seem right. But I don't know. I don't even know if all the window keys in the house are the same, so I have to make sure. I have to test each one. It is slow and laborious as well as risky, but it gives me a goal, and at the end of the day, when I have tested a key at least once, I have achieved a small target. It could take weeks, or even months. But I have the time.

I don't rely on the keys to be my saviour, either — I know all this might come to nothing. But I never stop looking for opportunities. This is exhausting but it will be worth it.

* * *

My heart jumps to my throat and sits there, choking me. I can barely breathe. I am in the dining room, where my job is to dust the cabinets, the drinks tray, the horrible paintings on the walls. Horses and more horses. Posh men looking proud in brightly coloured jackets. Sir is in his office with the door closed, Madam in the living room. I have a few minutes.

The key doesn't fit, as I expected. It doesn't even go in a tiny bit. The smaller keys, though they look like window keys, are not — or at least, they are not made for these locks. But I try the handle anyway, and to my great surprise, the window opens. The fresh air folds around me, the scent of cut grass filling my senses. I draw in a great breath, my head filling with the joy of it.

I close the window again with shaking hands, calm myself with an effort. I take the cloth and pretend to be dusting around the window frame, looking outside to see what is below, for my escape route. Beneath the window is a dense bush, beyond it some flowering plants. It is a good few feet to the ground, but the bush could break my fall. It might also hide me for a moment or two. At the side of the house, there must be gate or a fence.

Should I make my escape right now? Should I check where they are, or wait until she goes out — if she goes out? I don't know how long this window has been open. She used this room last week, when she had a group of women for lunch, so she probably opened it then and forgot to lock it. In which case, it has been unlocked for a few days now and she hasn't remembered, so a few minutes or even hours might not matter.

But I can't wait. I have been waiting for so long for a chance.

I gather my cleaning box and the vacuum cleaner and drag it into the living room, the next in my daily rounds. If I stay too long in the dining room, she might decide to check on me and remember the window. I check through the door — she is in the kitchen, music blaring, fiddling with her mobile. The office door is still closed and Matt is nowhere to be seen in the garden. I take a deep breath and turn the vacuum cleaner on, leaving it out of sight of either door, then I run to the dining room and wrestle the window open.

For a moment I am stuck with one leg inside, one leg dangling down the outside wall. Then all at once I am wriggling through, jumping, falling, into the bush, branches breaking and scratching the skin on my arms as I flail about. I land on my side in the foliage, the thump taking my breath away. To me, the clatter of my fall is deafening. I lie for a few moments, listening for a shout, the rumble of running feet. Nothing — not a sound. I detach myself from the clutching twigs of the bush, roll into a crouch and peer into the garden. There's nobody there. I reach one arm up and, with the very tips of my fingers, manage to close the window.

Then I am running, running, my head down, keeping as close to the ground as possible, round to the side of the house. There is a high wall stretching from the side of the house to the fence, a long, strong barrier. Even if I manage to climb it, I will still be trapped in the front garden, in full view of the house. I scuttle across, trampling the flowers in the border to reach the safety of the taller bushes up by the fence. I have to climb this somehow, and I must do it quickly. Madam will soon notice I am gone.

I am not tall, and the fence seems enormous, with creepers and climbing roses all over, making it even taller. I can't reach the top with my arms stretched high. But I am strong. This, now, is what I have been waiting for, preparing my body for, and I know I can do it. I gather all my fury, my frustration and my determination into an explosion of terrible energy and leap, forcing my legs to spring from a standing start towards the fence, like a frog leaping from the talons of a crow. One hand scrabbles at the wood and comes away with nothing, the other grabs at some foliage and takes hold while my feet flail around, trying to get some kind of grip on the fence. Rose thorns scratch at my arms, my face. The fence seems to bend and stretch as I reach my free hand high. The muscles in my shoulders strain as the tips of my fingers bend around the top of the fence. I am almost there — I can do this!

Then a heavy hand grasps my ankle. My hand rips from the splintered wood, my legs collapse and I land in a heap on the soft, dark earth.

CHAPTER FIFTEEN

Sofia

It was Matt who caught me, whose hand grasped my ankle. But when I scrambled upright from where I had fallen, she was right behind him, her face twisted, her precious heels sinking into the lawn. I screamed, hoping the woman next door would hear me, but Madam grabbed my arm and marched me into the house without a word.

"Where did you get it?" she roars, her porcelain face like a witch's mask. "Where was it?"

She waves the key in my face as I cower on the floor of my room where she has thrown me. I had left it on the windowsill in the dining room. She thinks it is how I escaped.

I shake my head. She slaps my head again, grabs my T-shirt. "Clothes off! Strip, little whore!"

I remove my T-shirt and my trousers slowly. I stand there in my underwear and socks, trembling, my eyes on the floor. She picks up the clothes and feels in the pockets. There is nothing else. It is all hidden away, though I pray she doesn't search my room properly.

I am glad the other keys are safe. The smallest is the most useless, and I don't care that she found it. I flinch from her beating but my mind is aflame. I hate her, I hate this place. I will get out. I will get my revenge.

"Where did you get it?"

When I refuse to answer her, she grabs my hair from behind and pulls down, hard, so my chin is within millimetres of hers. I can see her perfect white teeth, her pink, wet tongue, the false lashes on her upper eyelids, in sharp detail. For a moment I am strangely detached, observing her closely. The next minute the injustice, the indignity, the sheer cruelty of my situation takes over.

I shout directly into her painted face, snarling: "Take your hands off me!"

She recoils in shock, dropping her hand from my hair. I pause for breath, then shriek, spitting out the words in my own language: "Bitch! I hate you! Let me out of here, or I'll kill you!" I don't think she understands the words, but she can't miss the meaning.

"You little piece of — of — nothing!" she yells. "We give you home, food — protect you from police. You have nothing, not passport, not identity. You are — illegal!" The word is ugly, her Russian tongue curling awkwardly around it. "Illegal! If they find you, you go to prison! You never see family again — never!"

She slaps me around the head again and again, until I curl into a ball by the wall, protecting my head with my arms. She kicks me then, in the shins, as hard as she can, once, twice and again. I can see the intent in her face. The heel of her stiletto catches my shin, all the power of her long leg concentrated on a tiny patch of bone. The pain sears through me and I scream as loudly as I can, clutching my leg in agony. I want Matt to hear this, I want the neighbours, the whole world, to hear my pain, to know what she is doing to me. I carry on screaming until my lungs are empty, my mouth gaping wide, watching her face and waiting for the next blow, challenging her.

She hesitates. I take a breath and start again, my eyes on hers. She stares back at me now — she seems unsure what to do. There is blood on the floor. I watch her glance at it, then back at my face, at the cuts and bruises she has already caused. I don't bother to conceal the loathing I feel. It races through my veins, powers my heart, flows from my eyes. Time stands still for a fraction of a second, a heartbeat, while our eyes lock. In that infinitesimal moment I see it, I feel it. She turns without a word and leaves, locking the door behind her.

Fear. She is frightened of me.

* * *

Alone, I sit for a while, checking my wounds. My shin bone is the worst. An angry purple bruise is already puffing up around the imprint of her heel, blood still dripping down my ankle. I stand with difficulty, crying out in agony as my foot touches the floor. After a moment or two, holding onto the walls, I manage to limp to the bathroom, where I sit on the toilet and bathe my damaged leg with cold water. It looks and feels terrible.

I inspect my reflection in the metal cabinet. One eyelid is badly swollen and I can barely see with that eye. An angry red patch grows underneath, a horizontal cut leaving a trail of dried blood on my cheek. I look like a zombie in a horror movie.

Gently, I splash cold water on my face. I am glad it looks worse than it feels. Not that there is anyone to see it, only Matt and Sir, and neither of them seems in the least bit interested in me. But I vow to run to the front door if anyone comes. Surely a person would be suspicious to see this kind of injury — surely they would tell someone?

I am still buzzing from that brief moment of victory when I saw the fear in her eyes. I am triumphant, and the feeling is good.

But then, when I stop to think, I know what a dangerous thing I have done, and I am angry at myself.

It is better that she thinks I am weak and tame, a nobody who won't cause any trouble, who won't stand up to her. For months — years, now — I have kept up the pretence. But that has all changed. I have tried to escape — and so nearly managed to — and shown her my true self. She knows I hate her. She knows I am trouble, and I will do everything, anything to escape.

I tremble to think what she might do.

CHAPTER SIXTEEN

Beth

The pile of boxes in the garage has shrunk to just a few. All that's left is a handful of pictures that don't seem to fit anywhere in the new house, some barely used crockery destined for the charity shop, and the contents of the shed. That's a job for Adam, she thinks: the tools are his, and sorting out the shed is the kind of thing he enjoys.

Six weeks into puppy-training classes and Ruff is learning fast. He sits to order, comes to heel, and brings back a ball most of the time. There have been some incidents of ripping up magazines and cardboard boxes, Abigail's slipper has become a favourite toy and the wicker chair in the conservatory is in need of repair, but in general he's well behaved.

The biggest problem is what the dog trainer calls "recall". Ruff comes back when he feels like it, not when Beth or the children want him to. Though Beth diligently carries out their daily homework in the garden, letting him run off the lead, then calling him back with treats, the dog still suits himself. So letting him off the lead in the park is a risk, and often she waits and worries for what seems like an age before he reappears. The trainer says to persevere — terriers take their time and are notoriously stubborn. But he will get there. Beth isn't so sure.

He also loves to dig. The lawn looks good from inside the house, but close up, when she walks down the garden, she can see scrapes and holes. She's seen him scratch and scratch until there's enough bare earth to lie down in. He does the same in the flower beds, creating a mini-ditch for himself before flopping down for a snooze, usually when she's out in the garden herself. She can only hope he'll grow out of it. Anyway, she thinks, it will be winter soon, and the grass will have a chance to recover next spring.

* * *

Beth volunteers at the local charity bookshop. For two afternoons a week, she sorts, prices, stocks the shelves and mans the desk along with two other volunteers. It's well organised, and she enjoys the company of the other two women who help there, both of whom are local and retired. Though she'd prefer paid work, the hours work well for her and the dog, and she's always liked working with books. Her stack of unread books at home is growing at an alarming rate.

Her head is buried in a dusty box of ancient leather-covered tomes and battered paperbacks one afternoon when her mobile buzzes. Pushing her hair from her face, she sees Tom's name flash up on the screen.

"Mum, Ruff's gone." Tom is out of breath, his voice panicky.

"Calm down, Tom," she says, trying to keep her voice steady. "What do you mean, gone? Where are you?"

"I'm at home. I let him out when I got back from school and we played with the ball for a bit. I came back in to do my homework, and he stayed out — he was sniffing around. I forgot he was outside, and when I went to find him he was gone . . ."

"Okay, we'll find him," she says, sounding calmer than she feels. "Is there any chance he could have got out another way? Have you opened the front door at all since you got in?"

"No, Mum, it must have been the back."

"Right. What you need to do is check all around the fence, looking at the bottom for holes, or places he might have dug through. That's what we did last time. You remember where he got through before? Check Dad's repair. He might have managed to loosen it."

"Can you come and help? Abi's not home yet, I think she's got a club or something at school."

"Yes, she has. Don't worry, I'm just about to lock up, then I'll get home as soon as I can. Take some dog treats with you, and the lead, and keep calling him. I'll be there in about twenty minutes."

* * *

At home, all's quiet when she opens the front door.

"Tom? Are you there?"

Silence — and no welcome from Ruff either. Her shoulders tense as she hurries through the kitchen to the wide-open back door. There's no sign of Tom.

In the garden, everything seems normal as she walks towards the shed at the bottom, scanning the fences on either side. But then she sees it: the stepladder up against the fence, partly hidden in the ivy.

"Tom?" she calls again from the flower bed where the empty stepladder is propped. "Tom? Where are you?"

There's no answer, so she tests the bottom step with her foot. It seems pretty solid so she carries on up to the top, where a small platform allows her to stand, holding on to a narrow bar. The fence, or at least the ivy which spills over every part of it in this section, is as high as her waist, and she steadies herself as she leans over.

This end of Oksana's garden is dominated by large trees, with holly bushes and laurel growing beneath. It's at least twice the width of Beth's, so she can't see the whole of it, and there's no sign of Tom or Ruff.

She's about to shout to them when she recalls the conversation about Oksana and Keith. She's pretty sure they wouldn't like trespassers in their back garden, given the level of security at the front. She looks up at the windows of the house, staring blankly back at her. Everything looks dark inside, but she gets the distinct feeling that she's being watched. A prickle of fear touches the back of neck. Where can Tom be?

As she hesitates, there's a loud rustling noise and Tom appears, looking hot and dishevelled, holding Ruff firmly in his arms.

"God, Mum! He really didn't want to be caught . . . I've been running everywhere trying to catch him. Can you take him?"

Tom has to balance the dog on both hands and stretch high before Beth can reach him, but she grabs onto the lead, and then his collar, and after a moment with his legs pawing the thin air, Ruff is in her arms.

"Got him. Well done, Tom. Hang on, I'll tie him to a tree and help you over." She backs down the steps with some difficulty and ties the dog to a sapling at the bottom of their garden. Tom is taller than her and heavy, but somehow she manages to pull him back over, the step ladder lurching alarmingly as he wriggles over the top of the fence, ivy leaves scattering.

Tom stops to catch his breath as Beth wrestles with the stepladder.

"Little pest!" he says. "He's so determined. I'm shattered."

"Did you find a hole?"

"He dug through, Mum," Tom says, pointing. "It's not a hole, it's a tunnel."

Beth peers through a tangle of plants, following the direction of Tom's hand. Pushing the undergrowth to one side reveals a sizeable tunnel under the fence, leading into next door's garden. On this side it's hidden from view by bushes but it looks pretty established, as if it's in use by foxes or other wild animals. Adam must have missed it when he fixed the first hole in the fence. But it's not surprising that Ruff found it and went exploring.

Beth feels a twist of anxiety. They can't risk a confrontation with Oksana and Keith. If Adam doesn't have the time to do it properly, she'll have to fix the hole herself.

CHAPTER SEVENTEEN

Beth

"Who does it belong to, the fence on that side?" Beth asks.

"It's joint, unfortunately. We can't do anything to it without getting their agreement," Adam says.

"We can block the holes, though, surely?"

"Probably, though you said yourself it needs to be a proper job."

"I don't want to risk annoying the neighbours." Beth wonders why she feels so anxious when it comes to Oksana and Keith. "All that security has to be for a reason. They certainly don't want us running around their back garden."

"Bloody dog," Adam says, not for the first time, ruffling the soft fur on the top of his head. "Send him back, I say."

"No, Dad," Abigail says, jumping from the table to hug Ruff. "We rescued him. We're not sending him back, we love him. You are joking, aren't you?"

"Of course I'm joking. But this is awkward, and it could be expensive."

"It could be," Beth says. "It's quite a lot of fence, all the way round. We'd have to do both sides, and the bottom end."

Adam looks pensive. "Chain link might do it, but we might have to get someone to dig it in, like you do with rabbit fencing, to be absolutely sure he won't dig under it. He's turning out to be quite an expensive rescue dog."

"It was a bit crazy, climbing over to get him," Beth says.

Tom looks up, protest in his eyes.

"I'm not criticising you, Tom, I'm glad you did. What if he'd gone through to the next garden, and the next? We might never have got him back. It would be awful to lose him now we're all so fond of him. Actually, I've been wondering—"

"What?" Adam says.

"Do you think I should go round and apologise to Oksana, in case she saw something and wondered what on earth was going on?"

"I'll go," Adam says, winking at Tom.

"Dad." Tom gives his father a sideways look. "I know your game."

Adam's mouth twitches. "Damn. My dastardly plan has been rumbled."

"I don't think she's your type, my darling," Beth says, smiling. "And you're certainly not hers."

Adam looks comically offended. "How dare you. Some people think I'm a bit of a catch, actually."

"What, people like Mum, you mean?" Tom says. Adam gives him a fierce look.

"Of course, like Mum," Adam says. "But seriously, maybe it's worth keeping her sweet, Beth. We might have to negotiate over fixing the fence."

"True. Not that money is likely to be a problem."

"You never know. Often the people with the most money can be the meanest."

"Okay, I'll try," Beth says. "I'll pop round tomorrow."

"Better write her a note too, in case she's not there," Adam says. "We don't want the gardener getting suspicious of us."

"We didn't see him. It was all quiet as far as I could see," Beth says. "Quite spooky, actually."

"There was someone there, though." Tom pours himself a large glass of water.

"What do you mean, Tom?" Beth says. "Who did you see?"

"I was there quite a long time," Tom says. "Probably half an hour, chasing Ruff around the bottom of the garden. He's so quick! I nearly caught him a couple of times, but he got away and ran towards the house. That's when I saw her, looking out of a bedroom window."

"Oksana, you mean?" Beth says.

"No, it definitely wasn't her. It was a young girl, about my age, I'd say. She was small, with a pale face, and she didn't smile. She waved. . . kind of signalled to me, and put her hands on the window. She was trying to say something."

"That's strange. Oksana told me they don't have children. Did she look like a cleaner?"

"Too young, I'd say. Perhaps they've got people staying." He shrugged. "Have we got any ice cream?"

* * *

Dear Oksana,

Just a quick note to apologise for our dog, Ruff, who managed to escape into your garden again yesterday. If anybody saw a young lad in among the trees, running around the end of your garden, it was my son Tom, trying to recapture him. Ruff had managed to dig under the fence, so when Tom realised, he climbed over to fetch him back — but the naughty creature kept running off. There's obviously something very attractive about your garden!

Anyway, if anyone saw the drama, we apologise if they were alarmed and assure you it was all very innocent.

We hope to solve the problem of the escaping dog very soon. This may involve putting in a separate barrier on our side, like a chain link fence. We will of course discuss it with you before making any decisions. In the meantime, we'll be keeping a close eye on our dog!

Apologies again. Perhaps we can have coffee sometime?

Best wishes

Beth, Adam, Tom and Abigail (and Ruff!)

* * *

There's no reply when she presses the buzzer at the gate. She presses again, just in case, and when there's no sound from the speaker, she drops the note into the box below. In a way, she's disappointed. She doesn't want to be Oksana's friend, particularly, but she would like to know her a bit better, for when they need to discuss things like the fence. Also, she has to admit she wants to find out more about the mysterious girl in the window.

But here she stops herself. It's really none of her business who the girl is and why she's in Oksana's house. There's probably a very ordinary explanation. She could be a relative, perhaps a student staying for a few weeks, a friend's daughter, a niece. There could be a dozen different and completely plausible reasons why a young girl would signal to her son from a window. Perhaps the girl was beckoning him, wants to get to know him? Or it could just be Tom's imagination.

One thing is for sure: Beth isn't going to get involved. She's not going to risk that again. People are entitled to their private lives and she's going to let them be.

CHAPTER EIGHTEEN

Sofia

As I gaze from a first-floor window across the back garden, I see movement in the wooded area towards the far end. At first I think it is a squirrel; they are gathering food for winter at the moment, burying nuts and squabbling with each other. But this creature is not the right colour for a squirrel, it is black — and the wrong shape. A dog! Small, black and scruffy. Where can it have come from? Perhaps there is a gap in the fence that could be useful to me. He scurries in and out of the bushes, sniffing constantly, his little tail wagging, panting with excitement. He seems to be working his way towards the house. I want so much to see him properly, to say hello, to stroke his back. But all the doors are locked as usual.

Another movement at the bottom of the garden — a boy! He's about my age, dressed in dark jeans and a hooded jumper, with white trainers that stand out against the grass. He looks around for the dog, runs up the path with long, loping strides and tries to catch it.

I have to get his attention — but how can I do it? If he doesn't look up, if he catches the dog, he will never notice me. I bang my hands on the window but I am too high up; he doesn't hear. I am taking a risk. Madam is in the house, downstairs in the kitchen. Normally she will have the TV on, or some music — I hope she does right now. There is no time to waste. I run to close the bedroom door, hurry back — he is still there. I bang on the window with my open palms, wrestle with the handle, hoping against hope that it will give way, but it stands firm. I look around for something, anything, to signal with, but I see nothing of use. Only pillows and bedlinen and furniture. I stand with my hands glued to the window, helpless as the boy captures the dog in his arms and stands.

He looks up. My heart leaps, and I signal madly with my hands, mouthing "help me" like a mad puppet. Seeing me, he pauses for the smallest of moments, but I can't read his expression. I continue to jump and wave and scream my silent plea, but he turns away and walks quickly towards the bottom of the garden, disappearing to one side. My hands drop to my sides and I watch, helpless, as the dog is handed over the fence. A woman — his mother? — has appeared on the other side, her arms reaching out to take him. Then the boy clambers over and disappears from sight.

I sink to the floor, tears running down my cheeks, disappointment crushing me like a mighty weight. The best opportunity I've had since I got here, and I wasn't ready, I had no idea what to do. I beat my fist on the floor in frustration with myself. How could I be so stupid?

I've been in this room too long. I must not attract attention to myself. I hurry around with the vacuum cleaner, opening the door so she can hear me.

A feeling of deep despair comes over me. Even when someone sees me, they won't understand what's going on, they won't know I need rescuing. I am not wearing chains or a straightjacket, or holding a sign saying "Help".

That is what I need, for the next time, if there is one. A sign.

* * *

I keep my head down and say nothing. I do my work as quietly as possible, slipping away when Madam approaches, avoiding her as far as I can. I hope if I make myself invisible, she will forget I screamed at her, forget that I stood up to her. I know she won't easily forget that I tried to escape, though. I am still angry with myself for being caught, and for giving myself away.

Mostly, she ignores me, but I know she is watching from the corner of her eye. She speaks to me only once in the next week, and only because she wants the dining room prepared for a lunch event. She gives me exact instructions in her cold voice, without meeting my eyes. She makes me lay a place setting on the table just as she wants it, supervising my every move, before she leaves me to do the rest. At the door she says, her chin raised, "If you try anything again, ever — it will be bad for you. Very bad." She turns on her high heels and stalks away.

My injuries turn from red to purple to shades of green and yellow. There is nothing I can do to cover up the damage. My eye gradually opens but I look as if I have been in a boxing ring. When Matt sees me, he flinches. He steps forward as if to say something, but I drop my eyes and turn away.

My lower leg is worse. The cut on my shin is not healing well and the bruises have swollen right around my calf. The pain when I take a step sears through me. I limp around the house, though I try to hide it. I don't want to do anything to remind her of that day.

I wish I could take pictures of my face and my leg, as proof, to add to my journal, but I can't: I have no phone and no camera. So I do my best to describe what they look like. My journal logs every cruelty, every crime committed against me, as evidence for when I escape, for the police. If they believe me, which they probably won't. My word, an illegal immigrant — for that is what I am now, with no passport, no official status, no money — against the word of a rich British man and his beautiful wife?

The more I think about it, alone in my room with my smashed-up face and my throbbing shin, the lower my spirits fall. I am no more than a puppet on a string, kept here against my will to obey their every command. When she speaks to me, looking over my head, not in my eyes, I am the lowest form of life. I am not a human. She is not interested in my well-being — as long as I can still clean and wash clothes and iron and polish and lay tables. They don't see the need for me to have healthy food, fresh air or exercise. To bath, or wash my hair properly, or go to the hairdressers. To have nice clothes, young friends, to go to the cinema or a wine bar. Or to occupy my brain with learning, experience, relationships.

I grieve for all of this. I mourn my lost years. I was still a child when I came here. I believed my mother when she told me that I had a lifetime ahead of me. I had no interest in boys, not in any romantic sense — I thought I had time for that, once I had left my shyness behind, grown in confidence, turned into a young woman. It is all lost, left behind — falling in love, a first kiss, the late teenage years, full of possibilities.

I miss my family, my mama, my papa, my little sister, my lovely cousin Elena. The joy of a hug.

Human contact.

The anguish is a twist in my chest, a rock in my belly.

CHAPTER NINETEEN

Sofia

I can't give up. I am the only person who can change this situation. I must drag myself out of this ditch of despair and find a way to escape, or accept a life of drudgery and oppression, a life not worth living. I can't do that — I would rather kill myself. Only I have the knowledge, the motivation, the will to get out of it.

Somehow, as my body heals, my mind recovers its focus. I tell myself over and over: this cannot last forever. One day soon, if I stay sharp, an opportunity must come. The boy came, and that was an opportunity, but I missed it. The next time I must be ready with every brain cell I possess.

I start to plan again. To make a sign, I need a good pen and some paper. The pen I already have, but I must find enough paper or cardboard for the message to be seen. I still have the other keys, the screwdriver, my collection of odds and ends that one day I might use to escape.

Madam is out and I am cleaning downstairs, my mind in Bulgaria, picturing my family. I can almost smell the fresh bread my mother makes, the tomatoes left on the windowsill to ripen. I see her faded apron, her hands white with flour. I feel the clean Bulgarian air on my cheeks, the soft, rich earth under my feet. My father is out there, working on the soil, his back bent over lines of fresh vegetables ripening for market.

Back in the present, I pause to gaze into the garden. The sun shines on the autumn trees beyond the lawn, leaves glistening with last night's rain in a canopy of gold and yellow and rust. Suddenly Matt is there, outside the back door, his key poised, ready to enter. I start and turn away, but he is right beside me.

"It's a beautiful day," he says.

I nod, my eyes on the floor. What does he want from me?

"Would you like to sit outside for a few minutes while she's out?"

I am so shocked I drop the duster and stare openly into his face.

"Go on, the fresh air will be good for you," he says, holding the door open.

I shake my head. "I can't . . . if she . . . Madam . . ."

"Don't worry, she won't be back for hours. It's okay, I promise. It's warm in the sun."

I pull my sleeves down over my hands and step out onto the terrace, my feet uncertain on the unfamiliar surface. Matt nods, waving me over to a seat at the edge of the grass.

"Go on," he says.

I scuttle to the seat and sit, shocked at the sudden turn of events. Suspicion makes me tense. Is this some kind of trap, where Madam comes back and finds me, not only not working, but sitting lazing in the garden? She will surely kill me if that happens. But Matt carries on with his work as if he trusts me not to run.

I think briefly about escaping, but I am tired, my leg still painful from the kicking Madam gave me. If I run, Matt will catch me in a moment.

I think about the boy next door, so close to me now. Perhaps he might kick a ball into the garden by accident, and climb over the fence again. What would I do if he appeared right now? I wouldn't mess up again — I'd plead for help, even though Matt is here — I would have to. But there's no sound from next door, not even the dog. The boy must be at school, the dog curled up inside the house.

The warmth of the sun on my face is irresistible. The sensation of calm, the smell of damp grass and earth, the heavenly trill of birdsong: I surrender to it all, like a drug swirling around my body. I close my eyes and lift my face to the golden sunlight, absorbing its goodness into every pore of my dusty, deprived skin. If I decide to run, I am not sure my body will obey the order. I am more in the moment than I have been for as long as I can remember. My mind drifts and I forget, for a few blissful moments, where I am.

But it is over all too soon.

"You'd better go in now." Matt is at my side. "You need to finish your work before she gets back."

I stand and take one last gaze at the garden, drawing in the fragrant air with a deep breath. I want to capture it in my arms and carry its precious goodness to my stuffy, dusty room. Release it and watch as the room is transformed, as if by fairy dust, into a haven.

"Thank you."

There's a strange smile on Matt's face as he locks the door behind me.

* * *

I half-expect there to be trouble when Madam gets home, but she continues to ignore me.

I don't understand. Matt works for them, he is one of them. But it seemed a kind thing to do, to let me enjoy some fresh air and sunlight. He didn't have to do it, and there would have been trouble for him if Madam had found out. What is he doing? I am confused and still suspicious. I would like to think he is human after all, but there is danger in that. I can't suppose that one act of kindness means he will help me escape. He caught me last time and gave me up to

Madam, so he will do it again. He knows I am a prisoner and he does nothing about it. So he is not a good person.

But I note his kindness in my journal anyway. How wonderful it was to make that small, precious visit outdoors. It made me even more determined to get away.

I stay vigilant. I check the windows everywhere as I clean, quietly turn the handles on the outside doors to see if they are locked. I watch the front drive, and when the door buzzer goes I stand as tall as I can, straining every muscle to see who is at the gate, even though I know it is useless.

I haven't forgotten the sign. I know it's probably pointless, but at least I'm doing something to help myself. I need to make one big enough to be seen from a distance, but small enough for me to carry around every day without detection. The letters need to be big and black and clear. I have my pen, and I will use every drop of ink for this most important job.

Finding the paper is more difficult. I have plenty of opened-up envelopes, but nothing to hold them together to make a large enough sign. It may not be too difficult to find sticky tape — they don't hide it away, it is not obviously something that could help me escape. There might even be some in the kitchen drawer.

I swallow my impatience and wait for my chance, and after a few days I have gathered what I need. On the floor of my bedroom I carefully stick the flattened envelopes together into a big square of white paper.

Then I use the tiny nib of my pencil to draw the outlines of large letters, which I will fill in with ink. It takes a while, but I like the feeling of doing something useful, something that could really help me. When it's done, I sit back to admire my work. It's big and bold. "HELP ME" it says, in large black letters. You couldn't miss it, even from a distance.

I fold it carefully and tuck it into the waist of my jeans. There is no risk of it falling out there.

Now I am prepared.

CHAPTER TWENTY

Beth

In London, Beth's diary was always full. She loved to gather people around her, organise get-togethers over coffee or lunch, meet new people. At the school she made friends at the front gates and at events. The mothers from her children's year groups formed friendships, drank coffee together, had each other's children over to play. They were always in and out of each other's houses, helping each other with school runs, babysitting and homework dramas.

It was similar with the neighbours. Not all of them had children, but there were regular gatherings, Christmas drinks and Bonfire Night barbecues. Everyone was welcome.

She became firm friends with three women, all of whom lived within a few minutes' walk of her house. Annie, Rose and Jackie were around her age and lived similar lifestyles. Annie had a full-time job at the local council, Beth at the bookshop, while Rose and Jackie, who both had young children when Beth first met them, worked part-time from home.

Luckily the respective husbands also got on with each other, though the men weren't as close as the women. They worked full-time, often long hours — the women were the ones who dropped everything for a sick child or a forgotten book bag. It was the women who brought everyone together, who organised the social events, who opened up their houses, their cupboards and their hearts.

Beth had been at the centre of this social group and she loved it.

* * *

"How's the bookshop going?" Adam says one evening after supper. "Are you going to keep going with it?"

Beth puts down her book, stroking Ruff absently as he lies beside her. She'd been drifting anyway. The story wasn't gripping her and she was finding herself reading the same paragraph over and over.

"It's good," she says. "There are books coming in all the time, and they need a lot of sorting through, but I'm enjoying it. It's not the same as working in a proper bookshop, but it's keeping me going until I find something else."

"Any other options around? Not that I'm pushing you." Adam puts down his newspaper and takes off his reading glasses. Ruff yawns and stretches.

"I know you're not. I want to work — part-time, anyway, because of Ruff. Otherwise my brain will freeze. Problem is, there don't seem to be many jobs around here, apart from bar and cafe work. I might have to go a bit further afield. But I really don't want to commute."

"You should wait for the right thing to come along. I'm sure once you get to know more people, something will turn up."

Adam, though not as outgoing as she is, understands her need to be part of a group. He wants her to settle in here, to be happy like she used to be in Kingston.

"I've met plenty of people. None I could call friends, though, not yet anyway. The women in the bookshop are mostly retired: they're lovely, but a couple of generations ahead of me. I'm getting to know some of the dog walkers in the park, and I like Karen over the road — I think we'll be friends. It all takes time, though." She thinks wistfully of their former life in Kingston, the ease of seeing people when she needed company, the group of neighbours that she didn't fully appreciate at the time. They were lucky there, for a while. She misses it far more than she expected.

Adam watches her, a look close to concern on his face.

"Anyway, it's all still very new." She summons a smile. "What about you — how are your colleagues?"

"Yeah, they're all right, a good bunch. I don't expect they'll be friends, but that works for me. We'll get on fine." He reaches for her hand. "Are you sure you're okay?"

"Don't worry about me at all. You know me — I'll find my feet. It won't be long before I'm overdoing it again."

But her words sound hollow, even to her, and she turns away to hide the tears that spring unexpectedly to her eyes.

* * *

At the breakfast bar in her light-filled kitchen, Karen sets up the coffee machine. Beth perches on a bar stool.

"Are you okay? You seem a bit . . . flat," Karen says.

Beth sighs. "Adam's worried I'm not settling in, bless him."

It's difficult to hide, this sinking feeling. Waking up every morning wondering what to do with her day. The work at the bookshop is only four hours a week, not nearly enough to keep her occupied, and there's only so much dog walking she can do. She has no interest in fitness classes or the gym and she's reluctant to get involved in something she's not passionate about.

"So are you? Settling in, I mean?" Karen says, setting a mug of coffee in front of her.

"Not really. I don't feel settled yet anyway. The thing is . . ." She doesn't know Karen very well, but instinct tells her it's safe to confide in her. "The thing is, before, it was all very different. It was easier to meet people naturally — the neighbours in our row of terraced houses, other parents through school. That doesn't seem to happen at secondary school."

Karen smiles and sits next to her. "You're right about the school thing. I'm not allowed near the front gate. I have to drop the girls on the corner and they walk the last bit. Heaven forbid their friends see their mum. It's not you, Beth, it's a phase. When you've got young children, people get together because of them. It tails off as they get older. And the neighbours here keep themselves to themselves. But there are other ways to meet people."

"How? I can't find a job. The shop's all right but nothing will come of that. I'm no good with the fitness thing, it just isn't me. I used to think of myself as really sociable, but now I'm not so sure."

"You are sociable, Beth — you and Adam are the only people in the street who've ever managed to get the neighbours together."

Beth smiles. She's glad to have met Karen, at least.

"What about the kids, are they doing okay?" Karen asks.

"They're fine, they've both made friends and they seem to like the school, thank goodness. Adam's job's going well too. No, it's just me. I must sound ungrateful, moaning, when I've got a lovely new house and everything's going well for my family . . ."

"I completely understand. It's a new start for you, in a very different area. But you'll make new friends, I know you will. Apart from a job, you need something to occupy yourself that will also introduce you to new people. Come on, what are you interested in?"

Beth shakes her head. She's never been passionate about anything, really, except her husband and her children. And books. But reading is a solitary habit. It's unlikely to solve her problem.

"Books, I suppose. You know I used to manage a bookshop. I loved that. I read a lot. Mostly novels, but all sorts of fiction."

Karen slaps her hand on the worktop, startling Beth. "Well that's it, then," she says. "Set up a book club. I'll be your first member."

CHAPTER TWENTY-ONE

Beth

A book club! She stares at Karen with an unfamiliar flutter of excitement.

She's never been terribly keen to join a book group. Other people, even good friends, have different tastes from hers. She keeps a list of titles she wants to read and it seems a waste to spend time on books not on her wish list. But to start her own group? She could set the ground rules, expand her reading horizons and meet new people at the same time. Ideas begin to spark before she's even made a conscious decision.

"Genius! Why didn't I think of that?"

Karen laughs. "There you go! The perfect solution. We could ask Jenny, who came to your party? I'm pretty sure she'd be interested, and she probably knows other people who'd want to join. I could ask at the club. Perhaps you could put a notice in the school newsletter, ask people to get in touch? I assume there is a school newsletter?"

"I think so — an email one, anyway. And I could ask at the library. But aren't there already book clubs round here?"

"There might be, though I haven't come across one. There must be room for lots of them. I'm sure we'd get plenty of interest, especially as you have a background as a bookseller. You could even set up a website with the book choices, write a blog, put up reviews . . ."

"Whoa, steady on." She laughs. "I need to know it's going to work before I commit to things like that. But it's a great idea, Karen. Will you help me find people to join?"

"Of course. We can be the founding members. You make the rules, as you know what you're talking about. I'm happy to share the hosting — one month at mine, the next at yours?"

"Brilliant. I'll source the books and so on. I just need help getting started. Thank you, thank you! I feel better already. I'll go back and put some thoughts together — I'll email them to you. You can let me know what you think." Gulping down the rest of her coffee, she grabs her bag and makes for the door.

"Glad to be of help. Look forward to seeing your plans . . ." Karen's words fade as Beth strides towards her house, her mind alive with ideas.

* * *

So this is a "light-bulb moment". It certainly feels as if a new room has lit up in her mind. She can't imagine why she didn't think of this herself. Her mind whirls with bigger and more ambitious ideas.

A book club. A network of book clubs. A link with the local paper or even a radio station. Special deals at the local bookshop, events at the library. Perhaps, once the club is established and the members know each other better, they can watch films of the books, run theatre visits, go to see authors at book festivals.

She could start a literary festival. There are plenty around the country, but she's not aware of one here. They could add on a children's event, run it with the schools . . . It's a big idea, but surely she could get something like that going?

What about her own bookshop? Why hasn't she thought of that before? Adam would support her, she's sure of it. She knows how to sell books, and she would love to get back into the business. It can't be difficult to find a suitable place — there are plenty of empty shopfronts in the high street.

She imagines a small but characterful building, a large, warm room lined with beautiful wooden bookshelves, a corner with comfortable seating, a coffee machine always on the go. She could take Ruff with her, he would be the shop dog, welcoming people and snuggling up to them as they read. Her books would be well-chosen, a mix of fiction and non-fiction. There would be a cosy children's area. She would include new authors as well as best-sellers, invite local writers to talks . . . perhaps her book club could meet there, encourage more people into the shop . . .

But this is madness — her imagination's gone wild. She needs to make this happen first, start small with the book club, get people interested. She fires up the laptop and starts to type.

* * *

Beth's Book Club
A Proposal

A relaxed, welcoming book club for people local to the area who want to read and discuss books. A place to meet like-minded people who love literature.

Meetings to be held monthly on the first Monday of the month, alternately at Beth's house and Karen's house.

Beth will be Chair. She will nominate a replacement if she's unable to attend.

Starts at 7.30 p.m. and aims to be done by 9.30 p.m.

One book to be read per month.

Wine, soft drinks and nibbles (not supper) provided by Beth/ Karen. A small cash contribution from each member is suggested.

No more than 15 members at any one time (might be too many all at once but need to ensure enough people attend each month to make a good discussion).

Once the membership is full, current members can propose new ones to be put on a waiting list. All new members to be approved by the group.

Members must read at least 100 pages of the chosen book to attend (mustn't just turn up for the wine and chat!).

Beth to facilitate library involvement/discount at local bookshop.

The person who proposes the book to contribute a small amount of research on the author and/or the book at the meeting when their choice is discussed (nothing too time-consuming!).

No non-fiction, biography/autobiography or graphic novels.

A mixture of classics and contemporary from any genre.

Books should preferably not be too long for people to read in one month.

People's opinions to be respected and each person given the chance to make their point(s) without interruption (chair to control the discussion to ensure fairness).

Website, blog, reviews to be discussed as a group.

Marking system — do we need one, and if so, on what criteria should it be based?

Anything else?

CHAPTER TWENTY-TWO

Sofia

I lose heart with every day that passes. My paper sign is fading. The folded corners begin to rip, however careful I am with it. I make another one, just in case. It passes the time. Now I have two signs, one on each side of my waistband.

I think of the dog. I pray for it to find the hole again, run to me as I sit in the garden the next time Matt allows me — if there is a next time. I would hug it and play with it and it would lick me and nuzzle me and offer me all the love I am missing. Sometimes I hear it barking in the garden next door, the sound muffled by the windows. I wonder if it plays with a ball, or the boy.

I imagine the boy and his life. His clothes looked clean and new, he seemed strong and healthy, his hair was neatly trimmed. He was my age, possibly a year or so younger. Perhaps he goes to school: when I saw him it was late afternoon, so that would make sense. I wonder if he likes his school, what subjects he enjoys, if he is good at languages like me. Football, perhaps: he looked sporty. Does he have brothers and sisters? There could be many of them; perhaps they will all come looking the next time the dog escapes. I long to meet them, to make friends, to see their rooms, listen to their music, share their meals.

I never imagined I would miss school, but I do. My mind feels shrunken, as if there is empty space where my brain should be. Can a person catch up with all the missed learning after years of nothing? Does the brain lose the ability to absorb information, when the body finishes growing, perhaps? If — when — I get out of here, I will thank God every day for everything he gives me: my education, my family, my beautiful country. I will never, ever take anything for granted again.

But — will I thank God? Do I even still believe in God? I am not sure, these days. Probably not.

At home my family, along with most of our neighbours and friends in the village, are regular worshippers at the church. It is a beautiful building made of stone, set a little above the village, its tower looking out across the valley. Inside, a golden light flows through the highest windows. I love being there. A deep sense of calm falls on me every time I step through its carved wooden doors and every time, after the service, I feel refreshed. I wonder if I will ever see the church again, ever feel that peace.

I grew up believing that God is good. I believed He would be kind to me, He would take care of me and my family, and never desert me. The sad thing is, and I have only come to realise this in the past few months: my prayers were well rehearsed, but I am not sure I ever really meant them. Or even understood them, not properly. Perhaps God is punishing me for taking Him and His goodness for granted.

But if God is good, why would He treat me like this? Why cause me such terrible pain? What have I done that He would take me from my family, leaving them struck down with grief, as I know they must be? This is a great and ghastly punishment. It is hard for me to believe I am that bad — I have not killed anyone, been cruel to small children or animals, stolen from the old or the weak. I am not a criminal. Do I deserve this terrible punishment? It makes no sense to me.

I am losing my faith. I fear it might be another step towards losing my humanity. I steal and lie, I curse and plot against my captors. I want revenge — oh, how I want my revenge! I want to beat her, kick her like she kicked me, until she's bleeding and weeping and sobbing, I want to destroy all her beautiful clothes and her brash, flash jewellery. Smash and scratch and burn her smart, stupid sports car with its show-off number plate.

I want to lock her up and leave her somewhere with no food or water. No phone, no TV, no money, no smart bathroom, no slaves to do her dirty work.

Then perhaps I will get some peace.

* * *

Madam has two friends for lunch today and I must stay out of the way. I have set the table in the dining room, obediently carried the trays of food from the kitchen. I do not spit in the dishes, but I do manage to steal a sliver of fish, a mouthful of coleslaw and a couple of tomatoes for later. There is nothing cooked, just dishes of smoked salmon, green leaves, mixed raw vegetables, no bread. Madam watches her weight and spends a fortune on her skin. It is important to her that she looks good, no doubt. Sir needs a beautiful woman on his arm, not a fat housewife. And she wouldn't want her husband to stray, not with all that money.

I peep at her friends from the top of the stairs. They never look up. They are so like her they could have come from the same biscuit tin. They're glossy, beautiful and sharp-faced. They teeter on shoes worth more than my family home. Their hands flash with diamonds and other precious stones. Their smiles are stiff, as if they fear their faces will crack. They speak Russian in loud, confident voices, their laughter so shrill it could shatter the stone tiles of the floor. They smoke incessantly, the acrid stench of cigarettes drifting up the stairwell of the house, tainting the air.

Today I have been told to clean all the skirting boards. All of them, in every room in the house. I have to dust and wipe and polish and my work will be checked later. This morning, before her guests arrived, I had to rush through my normal work to make sure the downstairs was all done.

In the spare bedroom above the drawing room, away from where she is entertaining, I take a break. My back aches, my knees are bruised from kneeling on the unforgiving floors. I stand at the window, which today is spattered with raindrops. When I look through them, the garden is transformed into another place. It has been raining for some time, the sky just beginning to clear, blue showing through the grey-white trails of clouds. When I look up, I always think of home, because the sky is the same there, and my mama could even be looking at the same spot as I am now.

I am about to turn away when a movement catches my eye. I freeze, my eyes focusing on a place near the bottom of the garden. I gasp — there! The little black dog is back, running to and fro in excited circles, his nose to the ground like he is following a crazy rabbit in some strange animal dance. My heart beats hard, so hard I can't breathe. Please God, let someone come to fetch him. I will believe again, if only You have someone come, and they look up and see my sign. I fumble at my waist, pull out the flimsy paper, pushing it up against the window. The panes are too small, the words partly hidden. I try to position it so the words can be seen. With my other hand I wave, frantic, short movements to catch an eye, even though I see nobody.

I peer through the raindrops. Perhaps they don't know yet that he's gone, and I am waving in vain. But I don't have too much time, they must come soon, they must. I wave as if my life depends on it. A slight shiver runs down the fence — the creeping plant on this side is waving around, though there is barely any wind. Yes, there! A hooded figure appears, a leg straddles the fence, a flurry of movement in the bushes below. I can't see if it is the boy or someone else. I wave and wave, I move the sign from side to side: any movement at all to catch their attention. The dog is on the far side of the grass, in the low planting. There is no sign of Matt. He stops work in the garden when it rains, though he could still be here, fixing and repairing, as he does from time to time. This has to work, it has to!

The dog reappears, running in and out of the flowerbed on my right. The figure hurries after it along the edge of the grass— yes, come closer! I jump and wave and almost drop the sign, then clamp it to the window, willing it to be visible from below. The dog is cornered by a low wall; the figure bends to gather him up. It pauses for a moment as if to take breath, a hand pushing a lock of hair from a face, and the person looks up. A woman's face looks right at me — I can see her eyes register the sign, my waving hand, my urgent mouthing of the words, "Help me, help, help me, please help me . . ." The hand rises in a half-wave — she has seen me! I am frozen in position, both hands against the cold glass of the window as she turns away and hurries back down the garden.

I sink to the floor, shaking, my sign crushed in my trembling hand.

Someone has noticed me, at last.

CHAPTER TWENTY-THREE

Beth

"How does that sound — do you think it'll work?" Beth says.

"I do," Adam says. "It sounds really good. Not that I know anything about book clubs, really. It seems like a woman's thing to me."

Beth frowns. "No reason why it should be. It'll be open to everyone."

"I don't know many men who read novels — not as much as you and your friends do, anyway. Most of my friends read non-fiction, biographies, historical stuff. But there must be some who like fiction, I suppose."

"Of course there are. I'm going to add that it's open to everyone over eighteen. It would be great to have a mix of people — they'll bring different perspectives." She adds another bullet point to her book club guidelines.

"Hmm. It would take a brave man to join a group of . . . how many did you say? Fifteen women? . . . to discuss a novel."

Beth laughs. "Don't be so old-fashioned. Anyway, if it's open to all, we might end up with a good balance."

"You'll have to think about the mix of titles too. How will you choose?"

"We'll do it democratically. At the end of the year, each member will propose a title for the following twelve months and we'll vote. A mix of contemporary and classic — hopefully everyone will get to read something they wouldn't normally choose. So any male members can put their own suggestions forward. Even if they come up with books we wouldn't normally pick up, it'll be interesting. That's what a book club is all about: reading more widely."

"As long as everyone understands that, I suppose. Yes, I would go for it. They don't have to join if they don't agree with the principles of the group."

"True." She looks at her laptop, where the guidelines stare back at her, seeming suddenly too draconian. "You don't think I've overdone the rules, do you?"

"No, I think they sound entirely reasonable. Anyway aren't you passing them by Karen first, to get her input?"

"Yes, and I imagine she won't hold back if she disagrees."

But she's still unsure, an unwelcome feeling in the context of her new-found enthusiasm. She sighs. Perhaps she should keep the guidelines short, reword some of them so they don't sound too much like rules. Or maybe, if Karen agrees, they should check with the initial group and ensure everyone's happy with the guidelines before they start. That would be the most democratic way to do it.

She can't risk upsetting people before she even knows them. This time, with a new group of friends, she's going to be very, very careful.

* * *

"Come on then, Ruff, let's put you out . . . Ruff?" She's been upstairs tidying the children's rooms and hasn't seen him for a while. Did she let him out before? Sometimes he's a terrible fidget, asking to go out, coming in after a few minutes and then barking to go out again. Often she can't remember if he's in or out.

She checks the sitting room, then goes through the kitchen to the back door. It's a grey autumn day, damp and dark. All morning the clouds have been pressing down on the gardens as if to choke the daylight from them, and only now has the drizzle stopped. She peers through the window, her eyes searching the flower beds along the sides of the lawn, but it's impossible to see. Sometimes she wishes they'd bought a white dog — it would get dirty, but at least she could keep an eye on it more easily.

She has a bad feeling. If he's escaped, she's going to have to go next door yet again to retrieve him, on her own, clambering through the muddy flower beds to catch him. If she's seen it could be embarrassing, after all she would be trespassing, but she's reluctant to go to the front gate as she really should do. As usual when she's alone and doing the housework, she's not dressed for seeing other people — particularly not someone like Oksana. She imagines that even dressed casually, Oksana will be in silk and satin, wafting around the house like a model in the Paris fashion shows.

Today, Beth is in an old pair of jeans, muddy from this morning's walk, and a tatty grey sweatshirt that Adam wears when he's gardening, over a couple of layers of T-shirts that escape from the bottom of the sweatshirt. Her face is free of makeup and her hair is like a bird's nest from the damp air.

She grabs her dog-walking coat — also rather grubby — slips her feet into wellies and trudges down the garden to get the step ladder.

Though the fence is sodden, the top slippery with lichen, a splinter wedges itself painfully in her bare palm as she pulls herself over.

"Shit," she says quietly, sucking the flesh at the base of her thumb. It's a big splinter and has gone right in, but it will have to wait until she gets back.

Cursing, she heads for the bottom of Oksana's garden, where the winter trees drip into laurel bushes and holly grows in unkempt clumps. Everything is soaking wet. Calling and whistling softly, she ducks into the gloom, twigs clutching at her arms, her feet squelching through layers of rotting autumn leaves. There's no sign of Ruff. She's beginning to wonder if he's back in her own garden, digging a hole in some secret corner. She should have checked thoroughly first; how stupid of her. But after a few minutes of calling and listening, there's a scuffle a few feet away and Ruff appears, soaked through and muddy, his tail wagging furiously, his nose to the ground. He pounces, as if he's found something, then disappears into the undergrowth.

"Ruff, you rascal — come here! Come, I've got treats, come..." She doesn't have treats. That was another mistake. Or a lead. But she's here now and she must get him, or suffer the humiliation of being seen in this muddy and dishevelled state. She ventures after him into the bushes.

"There you are!"

Ruff looks up at her, his tail high, tongue hanging. He's panting with excitement. Dark earth is scattered around his mud-caked feet, the beginnings of a hole dangerously close to a well-tended shrub. He looks filthy — that's going to make things worse getting back over the fence.

"Come here, come!" She reaches for him, but he's too quick. He darts around her, trotting towards the house, dipping in and out of the flower beds. Cursing softly, she gives chase along the edge of the manicured lawn, keeping her head down, hoping there's nobody looking from the blank windows of the house. Her wellies make an odd flumping noise as she runs. She corners him by a low wall, and to her relief he surrenders and sits, his eyes full of guilt. She bends to gather him up. As she straightens, despite herself, her eyes are drawn towards the house.

Something's moving in a first-floor window. A young, white-faced girl, jumping and gesticulating, holds a sign against the window. She's trying to say something, her mouth wide with urgency.

The sign says, in big, bold letters: *HELP ME*.

Beth is transfixed, gazing upwards at the house while Ruff struggles in her arms. In the girl's eyes she sees despair, panic, hope. She knows, instinctively, that this is no teenage prank. She lifts her free hand in acknowledgement, turns and hurries back down the garden.

CHAPTER TWENTY-FOUR

Beth

She bathes Ruff, shutting him in the kitchen to dry. Her jeans are wet and filthy, her hair heavy with damp, but she barely notices.

Her mind whirrs with the image of the girl at the window. Who is she? Is she a prisoner there? What's happening to her that she should make such a dramatic plea?

She sits on the edge of the bed and tries to think logically. The girl saw her wave, knows she understood. Should she go round straight away, confront Oksana? But if Oksana denies there's anyone there, she will be forced to back down, leave without any idea what's going on. She can't demand to search the house. If the girl is in danger and Beth tells Oksana what she's seen, it could make things worse.

She could tell the police. On the whole, Beth believes in the police. She trusts them to be measured and sympathetic. She's pretty certain they won't overreact. No reason for them to get a warrant, just a polite visit, a chat on the front doorstep. It might not get a result, but they will keep a record, note the incident. If there is something going on, Oksana and Keith will be warned, and they may take heed.

But will that, by its very nature, endanger the girl? If Oksana and Keith find out she's been signalling, they'll surely not be happy. Even if the girl is staying with them legitimately, and the sign is a hoax, they will be angry with her for causing trouble. And if she's genuinely in trouble, what then? Could involving the police create an even worse situation?

Beth could go round on some pretext and — what? She could ask Oksana if they have guests, although that might at the very least sound strange, if not downright nosy. Memories of last time make her shudder. She could pretend to be looking for a cleaning lady, ask if Oksana uses one. Then, if the girl is some kind of domestic help, Oksana could say so and it would all be cleared up.

Unless, of course, the girl is indeed a domestic helper, and is being forced to work for them against her will. Beth has read the stories in the papers — immigrants being forced into domestic slavery, unpaid and isolated from friends and family.

But now she's being dramatic. It's hard to believe that here, in this middle-class, wealthy suburban area, anyone would need to abuse their staff. But maybe Adam is right: the more money there is, the easier it is to commit — and hide — a crime.

She could go round on a pretext and ask to use the bathroom. Once upstairs she could have a surreptitious look around. But the house is huge. It would be strange if there wasn't at least one downstairs toilet. She can't creep around someone else's house — what would happen if she was discovered? The embarrassment would be dreadful.

She will have to go to the police.

* * *

Feeling like a nervous teenager, she approaches the front desk. It's set behind a sliding glass window, like the one at the children's school, probably to protect the receptionist from unsavoury characters, or possibly assault. She can imagine what the place is like late on a Friday or Saturday night, when people have been drinking, tempers running high.

The policeman behind the window looks about sixteen, not much older than Tom, his forehead speckled with acne, his hands small and soft. He's dealing with an elderly man who seems confused by a form he's holding, and the young policeman is waiting patiently for him to read a section of it.

"When you're ready, sir, please sign at the bottom," he says, handing the man a biro. The blue lid is chewed and misshapen. Beth wonders if the pen belongs to him, if the teeth marks are his.

"I'll just take it and sit down," the elderly man says. "I need to get my reading glasses out and read it properly."

"Of course," the boy replies and, as the man shuffles away, looks at Beth with an expectant lift of his eyebrows. "Can I help you, madam?"

Taken aback by the formality, she wonders if it's only the police who still call people 'sir' and 'madam'. It feels oddly old-fashioned, out of place in this battered room, which must have borne witness to all manner of dramas.

She had thought about calling the police station rather than visiting in person, but she felt too agitated to explain on the phone, and she didn't want to be fobbed off. Having made the decision to report the incident, she needs to make sure they understand.

It's awkward, talking to this lad — little more than a boy — with the old man sitting within earshot. She leans forward over the grubby counter, trying not to let the arm of her coat touch the surface.

"Could I speak to your . . . er . . . manager, please?" A flush of embarrassment starts to crawl up her neck. Its warmth reaches her cheeks as, flustered, she tries to rephrase her words. "I mean, is there someone around who could take a statement, do you think?"

"Are you reporting a crime?"

"I . . . I'm not sure. I think so. It's a suspicion, really. It could be a crime, in which case it could be serious, but . . ." Now she's babbling. She closes her mouth.

The young man, with remarkable poise, says, "Can I ask what it's concerning?"

This causes her even more discomfort. She's underestimated him and she's cross with herself. "Ah . . . I'm worried — very worried — about a young girl. At a neighbour's house."

"Do you think she's in danger?"

"I think she might be, yes, but . . . I don't know for sure."

With an air of serious concentration, the boy writes this down in a small notebook, pressing hard on the paper. When he's finished, he tears out the page and indicates to Beth.

"I'll be one moment. Please take a seat."

She sits awkwardly on the seat furthest away from the old man.

It's not long before the door next to the front desk opens and the young policeman beckons her through. She follows him in silence through a maze of unadorned corridors, past partitioned offices, a set of toilets, a staircase to the upper floor. At last they stop at a door marked Interview Room 3 and she's shown into a shoebox of a room with a table and four chairs, nothing else. The young man withdraws, closing the door.

After ten minutes she's beginning to feel anxious and hot, wondering if she's done the right thing, coming here. But then the door opens and a slim man in black jeans and an open-necked shirt joins her, holding his hand out in greeting. When she takes it, his grip is firm and dry. His eyes seem to search hers for hidden secrets.

"I'm DI Thomson," he says, pulling out a chair. He sets a notepad in front of him. "Your name, please?"

He writes carefully in a box, adding her address, phone number, email address. His writing is large and clear. She reads upside-down almost as well as she reads normally, so she watches every word to make sure he gets it right.

"Now. I understand you want to report a possible crime?" he says, fixing her again with that intense gaze. He already looks as if he knows everything.

"Yes — at least, I'm worried it could be something suspicious," she says, stumbling over the word "suspicious" as if she's somehow guilty of a crime herself. This always seems to happen to her if she's dealing with a person in authority. It's a throwback to her girlhood: her father, a military man, instilled in her a respect for authority that spilled over into fear, and she's never grown out of it. She hopes the detective doesn't take her nervousness for guilt, or worse, a sign that she's lying.

She falters her way through the story, starting with the first time Ruff escaped and Tom noticing the girl at the window. When she gets to her own part she describes the girl's cry for help in some detail, looking for his recognition that she's right to be concerned. He nods and writes as she speaks, stopping to ask what the time was, approximately, when she saw the girl, what she knows about Oksana and Keith, whether she's been in the house. Most of the time, she looks at the top of his head as he writes, observing the short, no-nonsense haircut, the parting to the right, the strong, healthy hair of a young man.

He makes no comment until she's finished. Then he asks her to confirm that what he's written is correct, and reads the whole story out loud.

"Are you happy that this is a correct statement of the incident?" he says.

By now, Beth is getting impatient. She needs to know if she's being ridiculous, if this is really something to worry about, if the girl is in danger — and if that's the case, this is all taking too long.

He sits for a moment, contemplating the sheet in front of him.

"Anything else?"

"I want to know if this is serious," she says, in a rush. "If she's in danger, if these people are harming her. She looked so young, and frightened. I'm really concerned. What will you do to help her?"

"We'll pay them a visit," the detective says.

"You may find Oksana at home," Beth says. "But I doubt the husband will be there. There's a gardener sometimes too. I don't know his name."

DI Thomson makes a note.

"What happens if they're out?" she says.

"We'll leave our details, ask them to contact us to arrange another visit."

"Surely that will give them time to cover up whatever it is they're doing?"

He sits back, shrugs his shoulders. "There's not much we can do about that, I'm afraid, unless we have clear proof of criminal activity before we go."

"When will you go?"

"I can't confirm that right now, it depends who we have available. In the next day or so, I hope."

They will ask a few questions, say they've heard a young girl has been seen there and they've been asked to check on her well-being. Beth's torn between relief that they believe her and concern that they will find nothing.

A sudden thought occurs to her, shades of the past rising from the corners of her mind. "Will you have to say who reported it?"

"Not if you'd rather we didn't. Though I imagine they'll have a good idea."

"I would prefer it if you didn't. I don't want to seem like the nosy neighbour." She catches a look of scepticism on the detective's face. "Don't get me wrong, I'm pretty sure there's something untoward happening there. You don't hold up a sign like that for a joke — she must have prepared it in advance, and waited. It's not often members of my family climb over the fence and trespass in somebody's garden. And I wouldn't waste your time if I didn't think it was genuine."

He nods, closes his notebook. "I'm sure you wouldn't. Thank you for coming in. We'll take it from here."

"But . . . will you let me know what happens?" She's reluctant to leave it at that, if only to make sure something is done. It's hard to tell if the detective is taking her seriously or if the report will go to the bottom of a long list.

"If you'd like to call in a week or so, and ask for me, I will update you," he says, handing her a card. "Now, if you'll excuse me . . ."

"Of course," she says, fumbling with her bag.

On her way out the reception has filled up, and there's a queue for the desk. Many eyes follow her as she leaves.

* * *

"Are you sure that was wise?" Adam gives her a dubious look as she clears the table.

"Dad, the girl could be in terrible trouble!" Tom says. "We have to do something. I think Mum's right to involve the police."

"Yes, thank you, Tom," Adam says. "I was just making sure Mum was comfortable with what might happen with the neighbours."

"I know what you mean — of course I do," Beth says. "But we — I — can't ignore a cry for help. The girl looked terrified. What if something bad is happening and we ignore it? I'd never forgive myself."

"I know." Adam glances at the children, then back at Beth. "But we need to be prepared for their reaction."

Beth knows what he's saying. As she clears the table, she thinks back to that time in Kingston, when she made a similar decision and everything went horribly wrong. Disastrously wrong.

It is different here, though. They barely know Oksana, and they haven't even met Keith. If they have to move house again because relationships with the neighbours here have gone sour, then it wouldn't have the kind of impact it had before. There, they lived in each other's pockets — here, they barely see the people next door from one month to the next.

And yet Beth trembles inwardly at the thought. Neighbourly disputes can turn really nasty. If anyone knows that, it's her.

CHAPTER TWENTY-FIVE

Sofia

My room — if you can call it that — gives me no comfort, no sense of safety. It is just bare walls and floorboards. My prison cell.

I know every mark on the ceiling and the walls, I have lain on my mattress so often and stared at them. There is a long scratch on the sloping ceiling above my head. It has damaged the paint and on one side tiny cracks have appeared. I have often wondered how it got there. Next to me, there is a chunk of white plaster missing and some little scratch marks around it, as if someone has picked away at the hole.

Over by the window is a patch on the wall that reminds me of the shape of Africa. Sometimes I look at it and pictures of wild animals stroll across my mind, elephants and giraffes and lions.

The walls are not so much painted as covered up — a single coat of off-white paint, the brush marks clearly visible. The floor is not nice to walk on. I worry about splinters in my feet, and I have put an old towel on the floor by my bed so that at least when I get up in the morning I can step onto something soft. The little triangle of window at the top of one wall is so high I can't reach it, or see anything from it — except, sometimes, a lone bird flying high on the breeze. It does not open or let in much light, but I am glad of any daylight in this tiny space. One day I will find a way to see out. If I can find a sturdy box, or a waste-paper bin that would hold my weight, I might just be able to reach, if I stand on tiptoes. The only other light I have is a single bulb hanging shadeless from the middle of the ceiling. Its light is harsh, but at least I don't have to spend the evenings in the dark.

Apart from my journal, biting my nails and daydreaming, there is little else to do up here. I clean my room sometimes when Madam is out or busy on the phone. I bring the vacuum cleaner up here, spray some of her expensive fragrance around, if I am feeling brave. I wash the bedclothes and towels. I move the mattress to the opposite wall and sleep the other way round, just to be different.

But mostly I lie on my side and stare at the walls. Sometimes when this happens, I plan my escape. More often I am helpless with homesickness.

* * *

"What is wrong with your face?" Madam's voice cuts through the blare of the radio in the kitchen.

I am startled by the sound and spin around to face her. She rarely speaks to me, never asks a question. The word "wrong" sounds particularly harsh. She stares openly at my face as I stand, uncertain, the vacuum cleaner by my feet like a faithful dog.

I know what she's talking about. I have a terrible, flaky rash. It started a few months ago around my mouth, the redness spreading upwards to my nose, like a child with a permanent cold. My cheeks are rosy, as if I have a fever, and my chest itches beneath my old black T-shirt. When I sweat, which is often, my skin catches fire. At night it keeps me awake for hours. Sometimes I hold a damp cloth against the worst parts to cool it down, but it only dries it out even more.

This never happened at home. But in this house I breathe only stale air. I haven't taken a proper bath or a shower since I left home. I can't treat myself to creams and moisturisers to help my skin, so it only gets worse.

"I . . . it is a problem. It itches and I cannot sleep. I need creams, a doctor."

Madam frowns. "A doctor? That is not possible. Wait a moment." She turns to the kitchen, her heels tick-tocking on the tiles as she returns with her mobile phone. "I will take picture." She moves closer to me, her perfume wafting over me as she leans into my face. She takes photos from the front and both sides, moving my head to the light as if I am a dummy in a shop window. Her false eyelashes are perfectly in line, her lips painted a creamy pink that shines when she speaks.

I feel like a criminal in a police station.

"Your arms, your hands?"

My poor hands are examined: the ugly nails bitten to the quick, the skin around them dry and cracked, the rash a red river spreading towards my fingers. I look away as she takes more pictures, a look of disgust on her doll-like face.

"Anywhere else?"

I lift my T-shirt, look stonily ahead as she bends to get the right angle.

She steps away from me, lifts her chin as if there is a smell beneath her nose. "I will ask pharmacy." She turns and clip-clops back to the kitchen.

I feel like a circus animal, a workhorse, worth keeping alive only for my labour.

* * *

I lie on my mattress, a fog of despair swirling around me. It has been days since the woman came into the garden for the dog, since she saw my sign and waved to me.

She did not believe me. Nothing I do will get me out of here. My cry for help failed. What did she think I was saying?

Did she imagine it was some childish game, some hide-and-seek secret, that made me ask for help? She must know I was serious. *HELP ME* is as clear as I can make it without writing my story on every window of the house. I cry, beat my head against the wall, scratch at my skin until it bleeds.

In a frenzy, I pull out all my envelopes and receipts and arrange them into a bigger shape, the size of an entire window. Painstakingly I stick them together. My roll of tape is running out so I have to leave gaps, but when I pick it up it holds together. On it I write, with my fading stub of pencil:

I AM
A PRISONER.
HELP ME PLEASE.

I make the letters as big as possible, then darken them with the pen. But after only the first short words, the ink runs out. I wet the end with my tongue, shake it, scribble madly on a spare piece of paper. Nothing. I am overcome with exhaustion. My body aches. I collapse on the floor, all emotion draining away. I am empty, a void, a nothing.

Without bothering to hide my things, not even the sign, I crawl to my mattress and, fully clothed, pull the bedclothes over my head.

* * *

Madam has given me a tube of cream for my skin. For one tiny, impossible second, I imagine she has a streak of kindness in her. But she says, "Is horrible, your skin, ugly. I don't want your skin on bed, in bathroom. Pharmacist says use two times a day. It is expensive. Do it properly."

I take the tube, say nothing, stare into those beautiful, cold eyes, not bothering to hide my contempt. For a moment she hesitates, a hint of uncertainty crossing her face. She opens her plastic mouth as if to say more, then closes it with a snap, waves in dismissal and stalks away.

I put the cream in my pocket and carry on with my work. I bang the vacuum cleaner against the skirting boards in the hallway, against the legs of the horrible mirrored furniture in the living room. I spit into decorative vases, turn one ornament, a rearing horse made in bronze, to the wall. I make a scratch on the leg of the wooden dining table. Small things, but slowly my anger fades. When I bump the cleaner up each stair, taking no care to avoid the banisters, her head appears round the kitchen door and she glares at me while someone's voice chatters on from the mobile in her hand. I know I'm overdoing it but I can't help it. She can treat me like this, but I will never bow to her.

She returns to the kitchen and her telephone call. I stop my work and curl up on the top step. Her voice carries up to me through the marbled hallway, the nasal Russian words echoing clearly around the huge space. I listen idly for a few moments, challenging myself to understand. She is talking to someone about a dinner she's planning. They discuss the invitation list, the food, the possible dates, and I can tell she's looking in her wall calendar from the sound of the flipping pages.

I am about to return to my work when I hear her say, in Russian, "I don't know. I am finished with her. She is no good. She is . . ." I can't quite catch this word. ". . . I do not trust her. She tried to escape, and she will try again. I want someone more . . ." Another word I don't recognise. ". . . yes, soon. I will tell Keith . . ."

CHAPTER TWENTY-SIX

Beth

Thinking about that time always brings back the terrible sinking feeling that plagued her for months afterwards. Despite the nervous energy it took wondering how she could have played things differently, wishing she could go back, she still finds it hard to accept. Was it really so wrong to do what she did? Did she deserve the reaction she got? She certainly regrets the outcome, more than anything in her life, and for a long time she was devastated by the fallout.

It had been her day off from the bookshop and she'd been to a regular coffee morning with the mums from Tom's year at school. One of the other mothers had been selling cakes and she'd bought a delicious-looking carrot cake that she knew the kids would love. Carrying it back to the car carefully, she noticed a small coffee bar in a side street, in a little-known area of Kingston where she sometimes managed to find a parking space. By chance, she crossed the road opposite the window of the shop, so was looking directly into it as she approached the pavement. The place was half-empty, most of the tables clear, but one of the sofas at the side was occupied. A couple sat talking, their shoulders touching, their faces earnest. As she stepped onto the pavement, balancing the cake carefully on one hand, Beth realised she knew the woman sitting on the left. It was Annie, her neighbour from three doors down, one of her best friends.

She was about to wave with her free hand when something stopped her. Annie turned towards the man and took his hand, her eyes gazing into his face. The man's head bent towards her, and for a split second Beth thought it was Jack, Annie's husband. But in that moment she knew it wasn't.

Startled, she tore her gaze away and hurried off down the street, grasping the cake like a shield in front of her. She wasn't sure what she'd just seen, but the intimacy of the moment had shocked her, and the hand that rummaged in her bag for the car keys was clumsy. She dropped the keys twice before she was finally able to press the button.

In the car, the cake safely stashed in the boot, she took a moment to calm herself. Was that what it seemed to be? Why was Annie not at work on the other side of Kingston? It was the middle of the morning, after all. And who was the man she was having such a serious conversation with? Annie seemed such a stable, loving wife and mother, Jack a devoted husband who adored their two children. She couldn't be having an affair, surely — Beth didn't want to believe it. But the little scene she'd just witnessed had looked exactly like that.

What on earth should she do?

* * *

Beth had two brothers, both older than her. As small children, the three of them often played boisterous games involving physical contact. The boys accepted her as one of them and she never felt left out.

As they grew up, though, they drifted apart. Beth became close to two girls from her class while the boys had many friends, mostly those who enjoyed kicking a ball around in the garden or cycling around the industrial estate practicing wheelies. The girls became indoor creatures. Their idea of fun was locking themselves into a bedroom, painting each other's nails and faces, playing pop music and laughing until they cried over nothing.

Beth loved those long, relaxed hours spent with her friends, when they talked about everything and anything. Sex, holidays, books, their latest heartthrob on TV, how mean their parents were. Love. Nothing was sacred when the girls got together. Later on they discussed their wombs, the heartbreak of a broken relationship, or how to help a child struggling at school.

Nowadays the friends were different and the chats were governed by school hours, jobs and the grindstone of running a family, but the women were no less intimate as a result. Beth, Annie, Rose and Jackie met every week, either for a quick coffee in someone's home — they all lived in the same street, in houses that were startlingly similar — or in the cafe just around the corner.

There was no question of Beth confiding in Adam about what she'd seen. Adam would tell her she was imagining things, that she should stay out of it, and that would be the end of the discussion. No, she would ask Rose and Jackie, when Annie wasn't around, find out what they knew, if anything, about problems in the marriage, or anything else that might explain what she saw.

It wasn't difficult to arrange a get-together without Annie, as she was the only one with a full-time job. It seemed odd, leaving her out on purpose, and Beth felt almost guilty, but then they often had coffee without her and she'd never worried before.

Their eyes grew round with surprise as she told them what she'd seen.

"Are you sure?" Rose said, clutching her coffee cup as if for reassurance. "You're sure it was her?"

"Absolutely sure. Listen, I didn't mean to imply anything, I was just . . . surprised."

"Honestly, Beth, I don't believe in a million years that Annie would cheat on Jack," Rose said. "She adores him,

I'm sure of it. I'm often envious of how close they are. I just don't believe it."

"You're right, it was probably nothing." Beth wanted to believe it, but there was something niggling at her, refusing to go away.

"It is strange, though," Jackie said, with a thoughtful look. "Didn't she say she was going to a funeral this week, somewhere near Manchester? Perhaps it was something to do with that."

"Could have been. Whose funeral was it, do you know?" Beth said.

"I think an elderly aunt, but I'm not sure. Perhaps it was her brother you saw her with?" Jackie sat up and smiled, as if she had solved the mystery, but Beth shook her head.

"She doesn't have a brother. Just a sister," she said.

Rose shifted in her seat, glancing sideways at Jackie. There was an awkward pause. Then she said, the words falling out in a rush, "I'm sorry, Beth, but I'm uncomfortable talking about Annie like this. I'm sure there's a simple explanation. And even if there isn't, it's none of our business."

In an instant, Beth felt shame crawling through her scalp like an army of ants. "No, absolutely — I really didn't mean to jump to any conclusions. I love Annie. I would never—"

"But you did, though, didn't you?" Rose said, replacing her cup in the saucer with a little too much force. All three women flinched. Then, pointedly, her mouth set in a hard line, Rose stood, picked up her bag and left.

CHAPTER TWENTY-SEVEN

Sofia

I freeze. I listen for a few moments, but she says no more about me. I turn and run to one of the guest rooms, the vacuum cleaner bumping at my ankles. I close the door with shaking hands.

She wants to get rid of me. Those words, so expressive in Russian, so full of meaning for me, beat around my mind like caged birds. I am so afraid. I sink to the floor, my back to the wall, and sob helplessly, biting the back of my hand to muffle the sound.

But I cannot give in, I must not. It's an effort to stand but I walk up and down the room in a frenzy, hoping it sounds as if I am working. I can't face her now, not yet. If she follows me upstairs and finds me like this, I don't know what might happen.

What does she *mean*? Will they pass me on to another cruel 'Madam,' worse than her? Things are bad here — but my worst fear, the one thing that has always terrified me, could happen if they move me on.

From the little I know of war, poverty, drug abuse, criminals, it is clear as crystal to me that women, girls, even tiny child-girls, are cruelly used. Though I have been treated like the lowest human that exists, I have not faced that. Keith shows no interest in me. He treats me like a domestic appliance, an object too base to be worthy of his attention — and for that I'm grateful. Even Matt, so often left alone with me, has never looked at me in that way, though he is young and strong and could easily take what he wants.

I know enough about sex to know it can be used to threaten and control. I understand how, since the start of the human race probably, the bodies of women and girls have been used by powerful men to satisfy their worst imaginings. How they are used and thrown away, like dirty rags.

I know I have been lucky so far in this way. And I will do anything — *anything* — to avoid it.

I calm myself, continue with my work, my mind spinning. Though the horror continues, I am angry too. Angry at myself — that I let my guard down, that I allowed Madam to see that I am not a doormat. She does not trust me. I have made it obvious I plan to escape, and I will not give up. She knows I am strong, she saw it in my eyes, and I was stupid — stupid to let her see that.

Later, in my room, I can't be still. She said "Soon." How soon? She will talk to Sir about it first, she said. I don't know when he is back — how can I find out? She could call him today, even. I'm panicking, panicking, I don't have time to plan.

Forcing myself to think, I scrabble through my belongings. There is not much that can help me — if there were, I would already have used it. I still have the keys, hidden away in the laundry room, but it takes time to try them out and I will surely be caught. I stare at the mess I have made on the floor. Nothing falls from heaven to help me.

* * *

I creep around the house, doing my work. I do it well, to impress her, though I do not believe she will notice. Especially now. I doubt I can change her mind. Nothing in my power will influence her. I know she hates me.

In the bedroom, I dust the dresser, the windows, the huge bedhead. Madam's wardrobe is open, and it wobbles a little when I close it. It is attached to the wall behind to stop it falling forward, and I notice that one of the fixings has loosened slightly, its screw a fraction out of place. I run my fingers over it, wondering if my screwdriver will fit. Tomorrow I will try it out.

It is late afternoon when the buzzer goes. Someone is at the gate. Madam appears from the kitchen as I stare from the dining room. She puts the handset to her ear, flicking her mane of blow-dried hair to one side, arching her neck to make room for her hand. I sidle behind the door and peer out, straining to hear.

"Yes?" she says in English, her voice loud, arrogant like a queen. She waits, listening.

"Excuse me? Please repeat." Her body stiffens, all her attention on what she's hearing. "I am sorry, now is not good time." There's a pause as the handset crackles with a distant voice. "I am sick, I cannot see you now. Another day perhaps." Again, a pause. "Very well. Goodbye."

She replaces the handset slowly. As she turns, I step back into the shadow behind the door, but I cannot miss the expression on her face. An angry red patch has appeared on each cheek and her eyes flash with fury as she stalks back into the kitchen, slamming the door behind her.

I creep into the hallway, duster in my hand. Her voice through the kitchen door resonates, harsh, demanding. She is speaking English: I hear Sir's name. I almost faint with terror as the door opens again with a crash, and turn away just in time. She says, into the phone: "Wait," and runs, as far as her heels will let her run, up the stairs.

A moment later her bedroom door slams.

CHAPTER TWENTY-EIGHT

Sofia

This is a crisis — I know it. It's about me, it must be. My hands shake, my legs are so weak I can barely force them upstairs. When I have finished my work, or as much of it as I can bear to do, I go to my room. On the way, I take a waste bin from the spare room, holding it in front of me as I climb to shield it, in case she appears on the landing.

I wish I could lock myself in. Then I might feel safe, at least for a while. I lie trembling on my bed, waiting for her footsteps on the stair, the key in my door, the darkness. I can think better once she has gone to bed.

I have a choice: I can wait here, helpless, or I can make something happen. Whatever chance there might be, I have to take it.

I imagine Sir coming home, a heated conversation, Madam throwing words around, her arms gesticulating. The heavy tread of his feet on my stairs, my thin body grasped and forced downstairs, into a car and away . . . to what?

In my room, there is only one possibility. The walls are strong, the door sturdy. The window is my only option. I am going to get out, if it kills me doing it. I will climb across the roof somehow, down a drainpipe. If there is a way out, I will find it. If not . . .

I wait until the door is locked and the click-clack of her footsteps has faded before I turn the light on. The waste-bin is far too small to help me reach the window. I need a chair. I drag the mattress across the floor, put the bin on to it and step up. It wobbles alarmingly. I pile my few clothes under the bin but I am still nowhere near. I fold the mattress in half, puffing and sweating with the effort, hoping she is asleep and not able to hear my feet or the dragging sounds I am making. Almost there, so close! But not close enough. In the bathroom I grab the lid from the cistern. It lifts away easily. Surely I can use this to get just a little more height? It is not enough. But it might be, combined with the toilet seat! I wrestle and pull and scrabble with my keys to find the fixing, I brace my back against the wall and kick as hard as I can. It comes away.

Panting, I create a hill as high as I can with this strange array of objects. The mattress is rolled over, the toilet lid and seat arranged to give me extra height, the upturned bin on top. It is not stable, but it might be enough. I clamber up and get my balance, my legs working to keep myself from falling. My fingers grasp the wooden surround of the window and I peer over the edge.

There is nothing to see. The night is black and closed, even if I strain my eyes and gaze deep into the darkness. I clamber down and turn off the light. Climbing up in the dark is difficult but I have done it once and I am desperate. But even without the light behind me, even though my eyes have adjusted, all I can see is a single, silver star in the sky.

Panting, I climb back down. I can't do this tonight. I need to be able to see what is out there, find a way to break the glass, or scratch away at the window-frame until the glass loosens. I am exhausted and weak with emotion. I put everything back in its place, hiding the waste bin behind the door to the toilet.

Tomorrow I will find a way.

* * *

It is still dark when I wake to the sound of the key in my door. I drag myself around the house, keeping my eyes down when I see her. This morning she is preparing to go out, her coat draped over the banister, her favourite bag on the hall table, the keys jangling in her hand as she takes a final sip of coffee.

The metal heels of her favourite shoes clack noisily on the marble as she leaves, with a single, cold glance back at me as I shuffle towards the kitchen. The door slams.

I wait a few breathless moments for the familiar crunch of gravel in the drive, the click of the gates behind her. I need to do my work in the usual order, in case she returns. Everything must look normal. But today I will do it faster than ever, and then I will take a chair up to my room and smash that window. I must. I can't delay. I have no idea how long she will be out.

It could even be today, the day that she gets rid of me.

In the drawing room, on a display shelf in the cupboard where the wine glasses are kept, is a small sculpture of a woman cast in smooth, black stone. She stands about thirty centimetres tall and is naked apart from a coil of fabric that she holds to her private parts. She is small enough to hide beneath my jumper and heavy enough — I hope — to break a window. She comes with me to the attic, together with a chair from the guest bedroom. I leave the vacuum cleaner running while I sneak them up, my feet soft on the stairs, my back slick with sweat.

I put the waste bin on the chair and step up, the figure in my hand. This time, in the daylight, I can see out. A few trees, a patch of garden, the fence and the end of the garden next door. The roof slopes away at quite an angle and it seems impossibly high from here, but I am hoping there will be a gutter at the edge of the slope, a pipe for me to hang on to. There is enough light for me to see, though it is already fading, so now would be a good time to break the glass and climb out. I hesitate, the sculpture weighing heavy in my hand. Am I ready to do this? I tremble at the thought of slipping on the slate, tumbling two floors down onto the hard flagstones of the terrace. But time is slipping away, and I may never get the chance again.

I take a deep breath, closing my eyes in a silent prayer. I check my balance, brace myself and lift the statue. I hurl it at the window as hard as I dare, the head of the woman connecting with a terrifying crunch with the glass. But the weight of the statuette knocks me off balance and I fall, my knee hitting the chair back with a painful crack. I land in an awkward heap on the floor. Grasping my throbbing knee, I listen for a sound downstairs, but there is nothing. I wait for another minute or two, but all I can hear is the distant drone of the vacuum cleaner.

It didn't work — there is no glass on the floor around me. Did it crack? I grab the sculpture and clamber back up, my knee protesting. Perhaps if I try turning the figure? The woman stands on a small square plinth carved from the stone, sharp corners contrasting with the smoothness of her curved body.

The glass seems intact; it must be stronger than it looks. I examine every corner to check for weak points, but it is firmly sealed at the edges. Running my fingers along the frame, I feel a roughness there. Something is carved into the wood in one corner. I shift my weight and peer at the painted wood until the words become clear.

My heart stops. I stare in horror at the roughly carved letters. They spell *HELP JULIA*.

CHAPTER TWENTY-NINE

Beth

The regular meet-ups for coffee stopped with a sickening suddenness that had Beth checking her phone for missed calls every hour. When she tried to arrange a get-together herself, texting her friends as usual, there was silence. Not one of them replied.

It very soon became clear that Annie knew. Beth tried phoning, but the call clicked through to voicemail and she couldn't think what to say that wouldn't make things worse. She composed a text, deleting it several times before she was happy with it, saying she was sorry she'd hurt her and could they talk, but there was no reply. Beth was distraught. This had not happened to her before: she had never fallen out with friends. It was entirely her fault and she cringed with embarrassment and self-loathing. Her gut twisted painfully whenever she thought about it.

One Saturday morning, she found the courage to knock at Annie's door.

After a few moments, the door opened, leaving only a crack of a few inches. Annie's face appeared. She didn't smile or invite her in. Beth, already tense and terrified, tied herself into knots.

"I . . . I just . . . Can I come in?"

"I'd rather not, actually." Annie's ready smile was remarkable by its absence.

Beth felt a flush of mortification creep up her cheeks. "I just wanted to say . . . Listen, Annie, I'm so sorry, it was stupid of me . . . I was wrong even to mention it. I jumped to the wrong conclusion and made an idiot of myself, and I'm so sorry. Our friendship means a lot to me — you mean a lot to me."

Annie nodded slowly, but the door stayed firmly in place. "Thank you for the apology — I appreciate it," she said. Her voice was like a shard of ice. The door began to close.

"No — wait, Annie, please? Can you forgive me? You know I wouldn't hurt you, knowingly, ever. I don't know why I . . . what came over me. Please, can we forget it happened?"

Annie opened the door wider. But her lips were set in a grim line. "Unfortunately, Beth, I can't forget it happened. What you — assumed — was untrue, based on nothing. I was having coffee with an old friend, that's it. End of story. It was unforgivable to share your . . . suspicions with anybody else. If Jack and I didn't trust each other implicitly, the repercussions could have been disastrous. You could have split our family up. Did you think of that before you opened your mouth?" The door was closed before Beth had even absorbed the words. She was left gasping on the doorstep like the last fish in a disappearing lake.

* * *

That was the end of it, or so it seemed. No more cosy coffee mornings — even the school run was awkward. If she saw any of the others, they would turn away, or if they couldn't avoid her they'd nod and keep walking. Even the children seemed to distance themselves from hers, with no more invitations, no sleepovers.

"It'll blow over," Adam said.

"I wish you were right." She'd never felt so bad in her life. "But I don't think so."

"It seems a bit childish. You would have thought Annie would at least talk to you, let you explain."

"The trouble is, there's nothing to explain. I was completely in the wrong. I made an assumption, even if I didn't actually say it. I thought she might be seeing someone, having an affair, whatever you want to call it, behind Jack's back. And I told the others. It was unforgivable, and now I'm paying for it. Everything's changed. How could I be so stupid?"

"Listen, it was a mistake. Perhaps it was an unfortunate mistake, but it does seem to me that she's taking it particularly badly."

"I know. Sounds like she's told Jack all about it. Have you noticed anything different about him, or any of the other men?"

"Haven't noticed, to be honest. Though I haven't heard from them for a while. Look, don't worry, I'm sure it'll sort itself out and we'll soon have forgotten all about it."

"Thank you. I really hope so."

You don't know what you've got till it's gone. The words of the song resonated in her mind in a perpetual spiral, like one of those infinity gadgets that businesspeople used to have on their desks. Why did people like those? The annoying click clack of balls on strings, the eternal turn of a wind sculpture. Were they designed to annoy or to calm, with their mesmerising, repeating pattern? She couldn't rid herself of the tune, however much she tried.

She'd never experienced this kind of rejection, this absence of warmth, in her life before. All the confidence of having a close group of friends, always there, their doors open, the kettle on, the familiar kitchens, was gone. The children comfortable with their neighbours, their school friends within walking distance. What a gift it had been and what a loss she was suffering. She began to dread going out, in case she bumped into one of them. The bookshop was a temporary release — at least if they were avoiding her they wouldn't go there. But getting out of bed in the mornings became harder and harder.

She tried to hide it from the family, summoning a cheerful front for the children, at least. Luckily they had other friends at school. The barbecues had fizzled out with the arrival of cold weather and the open doors remained closed. But Adam felt her pain, and she could see the lines of anxiety deepen on his forehead when he looked at her.

So when the chance of a new job came up — a great opportunity for his career and away from London, it seemed like serendipity. Beth leaped at the chance of a new life, making new friends, and though at first the children were reluctant, they soon changed their minds when they saw their new school. It was easy to say they were moving for Adam's job, though if they'd really wanted to stay in Kingston, he would have happily commuted. No, they moved because she couldn't bear to stay any longer, with the daily reminders of what she'd done and what she'd lost.

There is a lasting effect, though. Before, she didn't hesitate about her perception of right and wrong, taking action when she thought it was the correct thing to do. Now, she teeters on the fence, unable to put a foot on either side in case she makes a wrong decision. And she knows what she could lose, now. She hasn't made many new friends here — she dare not make that mistake again.

When Tom saw the girl at the window, Beth's instinct was to go next door immediately and ask outright. But she stopped herself. She didn't trust herself — she'd got it so wrong last time. She couldn't run straight to the police, making wild allegations about a neighbour she hardly knew. She couldn't risk this fragile new chance to belong.

But perhaps she should have done. When the girl made that makeshift sign, waited for who knows how long, and finally saw someone who might pay attention, she must have been desperate. It wasn't a teenage prank, that's for sure. But still Beth wavered.

Going to the police station had taken all her courage. Was it the right thing to do?

CHAPTER THIRTY

Beth

"It's that woman again." His voice is muffled by a badly placed hand, but she can still make out what he's saying. This is only the second time she's called, and already she's becoming a nuisance?

She can hear a soft murmuring in the background, another voice talking. Then the man comes back on the line. "You wanted DI Thomson, right?"

"Yes, please. He said I should call." She feels her jaw set. He did say she should — well, could — call, so that's what she's doing.

"Can I ask what it's concerning, please, Mrs . . .?"

"Beth Grant. It's concerning a young girl who may be in trouble. She lives next door and . . ."

"Please hold the line."

She waits, holding back her frustration. They're busy, of course, but if this turns out to be a serious situation and the girl is in danger, they could be accused of negligence. What if the girl is being abused in some way? Surely the responsible thing to do is to check it out. That's all it needs.

"Mrs Grant? It's DI Thomson here. You're calling regarding your neighbours, I understand?" He sounds tired, as if he's making an effort to be patient. Or maybe she's being oversensitive.

"Yes — you suggested I check to see if you had been able to call in . . ."

"We did call in, but the lady of the house wasn't well and we weren't able to go in and talk to her. We will try again."

She imagines the scene. The tall gates, the entry phone, the imposing front door. Oksana could easily put the police off. It would be a simple matter to feign illness, to make some excuse not to open the door.

"What will you do if she won't let you in?"

"There's really not much we can do, except keep trying. Unless you have any evidence of any wrongdoing, of course?" His voice is calm, long-suffering. He must have dealt with so many cranks and busybodies. Perhaps he's beginning to think she's one of them.

"I . . . No, not exactly. I mean, no, not yet. So there's nothing else you can try? Can you call them?"

"We can call them, but it's better to do these things face to face. We can gather information from the owners' body language, their reactions and so on. And we might get more from being in the house itself."

"Of course. Can I ask when you'll go back?"

"We'll go as soon as we can. It may take a few days, we're rather busy at the moment . . ." His voice seems to fade for a moment and in the background there's a volley of shouting. "If that's all, Mrs Grant, then we will talk again in a week or so. Thank you for your call."

* * *

"Is there anything else we can do?"

Adam pauses by the kitchen sink, a glass in his hand. "Are you sure you're not getting yourself all wound up about nothing, Beth?"

"I don't know, Adam, that's the problem," she says with a sigh. "But I've thought about it a lot since I saw her. How many chances would she have to signal to someone that she was in trouble? She must have prepared the sign in advance, perhaps carried it around the house with her, or waited at her bedroom window day after day for someone to see her. And the chances of that were minimal. She could have been waiting months, even years, for the chance. And we would never have gone into the garden at all if it hadn't been for Ruff. She would have waited in vain, with her sign, and nobody would have known anything about it. She must be desperate — there's no other explanation."

Adam pours himself a glass of water, the tap gushing unexpectedly fast, casting a spray of droplets down the front of his jumper. He wipes it with his free hand. "Damn. Must fix this tap, it's getting worse. I do see what you mean, Beth, it does seem on the face of it like a serious cry for help. But we don't know Keith and Oksana at all. We have no idea what family they have, how they live. There could be another explanation."

"Like what, though?"

"Like, the girl could be mentally ill. She could be pretending, to get them in trouble. Look, we just don't know, do we? I think you have to let the police deal with it and stop worrying. Come here."

This is what she loves about Adam. The hugs, the reassurance, the sheer solidity of the man she shares her life with. With his arms around her she feels the comfort blanket of family life around her.

"You're right," she says, extracting herself from his embrace. "I should keep my nose out of trouble."

But she can't get her mind off the girl at the window. She can't help thinking that only a few feet away, through two narrow brick walls, something sinister is happening.

CHAPTER THIRTY-ONE

Sofia

I recoil in horror, my feet scrabbling — but I can't keep my balance. My head cracks against the sloping ceiling as I fall, pin-sharp flashes of pain fizzing. I lie in a heap, cradling the sudden lump under my hair. It takes a few moments for my mind to focus again.

Who is Julia? Why does she need help?

I can hardly bear to think it. Was there was another girl before me, locked in this room, desperate and lonely? Longing, like me, to escape, to return to her family, to a life with possibilities and a future? What other explanation could there be for the message? And where is Julia now? Did they "get rid" of her? Tears pour from my eyes, gathering in a stream at my jawline.

They have done this before.

I should have known. Oksana would always have had help in the house. She is not the kind of woman to do her own domestic work. Is it normal in England for people to be held against their will, treated like this? Does this country, that I thought of as friendly, full of possibility and opportunity, accept such cruelty?

I am struck with a terror so powerful it takes my breath away. I double up, my body shaking, my heart beating double time. I gasp like a fish out of water, sweat pours off my skin. I'm going to die.

But when the panic fades and the pain in my chest dulls to a soft ache, I hear the drone of the vacuum cleaner downstairs and I know I have to carry on. I drag myself to my feet and creep down the stairs. I turn the cleaner off, march about a bit to make it sound as if I am still working, move some furniture a little. I don't know where Matt is, but I am taking no risks. I leave my cleaning materials and run silently back to my room, closing the door. I climb back up to the window and beat at it with the statue with every ounce of my strength.

But I can't do it. I am exhausted, the window still in one piece. It will not give way. I slump, panting and sweaty, against the wall. Wretched with disappointment, I carry the chair and the statue back downstairs and return to my work.

But all day I can't stop thinking about Julia. Was she kept prisoner like me? How long was she there? She must have had a chair to get so high up and stay long enough to carve her name. Did she try to break the window as I did? Questions tumble through my brain like falling stones, but there are no answers.

Later, back in my room, I lie on my bed, staring at the ceiling. Perhaps Julia tried to escape like I did. She could have been frightened, like me, of what might happen to her if she was moved on. Or terrified for her life. A sudden thought gives me a burst of energy. I move my mattress to the centre of the room and inspect every inch of the wall, the wood around the door, the door itself. I send my fingers into every dark corner, every dusty nook and cranny. I pick more plaster off the wall where it is damaged. Like a mad person, I crawl across the floor on hands and knees, ignoring the prickle of splinters from the rough floorboards. I find nothing.

I do the same in the tiny toilet room, knocking the loose toilet seat awry with my shoulder as I squeeze into the darkest corner. And there, my probing fingers are rewarded. There are scratch marks. Something is carved into the floorboard, there is no doubt about it. There are letters, maybe numbers. I can't see, it is too dim, but if I contort my body so that my neck is twisted, my head against the wall, I can just reach far enough to trace them with my fingers.

Now I curse myself for my nail-biting habit. Though the letters are quite large, this would be so much easier with nails. I have to use all my patience and every nerve ending in the flattened tip of my index finger to identify each letter. Is that a B or an R? The one after it is a complete circle, so an O — or maybe a zero. Then what feels like a five, or perhaps an S. I am so uncomfortable I have to stop and shift my weight. This must have been hard to do, she must have had something long to carve in such an awkward place. And she must have been desperate to do it.

Throwing the thought from my mind, I settle back into position. The next letter is . . . an E. Then there's a single line. An I. Or the figure one. And another O, or maybe a zero. There are more below, but no more in the line I've been following.

BOSEIO? ROSEIO? Or B05E10?

Beneath I find what I think are R, or it could be another B, and H. Another S, or possibly a number five. RHS, or BHS, or RH5 or BH5. That's it, no more.

I trace them one last time and check the rest of the tiny room. Stretching out my sore muscles, I return to my bed and retrieve my stub of pencil and a piece of paper. I write down the letters and numbers. Whoever wrote this in that cramped corner did not want it found by the wrong person. To find it, you must look very carefully, as I did, and you need the time to do it. You need to be desperate.

What can it mean? It could be a code to help me escape. Maybe it's a warning, not that anyone held prisoner by Madam needs much warning of her cruelty. Or perhaps — a thought that clutches at me, sending a shudder down my spine — this person wanted to leave a message before they were taken away.

*　*　*

There is a mound of washing to be done today. I have hidden it from sight so that I can have some time for myself, but today I must get it done or risk a beating. I must not draw attention to myself by neglecting my work.

This morning I can barely drag myself around. I feel as if I am swimming through dark waters, my limbs slow and heavy. My head still thumps from the knock it took last evening. A lump has risen through my hair and I can feel dried blood. After I found the message, I couldn't sleep. My brain would not stop working, buzzing with questions, visualising the letters, the possible numbers, wrestling with imagined possibilities. When I did fall into a deep sleep, it felt as if only five minutes had passed before the bang on the door and the key in the lock.

I load the washing machine, watching my hands work as if they are separate from my body. Like a robot, I set up the ironing board and take a shirt from the pile. I pause to look out at a grey sky, heavy rain spattering the window, warping the image of winter trees and leafless bushes in the nearby flowerbed. Will it ever stop raining?

A warning hiss and a whiff of burnt cloth jolts me out of my trance and I look down to see a dark burn across the sleeve of Sir's white shirt. Panicked, I rub at it with a damp cloth, hoping the mark will come out, but the damage is done. The shirt is ruined. I curse, holding the shirt up to the light. I will have to hide it in the rubbish bin and hope he doesn't notice it is missing. He has so many white shirts, I might get away with it. Oksana never deals with his clothes, leaving me to wash, iron, fold and put everything away. His shirts hang in colour order in his wardrobe. I often wonder why he needs so many.

Anyway, it doesn't matter now, my fate is almost certainly settled. But then, as I stare at the burn, I realise there might be another way for me to change my destiny.

Taking my duster and the ruined shirt, I go to the kitchen, where a black bin bag awaits. Each day, I empty the waste-bins from every room into this bag and Matt calls in to put it outside. This morning I remember seeing paper, an envelope perhaps, discarded in the kitchen rubbish. I fish it out, hide the shirt at the bottom of the bag, and return to the utility room where the iron still hisses gently, steam rising from its cradle. I turn the dial to maximum, click the steam off and press the iron hard on a corner of the envelope.

CHAPTER THIRTY-TWO

Sofia

I think I have found a way. I have taken the metal bin from the office and filled it with bits of paper and fabric — some of my precious horde of receipts and envelopes, some rags ripped from old dusters, some discarded cotton wool from Madam's bathroom. I have almost lit a fire! I am going to finish my work and try again before I go up to my room. Hopefully, if I place the bin under the ironing board, with clothes on top hanging down, it will catch and the house will go up in flames.

I might go with it, I know, especially if I am locked in my room, and I am scared of that. I don't want to die that way. But I must do this, I have to. This will draw attention to the house, perhaps even get the police to come.

I wait, my shoulders aching with tension, for the end of my day.

In the afternoon someone comes to the house while I am upstairs. Madam lets her in, but I know it is not one of her usual friends because I hear what she says in the hallway.

"Shall I take my boots off? They're rather muddy. From walking the dog, you know." Muddy boots are not allowed here. No, this is someone else, and she is British, I think. In a flash I remember the woman from next door and her dog. Could it be her, trying to find me? If it is, I must do something, make her understand that I need help.

They go into the kitchen. I hear the rumble and crack of the coffee machine, then Madam's urgent feet on the stairs. She finds me dusting the dressing table in her room.

"Go to your room," she whispers, grabbing me by the shoulder, her talons digging into my thin skin. "I have guest. You keep quiet, you hear? Or it will be bad for you." She gives me a shake and pushes me towards the upper staircase, watching me climb to the top before hurrying back down. I go without complaint, hoping she won't follow me to lock the door, and I am rewarded. She rushes to return to her guest.

In my room, I close the door, but I open it again silently. Removing my shoes, I creep back out and sit as far down the stairs as I dare. The sound from the hallway echoes upwards, and when the coffee machine stops its racket I can hear the dim murmur of women's voices.

Should I make my move now? I don't know for sure who this woman is. If it is one of Madam's friends, and I rush in, that will be it, I will be in real trouble. If it is someone else, how can I persuade her, in the few moments before Madam drags me away and locks me up, that I am a prisoner, that I need her help, right now? I am so anxious, so tired and stressed and scared, I can't think straight. What should I do? I start down the stairs, then sit down again. I bite my thumbnail until it bleeds.

A moment later the kitchen door opens and the unknown woman comes out, followed by Madam's clicking heels, leading her to the downstairs toilet. I keep still and listen, guessing she will wait in the hallway for the woman to emerge. When the door to the toilet closes, I creep in my stockinged feet to the room above, looking around in desperation for inspiration. I have to make a noise, she has to hear me. At least she will know I am here, even if I am risking a beating. I will simply deny it. I know I can run without a sound back up the stairs before Madam, in her stupid designer heels, can follow.

There is nothing here to help me, so I thump my foot on the floor, three times, as loud as I dare, then run.

I am back in my room in a moment, the door closed, my hands trembling.

CHAPTER THIRTY-THREE

Beth

"Is your husband home?" Beth asks, having tried her only strategy to explore the house — asking for the bathroom — and failed. Oksana showed her there, waited in the hallway and accompanied her back, as if she had read her mind. Is she already suspicious of her?

"My husband is away on business. What can I say? Always business," Oksana says, indicating a bar stool at a vast kitchen island.

"What does your husband do?"

"He is businessman." Oksana's beautiful red mouth snaps shut on the last word. She turns away to prepare the coffee, ending the subject without apology.

Beth is awed by this house. The kitchen is huge, with shining surfaces and sleek cupboards, not a handle in sight. Everything gleams. A huge display of orchids stands in the centre of the kitchen table, more fresh flowers on the windowsill. Sparkling appliances are set discreetly into the walls. Oksana, dressed in figure-hugging white trousers, a shimmering blouse and gold heels, glides around the room pressing hidden buttons. Beth lifts herself carefully onto a plush leather barstool. She has to stop herself staring, compose herself before speaking.

"This is a fabulous kitchen," she says. "And a beautiful house, Oksana. Did you design it yourself?" Small talk, and awkward, but isn't this what anyone would say, here, in this palace of a house?

Oksana places an exquisite bone china cup and saucer before her. The coffee smells rich and strong. "Would you like some milk, or cream?" she says, posing like a celebrity in a gossip magazine, her hand on the enormous fridge.

"Just milk please." Beth is acutely aware of her socks, which have both worn thin at the big toes. And her trousers, muddy around the bottom from this morning's walk. She tucks her feet beneath her, on the rung of the stool.

"I am very lucky," Oksana says. She settles on a bar stool opposite Beth. "My husband had house already when we married. I changed all: kitchen, all bathrooms, everything. Decor everywhere."

"It's wonderful. You're obviously very good at it." Best to flatter her, Beth feels, though she doesn't feel comfortable here, surrounded by flamboyance, glitz and glamour.

"Thank you." Oksana takes a sip of coffee, her painted lips leaving a red ghost on the gilded rim of the coffee cup. "Now, what can I do for you?"

"I . . . Yes, I'm hoping to get a job soon, you see. I was a bookseller—" Beth pauses, expecting a reaction from Oksana. But her face doesn't move, the china-blue eyes unblinking.

". . . And when I do, which I hope will be soon . . ." now she's gabbling, repeating herself. She's really not good at acting a part. If she's not careful, she'll give herself away. "I'll probably be working two or three days a week. Maybe full-time, though I'd prefer not to, because of the dog."

Still no reaction.

Beth shifts her weight, uncrosses her ankles and crosses them again the other way. "Anyway, I wondered if you could recommend a good cleaner? Your house looks so — immaculate, sparkling clean, you must have a very good person."

Oksana smiles, showing a perfect row of teeth. Her lips move but no warmth spreads to those unblinking eyes. "I am Russian," she says, her chin jutting. "We know how to clean, my mother taught me well. I do everything, like I say. No cleaning person."

Beth takes a sip of coffee. It's strong, and very bitter. "Well, I must say you do a fantastic job — or perhaps your husband helps you when he's home?"

Oksana rises with a sudden, violent movement from her stool. Her heels hit the floor with a crack, her body unfolding to its full height. In those shoes she must be close to six feet tall. Around her the air crackles with latent electricity.

Startled, Beth scrambles off her bar stool, standing awkwardly in her stockinged feet while Oksana reaches across for her cup and saucer. A whiff of perfume — musky, powerful — taints the air.

"You must go now," she says. The look on her face could crack granite.

"Yes, I . . . I need to get back, anyway," Beth mumbles to Oksana's back as she leads the way to the front door. She's being dismissed in no uncertain terms.

"Anyway, thanks so much for the coffee. It was lovely to see your house — a part of it, anyway."

Oksana offers a limp hand to Beth as she leaves. Her eyes glitter behind the sweeping eyelashes.

When the door closes behind her with a thump, Beth realises she's been holding her breath.

* * *

"I definitely heard something upstairs," Beth says, on the way out for dinner with Adam. It's a dark, windy night and the rain sits in fat puddles on the edges of the country roads. "But she says her husband is away, and she doesn't have a cleaner. I don't believe that — you should see the place! It's like a hotel, everything sparkling, polished to a high shine. All marble and chrome and mirrors. Sumptuous is how I would describe it. And she looks as if she's never even seen a mop and bucket."

"Could have been a cat," Adam says, giving the windscreen a quick wipe with his gloved hand. "They have a habit of jumping off things with a thump. But I can see I'm not going to change your mind."

"Didn't sound like a cat," she says firmly. "Too regular. And I haven't been aware of a cat visiting from next door — I'm sure Ruff would have noticed. I know you're worried I'm interfering, but I can't stop thinking about it."

"Did you check with the police again?"

"I did, though they're beginning to think of me as an old busybody. I just wanted to make sure I wasn't about to arrive at the door at the same time as them, which would have been embarrassing. They were a bit off-hand with me, I have to say."

"They probably have more important things to do," Adam says easily. "Look, I think you're right to follow it up, but I also think you should leave it with the police now. It could look like interfering . . ."

She glances up, but he puts a reassuring hand on her leg.

"I'm not being funny or accusing you of anything," he says. "Just leave it with the cops. They'll send someone round, and that will be the end of it from our point of view — it will be out of our hands."

"You're probably right." She stares through the rain-splashed window, water running off it in glistening streams. The weather's been like this for days, the remains of a huge storm over the Atlantic. Her walks have been hard work, battling against the wind, returning home to bath the dog and clean the mud from the floor.

"First book club meeting tomorrow night," she says, as Adam guides the car into a parking space. "I'm looking forward to it. You hadn't forgotten, had you?"

"No, I'll make myself scarce, don't worry. How many are coming?"

"I think about six or seven to begin with, though you never know. Eventually it would be good to have about ten or twelve members, so that we always have enough for a good discussion. We'll do the meeting in the kitchen, if that's okay with you. It starts at seven thirty."

"Fine by me. Better warn the kids too."

As they walk towards the restaurant, avoiding the puddles on the wet tarmac, he says, "Did you invite Oksana?"

She's startled: the thought hadn't crossed her mind. "To the book club meeting? It didn't occur to me. I suppose it might have been a friendly thing to do. Although now I'm a bit scared of her, to be honest."

They're shown to a table at one side by a young waitress.

"Scared of her?" Adam says, surprised. "Why on earth would you be scared?"

"She's quite unnerving, believe me. She could break glass with a single look of those laser eyes. I can quite imagine her being cruel to some poor girl."

"Are you treating her as guilty before proven innocent?" Adam says, patting his pockets for his reading glasses. The restaurant is warm and candle-lit, blocking out the grim weather outside. Tempting aromas drift around the room.

His question brings back the sinking feeling. "Am I? Perhaps I am . . . It would certainly make it more difficult, if she is mistreating that girl, to have her as a member. But she doesn't strike me as someone who would be interested in a book club. I'm not being snobby, I just don't think we have much in common."

Adam peers at her over his menu. "On the face of it, I agree. But you never know what people are like behind the facade, do you? In her case, more than most."

He's right, of course. She is jumping to conclusions about Oksana without any proof. But the girl's pale face at the window keeps returning to her, and the poignant cry for help scrawled on the sign. That is evidence enough for her.

CHAPTER THIRTY-FOUR

Beth

The kitchen's tidy, the snacks are out, the dog toys cleared away. The children are banished, unable to keep their hands out of the food bowls. In the end she had to bribe them with snacks to take to their rooms.

On her way upstairs, Abigail says, "Mum, if you decide to read a book I want to read, can I join in?"

Beth strokes her daughter's soft cheek with her fingers, thinking of her "over eighteen" rule and deciding to relax it, and tucks a stray strand of hair behind her ear. "Of course you can, darling — that would be great. Tonight might be a bit boring for you, though. We're going to decide how it will all work. Then we'll agree on next month's book, and if there's time, the titles for the next twelve months. When we've got the list, you can have a look and decide when or if you want to join in. I'm sure there'll be something you'll like. In fact, if you want to suggest something, I'll even put it forward, if you want."

"Can I, Mum? Great! Do I have to decide tonight?"

"Just let me know in the next few days, if you think of something."

Abigail gives Beth a quick kiss on the cheek and disappears to her room.

It's not long before Karen arrives, and soon the room is buzzing with conversation. Karen has invited two friends who live nearby and are members of her health club, and her neighbour, who came to Beth's housewarming, has also brought a friend along.

"So," Beth says, tapping the table. "I'm delighted to welcome you all to our new book club. If anyone knows of someone else who'd like to join, do put them forward. We'd like to get the numbers up to around twelve."

A woman called Angela who works with Beth at the charity bookshop says, "What about the Russian woman — Oksana, is it? Doesn't she live next door?"

Beth is taken aback. She didn't expect anyone else to know Oksana. "She's a possibility. Do you know her well?"

There's a pause as everyone turns to Angela, who looks a little flustered. "Not well, no. She's a member at our club, isn't she, Karen?"

"Is she?" says Karen, her eyes widening with surprise. "I've never seen her there — and I go there a lot. Does she do classes, or the gym?"

"I don't know," Angela says. "I was introduced to her once in the spa. Her car's often there. You can't miss it, can you?" Oksana's car carries the registration OK 555. "I knew her predecessor, actually. Not very well. But Oksana is Keith's second wife. His first wife, Julia, was very different. Now *she* did like books — she worked at the charity bookshop for a short while, like you, Beth."

Beth nods. "Interesting." She files this in her mind for later. "But nobody actually knows Oksana?"

Luckily for Beth, who wants to avoid awkwardness of any kind this evening, nobody seems to know her well enough to invite her. "Why don't we wait until someone knows her a bit better? Then they can find out if she's interested."

They all nod, murmuring their agreement. Beth says, "Good. And if anyone does want to invite someone, I think they should put it to the group first, just in case."

"In case of what?" one of the other women says.

Beth hesitates, unsure how to describe in a diplomatic way her feelings about inviting Oksana.

"In case there are any objections," Karen says, closing the discussion.

* * *

"I think that went really well," Karen says, once the others have left. "We have a book club! Well done, Beth, you did a great job."

"Thanks for your support, Karen. I'm not sure I'd have wanted to do it on my own."

Karen gives her a quizzical look. "It's funny, you strike me as supremely confident — especially when it's to do with books."

"Well, thank you again. But I'm not, inside. I'm more insecure than I look." She says it with a smile, but it's true. Since that crazy, stupid mistake that changed her life, she's anxious around people, always worried she'll say the wrong thing.

Karen starts to dry the glasses lined up on the draining board. "So what do you think about Oksana?"

"What about her?" Is she sounding defensive? She hopes not, but she avoids Karen's eyes.

"The suggestion we invite her to join the book club. What do you think?"

Beth puts her cloth down and leans against the counter. Most of the clearing up is done. She takes a sip of water and thinks for a moment how to answer this. "To be honest, Karen, and strictly between you and me . . . I think joining a book club is not top of her list of priorities. A Botox party, maybe, or a champagne party in a Jacuzzi. And as to whether she'd fit in with the rest of us, I seriously doubt we'd last five minutes."

Karen laughs. "That is pretty honest. I gather she's not your type?"

"Let's sit down for a minute, finish our drinks. She's not my type, no, but there's something else." She's been wondering whether to tell anyone else about the girl. She had decided not to but her instinct is to confide in Karen.

"What is it?" Karen says. "Have you found out more about them?"

"No, though I have been for coffee with her. I went round on a pretext." She hesitates. "I wasn't there long, but . . . Karen, I might have to swear you to secrecy on this one. To be honest, I've been bitten before by making assumptions about someone, and I really don't want to put my foot in it again."

Karen's eyebrows rise. "I promise, I'm not a gossip. If you want to tell me, I'm all ears, but if you don't, I won't be offended."

She tells her the whole story: the dog, Tom seeing the girl, the sign at the window. The reaction of the police, the excuse to go next door for a coffee. And the noise upstairs.

Karen nods, looking thoughtful.

"What do you think?" Beth says. "Am I being ridiculous, worrying about this for no reason? Adam's being patient with me, but I'm sure he thinks it'll turn out to be nothing. And the police already think I'm a nuisance. I'd really appreciate an honest opinion." Anxiety, never far away, creeps into her voice, though she tries to keep it light.

"Do you know what?" Karen says. "I think you're absolutely right to be concerned. If more of us took responsibility for things like this, the world would be a better place. You absolutely should find out what's going on."

Relief floods over her like a warm shower.

"So what should I do now? The police are fed up with me, Adam thinks I should leave it to them, and I really don't want to get things wrong again. But I can't leave it, I can't stop worrying about her."

Karen drains her glass. "I see your point. It's tricky, because they live right next door. And they have loads of money, which could mean litigation wouldn't be an issue for them."

"God, I hope it doesn't go that far. The trouble is, if this girl really does need help — and I'm sure she does — then the longer we leave it, the worse things might get for her. I feel as if I should have done more already, not wait passively for the police to get their act together."

"Have you thought about asking Oksana directly, telling her about the girl?"

"That was my first idea. But then I thought — wouldn't that get the girl into worse trouble? If she's being kept there against her will, wouldn't they punish her for trying to get away? I really don't know what the answer is."

"Oksana isn't the easiest person to approach. What about the gardener, isn't he around most days?"

"I do see him there quite a lot. Seems to keep himself to himself. I could, though the same applies. If he's working for them, and knows what's going on, it might work out badly for the girl if I talk to him."

"What else is there? A charity? Social services maybe? If she's still a child, they might be able to help."

Beth frowns. "You're right. She did look quite young, not more than fifteen, maybe sixteen. So thin and pale . . . Perhaps I'll give that a try. They might be able to point me in the right direction, anyway."

Karen gets to her feet and stretches. "I'll keep thinking. Let me know what you decide to do. I'll back you up."

"Thank you so much, Karen, I'm glad I told you." Beth stands up too, feeling relieved at having confided in someone. "And thanks again for all your help tonight."

Waving goodbye to Karen at the door, she steps out onto the front drive and glances upwards to the house next door. The glow of a single light in an upstairs room is the only sign of life.

* * *

At the bookshop, Dorothy is with Beth on the shift. She has worked there for more than ten years. White-haired and talkative, she lost her husband a few months ago, and her life now revolves around the shop. Many of the customers are her friends. She belongs to a book club herself and is delighted to hear about Beth's plan.

"I wanted to ask you something, actually," Beth says.

"Anything, dear. About the book club?" Dorothy is pricing up a pile of books at the cash desk, while Beth puts them on the appropriate shelves.

"Not really. Just . . . someone mentioned my next-door neighbour. Well, the previous one, actually. She worked here for a short while. Her name was Julia. Do you remember her?"

"Julia? I don't think so . . . When was it?"

"It would have been a few years ago — maybe five, six, seven? Sorry to be so vague. I didn't know her, and I don't know what she looked like either. Her husband was called Keith."

"Ah, yes," Dorothy says again. "I do remember her — and I remember that Keith. She was a quiet woman, kept herself to herself. She was usually very reliable, always on time. It was strange, what happened."

"What did happen?"

"One day she just didn't appear, and I called her number to see if she was okay. But that man, Keith, was very rude to me on the phone, told me to go away in no uncertain terms. I never heard from her or saw her again. I was on my own in the shop for a whole day — and it was busy. Why do you ask?"

"Just curious. I've met Keith's current wife. She's Russian, called Oksana. Tall and glamorous — she looks like a model."

Dorothy chuckles. "That man needs a strong wife. He wants holding in line. A really unpleasant person — I'm not surprised Julia left him."

Beth smiles, picking up a pile of books. Interesting, to hear about Julia. Perhaps she did leave Keith, and that was the reason she left the bookshop so suddenly. But it seems strange, nonetheless. Beth can't help wondering what happened to her.

CHAPTER THIRTY-FIVE

Sofia

Madam's *trip-trap* grows louder on the stairs. Her visitor has left, the door resonating behind her, and she has wasted no time coming to see me. She must have heard my desperate attempt to make a noise, to get the attention of the stranger. Or maybe the woman, hearing the thumping, asked an innocent question about who was upstairs. Whichever it was, I am in trouble.

The door slams open, the handle meeting the wall with a sharp crack. "You made noise!" Her voice shakes with anger, her eyes narrow and dangerous.

She grabs me by the arm, pulling me up from my mattress, where I am lying under the bedclothes, trying to keep warm. When the door is closed, no warmth from below seems to reach my room.

My only option is to deny it all. "What noise?" I whisper, cowering, my hands poised to defend my face. "I was here, all the time. I was here — I did not move." I gesture at the bed with my free arm.

Her chin juts forward at me, her cold eyes searching, her fingers pressing deep into my flesh. I keep my gaze on the floor.

With a growl of frustration she tosses my arm away from her like a piece of garbage. "You are trouble — only trouble! Useless girl — get back to work!"

How much time do I have? Not long, for sure, but will it be hours or days before I am dragged away to an even worse life? I know in my heart that being sent from here will be bad. Madam cares nothing for me. She thinks I am lazy, I do a bad job. She won't try to find me a good place and she won't care where I go. If I get sent somewhere else I will have even less idea where I am, and maybe no chance to escape.

I have to make my fire tonight, though I am terrified. If the fire moves up the house and I am locked in my room, I am finished, unable to break the window or kick the door down. Nobody will know what happened to me.

But these thoughts are not helping me. I breathe deeply and banish the images from my mind. I am the only person who can create my future. Now I have to focus on my plan, however crazy it is. I have to set the house on fire, even if it kills me.

* * *

Sir is back. His huge car purrs into the garage before dark. Madam waits in the hallway as his key slides into the lock at the front door, her hair gleaming, the top button of her silk shirt undone to reveal the lace of her expensive underwear. Unseen, I watch from the stairs as he hands her his coat and kisses her smooth cheek. They exchange a few words in Russian — I don't catch what they say — and, leaving his bag in the hall, he goes straight to his study.

Since then, the house has an expectant air, as if it is waiting for something to happen. I feel the tension in my jaw as I tiptoe to the kitchen to find something to eat. I need energy to carry out my plan, to take my chances as the house burns. I stare into the fridge, filled to bursting for Sir's return. Steaks soaking in a dark red sauce — a bottle cooling on the bottom shelf. I find some cheese and a stub of bread, take an apple from the fruit bowl on the kitchen table. That will be my supper. Maybe my last supper here.

Sir's return is not going to deter me. In fact, it makes everything more urgent. Perhaps Madam will talk to him this very night about moving me on, finding some other poor girl to take my place. I take my simple meal to the laundry room, eating as I set up the ironing board and start on the pile of bedlinen. My mind is on the coming night. I must watch the time. If I finish too early, she will be suspicious and check on me — she might even put her head around the door here and see the strange mountain I am planning to create, the smouldering bin below.

Another two hours to wait before I set my world on fire.

* * *

Things are different this evening because of Sir's return. His bags need to be unpacked, his dirty clothes piled out of sight in the laundry room, his toiletries arranged in the bathroom as he likes them. I work quickly, for once glad to have more washing and ironing to do.

Madam seems nervous as she prepares dinner. She leaves the door to the laundry room slightly ajar so she can keep an eye on me, and I keep my head down as I load the washing machine and set the dryer. At one point she drops a glass, cursing in Russian as it smashes on the smooth tiles of the floor. Startled, I forget myself and glance at her. "What do you look at, stupid?" she says. "Stop staring like idiot — clear this up. Now!"

I take a dustpan and brush from the cupboard, crouching at her feet to sweep up the glass. As I crawl around to find every last fragment, she can't resist giving me a kick in the ribs. "Hurry up, girl," she says, her beautiful face contorted into a snarl. I scuttle around her, empty the pan in the bin and creep back to the laundry room, avoiding her glare.

Dinner is later than usual and I have to stay longer at the ironing until they move to the drawing room, where they will stay with the door closed until they go to bed. That is when Madam will push me upstairs and lock me in my room, so I must set the fire and leave the laundry room before she comes to find me. I prepare quickly, blowing softly on pieces of tissue and paper until they glow, adding them to a small heap at the bottom of the metal bin. My heart thumps so hard I think she must be able to hear it as I open the tiny top window a crack to encourage the flames. As I leave the room, a trail of smoke begins to rise under the ironing board, where pillow cases and shirts dangle as if I have placed them there to air.

My timing is perfect. As I switch off the light, leaving the door ajar, Madam marches into the kitchen. "Upstairs," she says, taking a bottle from the fridge. "Now."

I hang my head as I pass her and walk slowly up the stairs. Her feet thump on each tread behind me. The key rattles in the lock as she shuts me in my attic cage for the night.

I tremble to think what I have done.

CHAPTER THIRTY-SIX

Beth

She wakes with the girl's face in her mind's eye. The white pallor, the wide eyes, the desperate mouthing.

In those misty moments between sleep and full consciousness, she allows herself to imagine what the girl's life could be like. Perhaps she's not able to eat properly or keep herself clean. Perhaps she's being physically abused, or sexually . . . With a shock of realisation, Beth sits upright. How could she not have thought of that before? The thought sickens her. She shakes her head to dispel the image. But she's letting her imagination run away. Keith is so often absent, it seems unlikely. But when he's there . . .

Leaping from the bed, she dresses hurriedly, layering her clothes for her dog walk. Downstairs she grabs a quick cup of tea with the rest of the family, waves them off and leaves the house in a cloud of drizzle, her hat pulled down hard over her ears.

Today she will do something about the girl. She has to try or she will never forgive herself. Walking fast with Ruff at her heels, she figures out the options. Go back to the police? Yes, she should try again, even if she is making a nuisance of herself. Contact social services? A great idea. Talk to the gardener? Maybe, but she'll have to be careful.

But confront Oksana? No, not yet. That is a step too far, unless she can get more evidence that the girl is there and in distress. Check out charities dealing with modern slavery? Yes. Go over the fence when Oksana is out and investigate . . . ?

As she walks, she becomes more determined. After all, she has less to risk than last time. Then, she lost her friends and her comfortable social life. This time, there are no friends to lose — apart from Karen, who is on her side. If they fall out with Oksana and Keith over this, then so be it. They almost never see them anyway, and their houses are divided by walls, gardens and fences. It's not as if they're part of a social group, or ever likely to be.

So what is she afraid of?

* * *

She could make a hole in the fence, send Ruff next door and use him as her excuse for looking around. If she's found by the gardener, she can talk to him then. It seems extreme to trespass on purpose — Adam would certainly disapprove — but if she can't get something to happen any other way, she'll do it.

Confronting Oksana isn't an option. She's already suspicious and there's no way she'd let her in again without a good reason.

She starts at the easiest point. For the police to take her seriously, she needs to know what she's talking about. Opening her laptop, she types "modern domestic slavery" into a search engine. The first item on the list happens to be a charity helpline, so she clicks through.

Domestic slavery is the practice of exploiting and exercising undue control over a person or people to coerce them into performing services of a domestic nature.

> *Victims of domestic slavery typically live and work in their employers' household, performing tasks such as cooking, cleaning and child-care. They may work up to 16 hours a day for little or no pay, often in poor conditions and with limited freedom.*
>
> *In many cultures, it is considered the norm to have a 'house help' and, unlike trafficking for sexual exploitation, forced labour can be unrecognised. Often people are forced to work with no reference to UK law or basic human rights.*

There it is, in black and white. She delves deeper, becoming engrossed in real-life stories of domestic servitude. Some start with forced marriage or trafficking from other countries. Often young girls are lured into the trap with promises of good jobs, their passports and mobiles taken from them. Sometimes their kidnappers will use the phones to text their families false messages of reassurance. The girls are humiliated and forced into impossible situations, some sold into servitude, many raped. Often they are malnourished, surviving on scraps.

After an hour's research, Beth closes the laptop, moved to tears. Domestic slavery is far more common than she had thought. And far more dreadful. To be taken from your family, find yourself with strangers in another country, a foreign language . . . how frightening that would be for a young girl. Forced to do menial work, quite possibly without money, perhaps having to pay back her passage into Britain.

It could be happening right next door. A tiny, dark room, a dirty mattress on the floor. Nothing to do but work. Missing the teenage years, which Abigail has just entered, those wonderful, hopeful years of discovery, romance, learning, when you most need your family at your side to guide you. Being forced to say goodbye to childhood in a day, an hour, a moment. A chance turning, a fateful falling of the dice, a wrong answer, and a young girl's life is taken from her.

* * *

She sits, her eyes scanning the notices on the board aimlessly, waiting for DI Thomson. People come and go regularly through the security gate, flashing their cards at a reader on the way through.

After half an hour she asks how long he might be, and gets a long, pitying look from the receptionist. "I really don't know, madam," she says, with heavy emphasis on the last word. "They're all very busy right now, you may have read about it in the papers?" Beth nods as if she knows all about it, but she hasn't read a paper for days.

"Can I make an appointment with him then? It's important," she says. She looks the woman in the eye, hoping she looks more determined than she feels.

"Does he know what it's about, madam? Only it's hard to get a moment with any of them . . ." The uniformed woman taps her pen on the notepad in front of her. "I can give him a message, if you prefer not to wait?" She looks hopeful, as if wishing Beth would go away.

"He does know what it's about," Beth says firmly. "I have reported this before. It's a possible case of domestic slavery."

"I see. And have there been any developments since you first reported it?" The woman raises her eyebrows as if knowing the answer.

"Ah . . . no. Well, there might have been. But I don't know if he's been able to follow up yet . . ." The policewoman's face doesn't change. There's a long pause, as if someone has pressed a "stop" button.

"I'll leave a message then," Beth says.

With a grim smile, the woman passes the notepad through. Stiff with annoyance, Beth fills in her details in silence, then writes, in big letters:

> *DI Thomson, I'm most concerned about this girl now, and I suspect domestic servitude of a serious kind. Please can you update me as to any progress ASAP and advise as to what will be done next.*
> *Regards.*

The number for Social Services rings and rings. She goes through a long process of pressing numbers to get the right department, only to find she has to leave a voicemail. She wasn't expecting much, but she had hoped she might be able to speak to a person.

With a sigh, she remembers the newspaper in her bag. The moment she sees the front page, she understands why she got nowhere with DI Thomson today.

CHAPTER THIRTY-SEVEN

Sofia

Though I'm exhausted, I don't sleep. I can't get my mind off the writing on the floor. I try the letters as numbers, I write the sequence backwards, up and down. I try every way I can. I can't make sense of it.

All the time I am listening, listening so hard my ears almost hurt. I hear Sir and Madam tramp upstairs to their room, doors opening and closing and bathroom sounds for a few minutes before everything goes quiet. If there is smoke, they have not noticed, which is good — but if there is no smoke, then I have failed.

I sniff at the gap between my door and the floor but I can smell nothing different, just the dusty wooden flooring and the faint perfume of Madam's scented candles wafting up the stairs. I am determined to stay awake, so I walk up and down in the tiny space, do some exercises on the floor — anything to avoid falling asleep. In the end I give in and sit on my mattress with the light still on. If there is a fire I will scream and shout and bang on the door and maybe, just maybe, they will let me out and I can find a way to escape. Just in case, I have soaked a towel and left it in the basin. I will wrap it around my face when the smoke and the flames come. My journal is wrapped in kitchen foil, stolen from the kitchen earlier today. It is folded into my waistband for the police to find, a thick lump under my jumper.

I keep myself alert by imagining all the possible ways to escape when they open my door. Will I push Madam aside, slide down the banister as she tries to grab me, run to the front door? Will it already be open, with Sir outside waiting for the firemen to come? They are more likely to leave me to burn, but I dare not think about that. Once I am outside I will run to the fence and scream. The people next door will surely hear me. I will use every ounce of my strength to climb over. I will do it, I will.

* * *

The banging on the door gets louder — I wake from my dream with a start, standing up suddenly, still fully dressed. Has the fire taken hold? Do I grab the soaking towel and push Madam out of the way? My ears strain, every muscle tensed.

But the sound of her feet on the stairs is the same as always. She has unlocked the door and left me to get up and start work. There is no smoke, no fire, no shouting. Though it is dark outside, it is clear that the morning is here as usual. My plan has failed.

Disappointment washes over me like a fog in winter. I fall onto the bed, the energy draining from my body. Though it was not the best plan, I had put all my hopes on this. Stupid to hope when the chances were so small.

I had prepared well. I was ready to risk my life. But nothing I do to save myself seems to work. Everything is against me, every time. My eyes are closed but the tears flow freely, wetting the pillow. In that moment, my longing for home feels like a hole where my heart should be.

Madam's shrill voice from below drags me from my bed. Though I am filled with despair, I know I must go on, find a way, somehow. I pull my journal from my trousers, hide it as best I can in my room and drag myself downstairs.

* * *

In the laundry room, everything is as I left it. No sign of a fire at all. The clothes hang from the ironing board, neat and clean, not even singed. At the bottom of the waste bin are a few scraps of burnt paper, nothing else — the fire barely got going. I curse under my breath, empty the bin and go through to the study to return it.

There, something catches my eye. When Sir goes away, he always leaves the study tidy. Nothing is left on the surfaces, his desk is clear. He takes his laptop with him, leaves nothing around for me to tidy up. But today, though he has gone to work as usual, he has left a file on the leather surface, and I can't resist looking. I have nothing to lose, after all.

Looking over my shoulder, I half-close the door and switch on the vacuum cleaner. Pushing it to and fro with one hand, I open the blue folder with the other. In an instant, my heart stops beating. A list of names. Beneath the list, sheets of paper, forms completed in handwriting, a photo attached to the top of each with a single staple. There are ten or so of them, girls' faces looking out at me, sad, scared faces, their hair lank on their shoulders, dark lines and shadows beneath their eyes.

I know what this is.

An icy shiver runs down my back. With trembling fingers I riffle through the pages, my heart racing. The girls are from Bulgaria, Romania, Moldova, a couple from Belarus. At the top of each page there is a heading: Arrival in UK, and a date. There are no addresses, only names, countries of origin and ages. The numbers seem to shout at me: fifteen, seventeen, one is only fourteen.

My eye catches a movement at the window. I freeze, my heart thumping so hard it hurts. Matt passes without seeing me, a hood pulled tight over his head against the wind. I slam the folder shut, pushing the papers back in so they don't give me away. Nausea rises in my throat. I pull the cleaner behind me, away from the study into the living room.

She can't know I've seen this — she would certainly beat me until I begged for her to stop. It confirms my worst fears. They are involved in some kind of horrible kidnapping trade.

And I am on the way out.

***

I stand in the laundry room, my movements slow. The iron feels twice as heavy in my hand today, the mound of washing huge. I may try to start a fire again, but not today. I simply don't have the energy. I need everything to seem normal today. I must keep myself calm and out of Madam's way.

Later, I will focus on the message, try to work out what it says, and see if it can help me.

Placing the iron in its cradle, I lean over the cupboard to see better from the window. Strong winds pull at the nearby trees, grabbing the last leaves from branches. Shrubs and rose bushes scratch their bare twigs against the fence. Above my head there is an eerie whistling, as if the wind is calling me.

Clouds loom in dark mounds above the battered trees; raindrops lash the windows. I am surprised to see Matt heading towards the shed, his head bent against the wind. I wonder what work he can do in a storm like this.

Today could be the day they move me on. I know it is only a matter of time. I think about the file of girls. Has he left it there for Madam to pore over, to pick and choose her next victim? If he has, then perhaps I have a few more days. Or maybe she has already seen it, though I doubt she would leave it in full view — she is far too sharp. I can only hope I have a few more days to gather my strength.

I wonder again if setting a fire is the right thing to do. The thought of burning to death terrifies me more now I've spent time thinking it was going to happen. Perhaps it was right that my plan didn't work, and God still cares after all. But what now?

I could wait until they take me, and use the moment when they put me in the car to take action. But there is still the problem of the fence to climb. Or once the car is on its way, to whatever horrible place they are planning to send me, I could wrestle the door open and fling myself into the road. But the door might not open, and I have learned to my cost that windows are hard to break. There might be other chances, at the end of the journey perhaps, but all these are unknown. What if they drug me, like the first man did? What if they put me in the trunk of the car and I suffocate? In every scenario, I am weak. I have no strength, no weapon, no magic skill to free myself.

CHAPTER THIRTY-EIGHT

Beth

Human remains found in disused building.
The headline stands out on the front page in large letters, demanding attention.

> *Three teenagers broke into a derelict office building on the outskirts of Reading and got more than they bargained for on Tuesday this week when they came across human remains. It's understood they alerted the police and admitted to trespassing before being allowed home.*
>
> *"The offices have been unoccupied for a number of years," DI Stephens from Thames Valley Police said. "So the remains could have been there for some time. The building was boarded up and monitored by security systems, which appear not to have been operational."*
>
> *Anyone with any information is requested to contact Thames Valley Police. More on Page 3.*

So this is what the police are investigating. How does a person end up dead in a deserted office building? How come nobody noticed they were gone? Did they have no friends, no family? It's hard to imagine how this can happen here, in this age of smart technology, where communication is everything.

Her mind returns to the girl next door — she could end up like this. The girl's appeal for help has resulted in nothing. The police are too busy, social services don't answer the phone, the owners of the house deny her existence.

Suddenly the last option on her list seems much more attractive. Go over the fence when Oksana is out.

But the weather is against her. Fat raindrops spatter the kitchen window, shrubs and plants bow in the fierce wind, a plastic flower pot rolls around on the path. Everything shakes, bends and whirls in the angry gusts. In the last hour or so a storm has taken hold. She recalls the weather forecast on this morning's radio: a hurricane on the west coast of the US is heading towards Britain, unleashing the last of its massive energy on an already rain-soaked country.

Today is not a good day to climb the fence and go searching around next door. It's frustrating, but even the dog is reluctant to venture outside. Unsettled by the unfamiliar thumps and whistles around the house, he keeps running to the door to bark, only to back away when she opens the door.

"Too stormy for you, is it?" she says, ruffling the fur on his head. "I don't blame you. I don't want to go out in that either."

It's mid-afternoon but darkness already threatens, the sun hidden deep within the lowering skies. School will soon be out. Though it's November, the children left the house this morning without their coats. They're in jumpers and blazers, Abigail wearing a thin skirt. Beth wonders why she bothered buying them coats when it seems it's not cool for teenagers to wrap up.

It really is bad out there. Perhaps today she'll surprise them and pick them up from school.

* * *

Tom settles into the passenger seat, dampness rising from his shoulders into the warmth of the car's interior. Abigail brushes raindrops from her skirt and shivers. The short run from the school entrance to the car park has soaked them, and for once they're grateful that she has come to collect them.

Beth pulls the car out of its narrow parking space and joins the queue to the main road.

"Mum — you know that girl next door?" Tom says suddenly, startling her.

"Indeed I do. I haven't forgotten about her."

"Did you find out who she is? I never see her in the garden or going to school or anything." He stares out of the window as Beth slows the car for a group of schoolchildren to cross the road. Some of them are holding their jackets over their heads, others hunched against the wind and rain, their hair plastered to their cheeks. She drives slowly past them, avoiding a huge puddle that has gathered in the gutter.

"I've been trying, believe me," she says. "I am worried about her. If she's still there, of course."

"You said you'd go to the police . . ."

"I did. They said they'd look into it. I don't know if they've been to the house yet — they're pretty busy." For some reason she doesn't want to mention the human remains, even though the kids are unlikely to be upset by the story. After all, Tom murders fictional characters every day on his Xbox, and Abigail likes nothing better than a horror movie. But all the stories Beth has read about domestic slavery have unsettled her and she doesn't want to discuss it with her children. She wants them to be safe. Children should never have to face such horrors.

"Why do you ask?" she says. Tom isn't usually a worrier.

"I don't know, really. It seems weird not knowing the neighbours, like we used to. Anything could be happening next door, and we wouldn't know."

"Perhaps she's a ghost!" Abigail says from the back seat. "That would be so cool."

"I doubt it, in a modern house like that," Beth says. "But you're right, Tom, it does seem weird. It's different from where we used to live. Here, people want to keep themselves to themselves and not be friendly with the neighbours."

"Perhaps they're hiding something," Tom says.

"Ooh yes, let's go snooping," Abigail says. "We could climb over the fence and—"

"Don't even think about it," Beth says firmly. "Nobody's going snooping."

Though snooping is exactly what she's planning to do.

* * *

All night the wind batters the roof of the house. Strange sounds keep Beth awake into the small hours. Normally she sleeps with the window cracked open, but tonight it's too noisy, and there seems to be plenty of fresh air around, draughts creeping under doors and round window frames. She reads for a while until her eyes droop, then falls into a deep sleep, her dreams full of noise and chaos.

Waking into a dark room, she pads downstairs to put the kettle on. Ruff is still sleepy in his bed in the kitchen, only raising his head when she goes in and snuggling back down when she leaves carrying mugs of tea. By the time Adam stirs, it's brightening outside and he opens the curtains to let the light in as he gets dressed. At the window, he pauses.

"Still pretty windy outside," he says. "Looks like we've lost part of the fence on this side."

"Really?" Beth clambers out of bed to join him at the window. A long stretch of fence lies in Oksana's garden, the remainder twisted and rocking in what's left of the storm.

As she goes to call the children, she realises that fate is on her side. This is the ideal excuse to trespass in next door's garden, even to have a chat with the gardener. Adam will be out at work, and it will take a while to get the fence fixed. It's perfect timing.

CHAPTER THIRTY-NINE

Sofia

Most of the bedrooms are cleaned by the time the weak light of the sun reaches inside. My sign is under my jumper.

When I open the curtains in Madam's bedroom and look down into the garden at the back, I can't believe what I see. The fence is down, blown flat by the wind, leaving a huge, gaping hole. I can see right through into the neighbours' garden, where the boy and the woman live, the ones who saw me at the window.

Excitement gives me energy, my mind racing. But I must not give myself away by rushing — everything must seem normal. This is my first lucky break and I am going to make the most of it if it kills me.

I finish in the main bedroom and go to the guest room, to the same window as before. Madam is in the kitchen finishing her breakfast, so for the moment, I am safe. A duster hanging limp in my hand, I gaze into the garden. The heavy rain of yesterday has turned to drizzle and the fallen fence lies like a wide brown pathway across the flower bed. The garden next door is clearly visible now, with its matching beds beside the fence, its old wooden shed still standing despite the night's storm. Twigs and leaves litter the ground, the trees swaying in the wind.

I pray for the woman next door to come to inspect the damage. Surely she'll come out soon? If she opens the door, not realising the fence is down, the little dog will escape and she will come looking for him.

Please, God, I pray, *let this be the day luck is on my side. I'm so sorry to have turned away from You. If You just listen to me today, take pity on me, I will love You with all my heart, forever.*

There may never be a moment like this again. Please let that woman, or her son — anyone — be at home, let the rain stop, let her come outside and walk into this garden, look up at me and see my pain. Let her rescue me. Please, God.

Matt appears from the side of the house. Startled, I ease back into the room, away from the window, still watching. He approaches the broken fence, bends down to lift it up with both hands. But it starts to break as he does so, and he lowers it back down to the ground.

Then — I gasp — the dog is there, wagging its tail, bounding over the fallen fence to greet him, the woman following him. She wears a bright yellow raincoat, the hood up so I can't see her face, but it is her, I am sure of it. She steps slowly over the fence and approaches Matt, while the dog runs to the end of the garden, disappearing into the bushes.

From the bedroom door, I can hear Madam's shrill voice resonating from the kitchen. She is mid-conversation. With shaking hands, I pull out my sign and hold it up at the window. Matt will see it, but I have to take the risk. This has to work, this time.

Please look up — *look up, please.*

The two inspect the damage, lifting the fence a little to check what is underneath. Meanwhile, unnoticed, the dog is digging a hole in the flower bed on the other side of the grass, the black earth spraying out into a fast-growing mound of mud behind him. The woman turns and steps towards him, but he skips and runs back to the bottom of the garden, his tail wagging. She turns and speaks to the gardener again.

Then they look up at me — together, as if it was planned. My heart lurches in my chest, my fingers gripping the sign as if it is a lifeline. I point at it from above, wave an arm, the sign slips. I rescue it and hold it up high with both hands. I can see they are talking about me, the woman indicating me with her hands. Then Matt raises his arm and gestures for me to move away from the window, I know that is what he wants but I can't, I need this to work, the woman must know I am desperate. Please, God.

Matt's gaze moves towards the kitchen window, perhaps checking if Madam has seen. I whirl around, run on tiptoes to the door again, my sign flapping against my legs. But I can still hear her talking, I am safe — as long as she is not looking out of the window. I hurry back. Matt walks away, towards the bottom of the garden. The woman looks up at me. She nods her head once, twice, and gives me a 'thumbs up' sign. Her mouth moves, as if she is talking to me. Then she signals for me to move back. She turns and follows Matt.

I sink to the floor, clutching my chest, my heart thumping so hard it hurts. But my spirit soars. She saw me, she knows I need her, she will surely do something to help me now.

* * *

I try to act normally for the rest of the day, but my mind is elsewhere, my hands trembling, clumsy. When Madam comes upstairs, I freeze, certain she's coming for me, but she goes to her bedroom and closes the door. I hear her moving around, opening and shutting wardrobe doors and drawers. With luck, she will go out and I can breathe. It is hard for me to focus after what has happened.

I wonder what the woman will do now. Will she call the police? Will there be sirens, flashing lights, a sudden violent banging at the door? They'll search the house, break down my door, find me in my tiny room at the top. I am going to tell them everything, from the kidnap to imprisonment, the beatings and the near-starvation. I will give them my precious journal, with its dates and details. Sir and Madam will go to prison. Then, maybe — just maybe — she might understand what she has done to me.

I am worried about Matt. I don't know whose side he is on. He is employed by them, he does what Madam tells him to do — but there have been times when he has been kind to me. He doesn't talk much, going about his work in the garden, but when she is out he leaves me alone now, even when he is supposed to be watching me. It is possible he has no idea what my life is like, though that is hard to imagine. He can't think I am doing this willingly, surely. Perhaps he doesn't want to get involved.

But the woman does, I am sure of it. For once, I find myself smiling as I dust and polish and clean.

CHAPTER FORTY

Beth

From the bedroom window Beth can see the gardener already out there, inspecting the damage to the fence. If she's quick, she can catch him.

Ruff bounds about under her feet as she grabs her boots and coat. Opening the back door, she lets him run. He makes a beeline for the broken fence, trotting straight across it and into Oksana's garden before Beth has even stepped outside. It's still drizzling and gusts of wind tug at her hood as she follows him across the grass, tiptoeing gingerly over the broken fence.

"What a storm," she says to the gardener, who nods as she approaches. She smiles, hoping she looks friendly and unthreatening. He's younger than she remembered, his shoulders broad, his skin a deep brown. Dark hair brushes the collar of his oiled jacket. "I'm not surprised there's some damage."

"It's not finished yet, either," he says, squinting at the sky. "Looks like more to come."

"I'm Beth," she says, holding out her hand. "We're new next door. My husband is Adam. You work here?"

"Matt." He removes a muddy glove to shake her hand. His own is rough, the nails grubby. "I look after the garden, do a bit of maintenance, that sort of thing."

"Sorry about the dog," she says, turning to check on Ruff. "He seems obsessed with this garden." She turns to see him digging frantically in the flower bed beyond the lawn, earth flying into a heap behind him.

"Ruff, no!" Ruff looks up at her voice and as she steps towards him, skips a little and runs off towards the end of the garden.

"He's a bit of a rascal, I'm so sorry. That rose bush might need rescuing," she says, turning back to the gardener. As she does so, her eye is caught by a movement in the house.

The girl is at the same window as before, holding the sign. She raises one arm above the sign and points down towards the words. HELP ME.

Matt turns, his eyes following Beth's gaze. For a moment, a look of surprise crosses his face, then he raises an arm, gesticulating at the girl. His meaning is clear: she should get away from the window.

"Who is she, Matt?" Beth says, carefully. "I've seen her before. But when I asked Oksana, she said there was nobody else in the house. What's going on?"

Matt takes a searching look at the kitchen window. "We can't talk here," he says. "Follow me, let's go and find the dog."

He starts walking towards the end of the garden, into the area where bushes and trees provide cover. Beth turns back to the house where the girl still looks out, half-hidden by a curtain. Beth nods at her slowly, gives her a thumbs up.

"I've seen you," she whispers. "I'm going to help you."

* * *

Matt stops by a large chestnut tree, its trunk dark with rain. Fallen leaves form a mulch beneath, soft and slippery under Beth's feet. Great bubbles of water drip from above as she follows Matt's back into the cover of the tall trees. Ruff is nearby, exploring the undergrowth, lifting a leg every so often. Glancing back towards the house, Beth sees the girl has gone. There's no movement in any of the other windows.

"Who is that girl?" she says again. "Do you know anything about her?"

Talking to Matt could be disastrous for the girl, but it's a risk Beth has to take. If she doesn't, and nothing happens, then she daren't think of the consequences.

Matt glances towards the house again, his eyes nervous. "Look," he says. "I don't know what you know about these people, but they're not what they seem. You need to be very, very careful."

Beth feels her eyes widen. "What do you mean, not what they seem?"

"It doesn't matter. Just . . . take my advice, don't get involved."

"But the girl — she needs help! Somebody needs to find out—"

"I know she needs help." He looks into Beth's face, his eyes questioning. Then he takes a breath. "Look, can I trust you?"

"Of course. I could ask you the same thing — you do work for them, after all."

"I'm working as their gardener because of something that happened here that I don't understand yet. I think that girl is being held against her will, but I can't prove it. She's too frightened to talk to me. But there's a lot more to this than you'd imagine."

"I don't understand. What happened here? What do you mean?" Panic begins to rise in her throat.

He gestures for her to keep her voice down. "Listen, we can't talk now. I'll help you catch the dog. It's probably not a good idea to let him come back here until the fence is fixed." Beth opens her mouth to object. "Yes, I know . . ." He grasps her arm, his voice urgent. "I know we have to do something to help her. Can you meet me this evening?"

CHAPTER FORTY-ONE

Sofia

The house is quiet. Madam has gone out. My belly is tight, and not from hunger. I have eaten the leftovers of last night's supper, some kind of meaty Russian pie. I had to force it down cold — it would have tasted okay, I think, if it had been warm, but I don't have that option. I took an orange too, which looked past its best but was edible. The food sits heavy in my stomach.

Sir has been home for a few days now, too long for my liking. Signs of his presence are everywhere — his coat on the rack in the hallway, the well-stocked fridge, the increase in laundry. He leaves early and returns late. I wonder again what he does that earns him so much money. I think he is buying a new boat, because there are new glossy magazines and brochures in the sitting room with markers on some of the pages. I skim through them, looking at the pictures. Enormous yachts, bigger than this house, float on sparkling seas, the sun reflecting from their shining paintwork. Some have their own swimming pools and helicopters, and smiling, uniformed staff, their shirts white as snow. The owners look relaxed and proud, their wives beautiful, glamorous, showing off their tans and their jewellery.

How does anyone become that rich?

I am still in a dream of boats and beautiful sunshine when Matt walks in, startling me so much that I drop the magazine from my hand. It lands with a slap on the polished floor. Flustered, I reach down to pick it up, turn to carry on with my work.

"Sofia." His voice is soft behind me. "Don't be scared."

Slowly I turn to face him, swallowing the bile that has suddenly flooded my mouth. I am terrified. It was a huge risk showing the sign when he was there. If he chooses to tell Madam, I will be out for sure.

I step behind the coffee table, just in case.

"It's okay," he says. "Listen carefully. I — we — saw your sign. No—" I gasp and shake my head — "I'm not going to tell them. You need to trust me, I'm not . . . who I seem."

I wait, ready to run if he comes close. I don't understand what he means. This could be a trick. Oksana could have told him to get rid of me, to force me into a car and take me away.

"Don't be scared," he says again. "I'm going to try to help you. But I need to be sure . . ." He asks me something, but I don't understand, so I say nothing. "Do you want to go home?"

I nod and, to my surprise, tears spring to my eyes. My throat swells. I don't trust myself to speak.

"It's going to be okay," he says. "Help is coming soon. Do you understand?"

I nod again.

"Trust me," he says, and strides away.

I sink to the floor, tears running down my cheeks. They drop onto my chest, making damp patches on either side of my T-shirt. At the mention of home, all my emotions, hidden for so long, rise and swell, overwhelming me. I recognise what I am feeling. It is hope.

My hands shake for a long time after he leaves.

* * *

I have refused hope a place in my heart for a long time, and for good reasons. Hope, when you have no control of your life, leads to desperation. If you have hope, every small disappointment, every single, tiny failure builds and grows into a huge mass until your mind can't deal with it anymore and you go mad.

It doesn't help to have hope when you are a prisoner. I have worked on myself until any trace of it has transformed into a different emotion: rage. Rage, when you have no control, is a much better emotion. It gives you strength to carry on, it helps you plan your revenge. It has far more power than hope.

So that is why I try not to hope, even this time. There are so many ways it could go wrong. My prison is very strong, the warders clever and watchful, always. Matt could be lying, waiting for Madam to give him the word later today. The woman next door could try to help me, only to have Madam tell her I am not here, that I have never existed. She can refuse her entry if she comes to the door. Perhaps the woman will contact the police, as I imagined, and they won't believe her. They will believe Madam. She is beautiful — and she can be very charming. Beautiful women have a way of making fools of men, even if they are policemen. Even with my small experience of life, I know this.

They could take me away today, tonight, in the dark, and nobody could do anything about it. Even if Matt is my friend, he would not be here to help me. And Madam knows I won't go easily. They will probably bring other men to hold me down, drug me, bundle me into the boot of a car, and I won't be able to do a thing about it.

Once again, I am helpless.

CHAPTER FORTY-TWO

Beth

There's a pub on a corner close to the small row of 1960s shopfronts, unremarkable in design, faded and greying now. A dry cleaner's rubs shoulders with a newsagent, a charity shop and a hardware store. The one redeeming feature of the drab frontage is a small cafe fitted out with cheerful colours and comfortable chairs.

The Crown pub, however, has not been refurbished recently. It looks dejected, its grubby brick exterior far from inviting. Beth has never been inside before. She feels instantly out of place as she pushes the swing door open a crack to see if Matt is there. She's brought Ruff with her for moral support, and she's glad he's with her as three men, she guesses builders from their plaster-and-paint-strewn clothing, turn to look as she approaches the bar. The soles of her shoes stick slightly to the brown patterned carpet as she walks.

There's no sign of Matt, so she orders a drink and carries it to a small table beneath a dusty window, settling Ruff down on the carpet beside her. She's not surprised to be the only other person in this dim place on a Thursday evening. Although it's early, only seven o'clock, she doubts it will get busy. The room is far from welcoming, with its dark wood furniture, old-fashioned decor and draughty doors. She keeps her coat on and her collar up.

A few moments later, the door swishes open, cold air gusting into the room. Matt gives her a nod and goes straight to the bar, returning with a glass of beer. He sits opposite her on one of the battered stools scattered around among the tables. Ruff greets him with a wagging tail.

"He's a nice dog. Sorry about this place. Terrible pub, but it's convenient," Matt says, scratching Ruff behind the ears. She nods. The sooner they can get out of here, the better. Adam is out at a choir rehearsal and she wants to be back before he returns. She hasn't told him what she's doing, he'll only disapprove.

"I haven't got much time," she says. "What's going on, Matt? Who is that girl — what's she doing there?"

Matt takes a sip of his drink, wiping the foam from his upper lip with his hand. "I'll tell you what I know — and what I suspect. It's a bit of a long story, but I'll try to make it quick."

She nods, her eyes on his.

"I've been working there for about six months," Matt says. "I'm not really a gardener. I'm undercover."

"You're . . . what?" She wasn't expecting this.

"Doing a bit of detection work, undercover," Matt says, with a wry smile. Beth tries to reorganise her face. She's beginning to feel like she's in a crime movie.

"What's it all about?"

Matt sighs, gazing down at his hands, sadness sketched in the lines of his face. "My younger sister, Julia, got married a few years ago to a man I never met — no one in our family did. He was a wealthy, older man who turned out to be very controlling. Soon after they married — it was secret, none of the family was invited — they moved south and settled here. He wouldn't let her see her family or friends, and though she said she was happy with him, we suspected — we just knew — she was being manipulated. That man was Keith."

"It was Keith? So . . . your sister was his first wife?"

Matt nods. "My parents were devastated. She begged them not to contact her, because Keith would be furious if he found she was in touch with any of her old friends or family. We all tried. We sent gifts and messages at Christmas and on her birthday, but we never knew if she got them — there was never any response. In the end we didn't want to cause trouble for her, so we had to accept that she wanted to cut herself off." He picks up his drink, then puts it down without sipping. "It was difficult for all of us. But then Mum got cancer and begged me to find Julia. I tried all the contacts we had, but there was no response — nothing on social media, no reply to texts or emails, her mobile number didn't work. She just seemed to have disappeared. I tried contacting Keith, but that didn't work either."

"Did you talk to the police?" Beth says.

He nods. "We reported her missing a couple of years ago. They followed up with Keith. He told them it was her choice to cut off her family, and that he's not in touch with her any more. They don't seem to be taking it any further."

"So you came here to find her?"

"I was hoping to reach her before Mum got any worse. Sadly, she died a year ago. I know Julia would have gone to see her if she'd known about the cancer — she would never have abandoned her. But she didn't even come to the funeral. That's when I got really worried. So here I am."

"What do you think happened to her?"

He shrugs, his index finger tracing around a circular stain on the table. "I don't know yet. When I arrived, Oksana was already here and, I presume, married to Keith. I suppose it's perfectly feasible that Julia and Keith broke up, they divorced and he remarried. She may not want to have anything to do with him. But once she was away from him, why didn't she get in touch with us? Nobody's heard from her since shortly after they married. We worried she might have had some kind of breakdown, but . . . there's no trace of her in the house, as far as I can see. I can't ask Keith, he doesn't speak to me and obviously he doesn't know who I really am."

"Perhaps she's too ashamed to contact you? If she had a breakdown, I mean?"

"That's possible, I suppose," Matt says. "But I don't think so. It's been a few years now — there's been plenty of time for her to get in touch. I'm thinking the worst, I'm afraid. I'm beginning to suspect that Keith is involved in something very nasty."

Beth feels suddenly cold. "What kind of nasty?"

"I don't know exactly what he does. Money isn't a problem, though — his wallet's always bulging with cash. Oksana splashes it around too — clothes, jewellery, expensive art on the walls. Julia didn't know what Keith did for a living when they married, he didn't like her asking. That always seemed strange to me. He travels a lot to Russia and Eastern Europe, and all the people around him seem to be from there too. It could be genuine, but . . ."

"It does seem odd, not wanting your wife to know what you do. Even if he was very controlling, you'd have thought she would need to know."

"I might be wrong. I have no proof of anything yet, though the girl might be the key."

"Do you know anything about her? Her name, where she's from?"

"Her name is Sofia, but I don't know where she's from. Possibly Russia, like Oksana, maybe Eastern Europe. She doesn't talk much at all, she's too scared."

Sofia. At last, she has an identity. Now she has a name, Beth feels closer to her somehow.

"So, why haven't you done anything to help her?"

"I wasn't sure at first — it wasn't obvious what was happening. I didn't know if she was a relative of Oksana's, or if she was being paid properly. But recently it's become obvious that she's a prisoner. She tried to escape a few weeks ago, climbed out of a downstairs window. I was right there, and Oksana saw her straight away. I had to make out I was stopping her. She didn't have a chance."

"Why didn't you help her then, confront Oksana?"

"You don't know Oksana. She would have sacked me on the spot, and that would have got me nowhere. Anyway, Keith was in the house, and I didn't want to face up to him — he's pretty unpleasant at the best of times. I have to find proof before they find me out."

"Poor Sofia! I mean, this is inconceivable. Awful."

He nods, his mouth turning down in agreement. "I doubt she's ever given any money, let alone allowed out of the house. Oksana sometimes asks me to keep an eye on her. She's not even allowed in the garden. I let her sit there sometimes when there's nobody in."

"But why are you letting it go on — the girl clearly needs help!" Beth begins to feel angry with this man. If he had only helped Sofia, she would be home with her family by now.

Matt looks over his shoulder before he speaks.

"It's obvious now that she's in trouble, but as I say, I didn't know at first. I'm not in the house very much, and I couldn't be sure she wasn't there from choice. But I'm not a totally irresponsible person — I've been keeping an eye on her, as far as I can. The only reason I've delayed is to get some evidence."

"What do you think happened to Julia?"

He lowers his voice. "What do I think? I think . . . that she's been . . ." He swallows, looking suddenly vulnerable. "Got rid of."

Beth gasps, her hand flying to her mouth. "Got rid of — as in, murdered? Oh, my . . ."

"It all points to that. There's absolutely no sign of her anywhere. Nobody can tell me where she's gone. Why wouldn't she contact her family? Why won't Keith cooperate? Something must have happened to her — it's the only answer."

"But surely it's a matter for the police?"

"We tried that and got nowhere. We have to find some evidence. If I'm right and they got rid of her, my only chance is that house and staying close to Keith and Oksana. Otherwise it's a dead end."

"But Matt, in the meantime, Sofia could disappear too — she could be murdered, just like Julia! We could save her life if we go to the police now. You saw the sign, you're a second witness — they have to believe me now. We can insist they search the house. They'll find Sofia, and who knows what else? It could turn up the evidence you need. Oh . . ."

"What?"

"We should have taken a photo, of her with the sign. But you saw it, and you can back me up. Will you, Matt?"

"No, you're right," Matt says. "It's been long enough, and I've come up with nothing. I agree, Sofia is in danger. If we can persuade the police to go in . . . Perhaps she can tell them something about Julia. She will certainly give them a reason to investigate."

"We mustn't give Oksana and Keith any warning," Beth says. "If they've hidden it for this long, they'll be suspicious, and we'll put her in even more danger. The police have tried before — I asked them to go round, but Oksana put them off."

"I'm not surprised, she's a tricky one. I'm not sure who makes the decisions there, but she's certainly not kind to the girl. And she can be very persuasive."

"I'm sure she can. Will you come with me to the police tomorrow morning, first thing?"

"Let's do it," he says.

CHAPTER FORTY-THREE

Sofia

I sit on the worn-out mattress, biting my fingernails until they bleed. My whole body is tense, my ears aching, listening for feet on the stairs. My neck and shoulders hurt too. They have been knotted all day — every muscle taut as a guitar string. When I stick my fingers into my shoulder, I feel iron-hard lumps and sinews that refuse to relax even when I try my hardest to rub them loose.

I go back to the coded message from the washroom.
BOSEIO? ROSEIO? B05E10?
Then, BHS. Or RHS or RH5 or BH5.

What does it mean? Is it a name? The first letters of each word in a message? I have never heard of anyone called Bose, but Rose is a possibility. Perhaps another girl was here before Julia. But what do the other letters or numbers mean? I try all the different combinations of letters and numbers until I can't see them anymore. I was never any good at crosswords, and this clue has beaten me. I go back to the washroom and trace the letters and numbers once again. It is no good. I am still not sure of the Bs and the Rs, or whether the Os and the Is are numbers or letters.

I write a page of my journal, about what has happened today. It takes a long time, and by the time I have finished my eyelids are drooping.

Praying for sleep, I climb under the covers and close my eyes. I allow my mind to drift. I have done what I can — I can't guess what will happen next.

* * *

I wake to the sound of the front door slamming. The crunch of gravel in the drive forces its way into my strange, frantic dreams. With the final click of the gate I am awake, my eyes opening into a darkness so thick I wonder for a moment if I am somewhere different. Panic draws my body up to sitting, and gradually, as I stare around me into the blackness, I make out the familiar triangle of the window above me, a dim glow under the door. I never thought I would feel relieved to wake up here, but I am. In the last weeks I have started to worry that they will take me in the night, put something to my face to knock me out and spirit me away.

It must be very early, or Madam would have woken me already. There's no sign of dawn outside, no sounds of traffic. Nothing within the house to show that Madam is up and about. Perhaps Sir has left on one of his trips again. If he has, I will be glad. He scares me. She is smaller — against her, I have a chance. My work keeps me fit, I can see the muscles in my arms and legs, and though I am thin, I am still strong. And my rage gives me extra power.

When I hear the sound of her slippered feet on the stairs, the scrape of metal on metal as the key slides into the lock, I ease out of bed and turn the light on. I feel lighter, full of expectation, as I dress. But again I have to warn myself against hope.

I look for signs that Sir has left again. His bag of toiletries has gone from their bathroom. I look into the wardrobe, but it is hard to tell if he is away: sometimes he takes only a couple of jackets, shirts and trousers, and there are so many, some could be at the cleaners or in the laundry basket. His coat is not there in the hall, but that may not mean he's travelling. I will only know when he doesn't come back tonight and in the next few days. I cross my fingers and bite my lip until it bleeds.

In the hallway, Madam's bag is on the table. A beautiful red coat hangs at the bottom of the stairs. I pray that this means she is going out.

For the next hour I scrub and polish and dust as if the British queen is coming to stay. I have too much nervous energy today, I need to work it off before it explodes. Madam spends a long time getting ready, but suddenly she is there on the stairs, carrying a pair of red heels in her hand. She sits on the bottom step to put them on. When she stands, she towers over me, glossy, every part of her perfectly groomed. I feel like a mouse next to her.

"You must polish kitchen floor. Properly. There are stains," she says, gazing at her image in the mirror. She eases her graceful body into the coat, flicking her hair from under the collar. It falls in a silken swathe down her back. "When I get back, I want stains gone. And drawing room is dusty. I see horrible dirt in corners. Clean properly today. Polish all. You hear?"

I hang my head, say "Yes, Madam," my voice meek and soft. No challenges to her today.

Only, I hope with all my heart, the big one.

CHAPTER FORTY-FOUR

Beth

It's past eight by the time Beth gets home after meeting Matt. The house is quiet, Adam still out, Tom and Abigail in their rooms. She calls up the stairs to them, but all she can hear by way of reply is Tom's voice chatting to his friends on a computer game and the faint strains of Abi's music.

In the kitchen, Ruff is curled in his bed. He wags his tail when he sees her but doesn't move. She pours herself a glass of water and sits, her mind racing. So Matt is not a gardener at all. Keith might have murdered his first wife. Sofia is terrified and could be in dreadful danger. It all seems unreal. She wonders what Adam will say. He'll be sceptical at the very least, if not disbelieving. He definitely won't want her to get involved.

But this time, despite the terrible consequences she experienced in the past, getting involved is the right thing to do. In some ways, she feels even more compelled to act. Interfering in other people's lives may not always be the right thing, but there are situations where it is crucial. She will never forgive herself if she has the chance to help but does nothing.

What if Julia was murdered? Are they really living next door to a hardened criminal, a danger to them, to their children? The thought is just terrifying. She feels her breathing quicken, her heart thump, the beginnings of panic in her belly.

She really has to do something. And it's better if she doesn't get swayed by Adam's sensible reasoning or her own past experiences. The girl could be in danger right now.

She's not going to tell Adam.

* * *

As Beth approaches the traffic lights close to the centre of town, cursing the rush hour traffic, it starts to rain again. Big, fat drops drum on the roof of the car. She swears out loud. This will make the traffic even worse and she's already late to meet Matt.

She almost runs the short distance from the car park to the imposing red-brick building that houses the Thames Valley Police. Matt is waiting on the steps outside, sheltering from the rain in the entranceway. He's in his usual gardening clothes, a hat pulled down over his forehead, muddy trousers tucked into sturdy boots. He nods as she approaches, turning to hold the door for her.

"Sorry I'm late," she says, shaking her umbrella and dropping it in a stand by the door.

The young policeman she spoke to on her first visit waits behind the desk. He gives her a nod of recognition.

"We'd like to see DI Thomson please," she says.

The young man hesitates, glancing at Matt.

"There's new evidence regarding the report I made recently," Beth says quickly. "This is Matt . . ."

"Davies," Matt says.

The policeman notes his name.

"One moment please. Take a seat."

After only a few moments, DI Thomson waves them through and they follow him to an interview room deep in the maze of corridors. Matt's face is grim as he describes why he's there.

"And you're the gardener, you say?" DI Thomson gives Matt a piercing look. "How long have you worked there?"

"A few months, part-time. I do two to three days a week, depending on the weather and the time of year. Plus a bit of handyman work, fixing things around the house. But there's not much of that."

Beth wonders if Matt will tell the police his real purpose for being there. So far, he's holding back. Perhaps he's deciding whether to trust them. Perhaps he's hoping, if they search the house and find Sofia, they will look further into Keith and Oksana and discover the truth about Julia.

"So, you both saw the girl, Sofia, holding a sign to the window. The sign said, 'Help me' — right?" the detective says.

"Yes," Matt says, and Beth nods.

The detective focuses on Matt. "And the girl has been there all the time you've been working there?"

"She has."

"What do you think is her situation?"

Beth starts to speak but DI Thomson indicates for her to let Matt respond.

"At first I wasn't sure if she was the paid help, or perhaps a relative living there in return for help around the house. Oksana is Russian, and Sofia could be Russian, or maybe Eastern European. She hasn't got a British accent. But I don't think that's the case. They don't treat her nicely."

"By which you mean . . ."

"She never goes out, not even into the garden, or at least, only when I let her sit outside when they're out. I've never seen her leave the house or have friends round. She seems very frightened, doesn't say anything, avoids me when she can. She recently tried to escape — climbed out of a window — but she didn't get far. Oksana hit her across the face. I've seen her with bruises at other times too."

DI Thomson notes everything down, nodding.

"And why haven't you reported this before?" he says.

"As I say, I wasn't sure at first. My employers are not easy people to talk to, and we never have a proper conversation. It makes it difficult to ask questions. It's hard to accuse people when you don't have any concrete proof." His manner is calm and confident. Beth is reassured that with his evidence, DI Thomson might believe her now.

He sits back, pondering for a moment. Then he slaps his pen down on the table with a crack, scooting his chair forward. "Thank you for that," he says. "I believe we have enough now to get a warrant to search the house." He nods at Beth. She returns the nod, breathing a sigh of relief. "I'll do my best to speed up the process. I know it's been a few weeks since you first reported it, Mrs . . .?" He shuffles the papers in the thin file in front of him. "Mrs Grant, yes, apologies." He stands and opens the door.

"Will you let us know what happens?"

He nods. "We may need to interview you again, both of you, depending on what we find out. We'll be in touch."

* * *

The day passes slowly after that. Beth can't help watching the house next door, but nothing seems to be happening. There's no movement from the inside that she can see, no sign of any cars coming or going.

After lunch the rain eases and Matt's dark shape appears by the fallen fence with a wheelbarrow, a saw in his hand. It looks like he's starting to clear the broken panels away. She takes the opportunity, putting on her coat and calling Ruff to the door. Attaching his lead, she heads out to the garden and strolls around while the dog sniffs and wanders. Approaching Matt as he bends to clear some more wood, she says, keeping her voice low, "Has anything happened?"

"Nothing yet," he says, straightening up. "Oksana isn't back yet either. I'm hoping they'll come while she's out. Then I can say they insisted, and let them loose in the house."

"I hope they do insist," Beth says. "Surely if they have a warrant, she'll have to let them in?"

"Of course. But it's better if she's out."

"Any sign of Sofia?" she says, gazing up at the blank windows.

"Not that I've seen," he says. "She's probably lying low, hoping something's going to happen. Poor girl, she must be terrified."

"I hope they come today," Beth says. "Though they seem very tied up with this latest discovery . . ."

"What's that?"

"Some kids broke into a derelict building — they found remains . . ."

"Remains of what?"

"It was in the paper—" Beth's hand flies to her mouth. "Oh, my God. Human remains, Matt — they found human remains."

Matt's face turns pale. He stares at her, shock registering in his eyes.

"What?" he says. "How long had they been there — was it a woman? Do they know who it was?"

"I'm so sorry, it didn't occur to me — hang on, I'll get the paper for you. Come with me."

He reads the story with shaking hands. "I have to go," he says. "I need to call the police."

"Of course — good luck," she says to his departing back, immediately wishing she hadn't. Whichever way it turns out won't be down to luck, and it won't be good.

CHAPTER FORTY-FIVE

Sofia

Madam is still out, the doors locked, everything's quiet. Nothing is happening. There is no sign of Matt in the garden, the dog or the woman. I keep thinking about the woman and her sign to me, the thumbs-up, showing me she understands. But will she be able to do anything about it? Will the police come and be fooled again by that witch and her charms?

I decide to be ready. I wrap my journal in a plastic bag, hide it in my waistband, under my top. It is the only thing I want to keep from this prison. I have been here for almost three years. Three years of my life stolen from me.

A thought strikes me. I go to her bedroom and open her jewellery box, with its three hinged drawers, bursting with rings and necklaces, bracelets and earrings. The contents sparkle and glow, inviting me in. I wonder what they are worth. I bet one of these pieces could feed my whole family for months, if not years.

I want to take something that will really upset her. But if nothing happens today or tomorrow, she will notice, and I fear that will be the end of me. So I must prepare to leave in a hurry, and make it easy to take things with me. In the lowest level, in a divided velvet cushion, is a line of beautiful rings. There is one with diamonds, another with a large blue stone surrounded by smaller ones. They look like the adverts in her magazines. I move them up to the top level, where I can grab them easily.

I turn my attention to her clothes. That soft cream coat hangs alongside others in the wardrobe. I stroke the arm and whisper, *I choose you*. I ignore the rows of shoes, their sharp, pointed toes and heels lined up like weapons ready to strike. But the cashmere jumpers, those I will raid, if I get the chance. My mama would love one of those.

At the thought of my mother, I enter a dream. I see myself arriving back, walking towards my home, my parents running towards me, my little sister jumping up and down with excitement. We hug and cry and laugh all at the same time. My little sister — she will have grown so much! — will carry my bag inside, and I will hand out presents to everyone. Those diamond rings will pay for everything, and we will be rich.

But then I stop. I don't want us to be rich. We have riches enough in my family. We have joy and laughter and love. We have animals and beautiful countryside and sun. And once I'm back I will never leave again.

* * *

There is something else I need to do. The timing is crucial. It mustn't be too soon, in case everything carries on as normal for a few days. I need to do it at just the right moment. I plan carefully, moving around the house, noting every possibility.

I have had the time to think about this — I know this house so well now. Every step on the staircase, every piece of furniture, all the ornaments I have dusted and polished and put back in their places. I know about Keith and Oksana's private things: their underwear, their expensive clothing, his aftershave, her scent. The contraceptives she keeps in a little box in her bedside table. The porn he watches on his laptop. There is almost nowhere I haven't been, cleaned or investigated.

The only exception is his office — his desk and the safe. That is surely where they should concentrate, when they come. There will be secrets there he will not want seen.

I also have detailed knowledge of her routine. What she does when she comes through the door, how she throws her coat on the post at the bottom of the stairs for me to hang up, abandons her shoes for me to put away. I know the rooms she visits regularly and those she does not.

It is not a good idea, I think, to have a routine when your enemies are close.

It doesn't take long for me to decide on my plan. It is simple. It won't take long and it won't be noticed. Not until the crucial moment, that is. All I need is my screwdriver.

When I have finished I go back to the laundry room, where a large pile of creased clothes and bedlinen waits. I get the ironing board out, fill the iron with water and take the first item, a shirt. But I am not concentrating. I dream about home, my family, the things I will do when I get back. The sun in summer, the snow in winter. Even the fog will seem beautiful after living as a prisoner. I will spend as much time as possible outside, read books and study hard to finish my education. I will run free in the fields and on the hills behind our house. I will play with my sister, I will dance and jump and swim, hug my mama and tell her I love her all day long. I will help her in the kitchen, labour in the fields with my father to show him how much I care. I will go to the church every week to thank God for saving me, for showing me that my country is beautiful, my village is beautiful, that life is beautiful.

CHAPTER FORTY-SIX

Sofia

When the buzzer at the gate goes, I am so startled, I almost drop the iron. I feel a shock wave rising from my gut to the hairs on the top of my head. I start to panic, I don't know what to do — but then I see Matt heading around the side of the house towards the gate. Perhaps he will let them in. I turn the iron off, tiptoe to the front door and pick up the handset as quietly as I can.

I hear the sounds of cars passing, a male voice. I peer through the window beside the door and see Matt at the gate, which is opening slowly. Beyond the gate is a man in a dark uniform. A police car creeps into the driveway — I hear car doors opening and closing. I stand like a statue, waiting for the front door to open, but nothing happens. Then I realise they are going round the back to the kitchen door. I hold my breath at sounds in the kitchen, boots on the floor. Cold air wafts towards me as I stand, unable to breathe or move my feet, rooted to the spot.

"This way," I hear Matt say. Suddenly they are here, Matt in his big, dirty boots that he is not allowed to wear in the house. A policeman follows him — he seems to fill up the entire hallway. Feeling the blood drain from my face, I can only stare at him, terrified by his size, his black uniform. Is he here to arrest me? I have no ID, no passport, no way to defend myself if they want to put me in prison. Then I notice behind them a policewoman, the men stepping aside to let her through.

"It's all right, Sofia. Don't be scared," Matt says. I can't speak. Even my legs are trembling. I am frightened I might collapse. The woman moves forward. She has a round, open face, kind eyes.

"Hello . . . Sofia, is it? My name is Margaret. We're from the police," she says, her voice soft and calm. "We'd like to talk to you, if that's okay?"

I nod. My throat feels as if I have swallowed a stone.

"Shall we sit down somewhere?" The woman looks towards the drawing room.

I shake my head. "No, no . . ." I turn to Matt, hoping he understands. "Madam, she . . ."

"It's okay, Sofia, she can't hurt you now," Matt says.

"But . . . she . . . coming back . . ." Even my English is deserting me. I need to get away, now — I can't see her, ever again. "Please, we must go now — please!" I grab the woman's arm — she puts a hand over mine to reassure me.

"Okay, Sofia, we will go. Just answer me one thing, if you can. Are you here against your will? Are you a prisoner here?" She speaks slowly, as if to a child, leaning towards me. "Do you understand?"

"Yes," I say, my voice breaking. "I am prisoner. They take me, make me work. Lock the door. No money. Madam, she beats me. Three years . . ." The woman straightens up, turns to the policeman, a look of satisfaction on her face.

Matt nods at me and smiles, and I feel a little better.

"We will take you to the police station. We can talk there. Don't be frightened. Is that okay with you?" the woman says.

"Yes, yes," I say. "I just get — my coat . . ."

The woman nods and I leap up the stairs, my legs suddenly full of energy, my mind racing. I return wearing the cream coat. I stare ahead as we leave, but I think Matt has noticed. I don't care, and I am sure he does not either, because he says nothing.

Once in the car with the engine running, I start to breathe again. I don't look back, not once. For the first and last time, I am in the car that makes the crunching noise on the gravel as it leaves.

CHAPTER FORTY-SEVEN

Beth

Beth's mobile buzzes on the hard surface of the kitchen table, like an angry wasp. She's hoping Matt will call, tell her what the police have found out about the remains. She's been in a turmoil of anxiety all day, what with Sofia and now the possibility of Matt finding Julia.

"Mrs Grant? It's DI Thomson."

"Did you go in?" She can hear the desperation in her voice. "Did you find her?"

"We have her. You were right, she was being held prisoner."

"Oh thank goodness," Beth says, all thoughts of Matt and Julia gone. She sits abruptly, her legs unable to hold her up. "How is she?"

"She's scared, of course. We're having a doctor check her out now. But she's asking for you."

"For me? Are you sure?"

"I'm sure. She doesn't trust the police — it often happens. She knows you helped to get her out, and she says she'll talk once you're here. Are you able to come to the station in an hour or so?"

That poor girl. It's not surprising she finds it difficult to trust people.

"Of course I'll come. Do I need to . . . bring anything? Food for her, clothes, anything like that?" She's already working out which of Abigail's clothes might do for Sofia, trying to remember what she has in the fridge.

"No, we'll give her something to eat and drink now. As for clothes, I think that can wait." He sounds amused at Beth's mothering instincts. All she can feel is deep sympathy for the girl and relief that it's over. Relief for herself, that this time she got it right. And that she can tell Adam.

She wonders what will happen next, if Sofia will be taken into care. Maybe she's an adult, though. She seemed so small and childlike at the window, but she could easily be over eighteen. What will happen to her now? Beth is determined not to abandon her, she'll do her best to make sure she returns to her family as soon as possible, if that's what she wants, and until then is looked after properly.

Adam picks up her call immediately. "Hi. You okay?"

She so rarely calls him at work, he assumes it's something urgent.

"I'm fine. But something's happened at last, next door. The gardener — his name's Matt — he saw the girl with the sign too, and we went and told the police, and now they've come and got her and she's asking for me. I'm going to the station in an hour." The words fall out of her mouth in a flood.

There's a shocked pause at the end of the line. "Wait, hold on. Slow down a minute. Are you all right? Have the police arrested Oksana?"

"No — well, not that I know, anyway. They've rescued the girl. Her name's Sofia. The girl at the window. She was a prisoner and now she's free. Well, she's at the police station at the moment, but she will be free, soon. Oksana was out when they went in, I think. Matt helped. I'm so relieved, Adam . . ."

"Wow, okay." Adam sounds stunned. "Listen, I've got to go, I'm in a meeting. But I'll be home as soon as I can so you can tell me everything."

She says a silent "thank you" for a husband who doesn't always need to be right.

* * *

In her bag is a home-made sandwich with cheese and salad, some fruit and an oat bar. She simply couldn't leave the house empty-handed, knowing that the girl was frightened and alone. There's also one of Abigail's jumpers, just in case.

The man at reception recognises her. She's barely sat down when DI Thomson appears on the other side of the security gates and waves her through.

"How's she doing?" Beth says as they walk through the maze of corridors and up a flight of stairs. Each time she goes to the police station it seems to have grown, a never-ending labyrinth of corridors and stairways.

"The doctor's seen her. He says she's too thin, possibly malnourished, but apart from a skin condition and some old bruising, she seems okay. Mentally, who knows? She's fragile and confused. She's been a slave for three years. I think she'll be happy to see you."

"Three years? She's been kept inside for three years?" If only they'd seen her earlier.

The detective shows her into a room. She's surprised to see there's nobody there.

Anticipating her reaction, he says, "I need to tell you about the procedure before you see her. Her name is Sofia."

Beth nods. "Yes, Matt — the gardener — he told me."

"As it's pretty clear she's been a victim of domestic slavery and held against her will, we've put her case forward to the National Referral Mechanism, a Home Office system that makes sure people like Sofia get the right kind of help. At this stage, the Salvation Army gets involved. They provide specialist support for victims — they'll be with her at the interview."

"Can I be at the interview too?"

"I'm afraid not."

Beth opens her mouth to object, but he holds up a hand. "It's the law. It's to protect her, in case you've been influenced by her captors, or are one of them . . ."

"But . . ."

"You do live next door, and you know Oksana, so you can see how it might happen."

"So what can I do to help her?"

"You can see her now, maybe talk to her for a few minutes to reassure her, with others in the room. Perhaps you can explain to her that she's safe now, and the reason why you're not allowed to help with the interview."

"Okay . . . then should I wait? What will happen to her afterwards?"

"The Salvation Army will help her with whatever she needs: legal advice, accommodation, protection, practical help. You can wait if you like — you'll be able to see her when the formal interview is finished."

"I'm happy to help too, in any way I can."

"Let's see how she responds. At the moment she seems shell-shocked, too scared to talk to us. She might open up once you're there. We need to go gently."

"Can I ask you something before we go in?"

"Of course."

"What will happen to my neighbours? Have you arrested them?"

"We have surveillance on the house, and we'll bring them both in as soon as we can."

"And what about Matt, the gardener? He wasn't part of it, you know — he helped me when he realised what was going on."

"He's making a statement right now. We'll need to take a statement from you too, after you've seen Sofia." He turns to open a door. "Right, let's go and see her."

"Wait a minute — there's one other thing," she says, stopping abruptly. He turns, surprised. "Matt spoke to you about his sister?"

The detective nods.

"Was it her? The remains, in the derelict building?"

"We don't know yet, I'm afraid. But we're looking at the possibility."

* * *

This room is bright, large picture windows looking out over the streets, sofas and chairs arranged round a coffee table. It's not a beautiful room, the furniture is sparse, the walls bare, but it's a lot better than the interview rooms Beth's seen before. DI Thomson stands to one side, leaning on the wall. He gestures to Beth to go forward.

In one of the chairs is a woman she hasn't seen before. Sofia is perched on the edge of a sofa, her arms curled around her waist, head down, her body taking up so little space she's almost not there. She looks up when Beth walks in, her eyes red-rimmed, the skin of her cheeks pallid.

The woman jumps up, holding her hand out to Beth. "I'm Sandy Kerr, from the Salvation Army," she says, smiling. Her handshake is firm, her voice reassuringly warm. "You must be Mrs Grant. Good to meet you. Come and sit with Sofia." She indicates a place on the sofa next to the girl.

"Call me Beth, please," Beth says, sitting down, leaving a space between herself and Sofia in case the girl is frightened.

"Hello, Sofia," she says softly. "I'm so pleased to meet you at last."

The girl glances sideways at her, looks quickly back down at her hands.

"I'm Beth. I saw you at the window." She watches the girl's fingers. They are gripped tight together but still they tremble. Her nails are chewed to the quick, the skin around them red and sore. Her face is in shadow behind strands of lank, greasy hair.

"It's all right, Sofia, you're safe now," Beth says. "We're here to help you. You are free, you can go home very soon."

At that, the girl looks up at Beth, her eyes full of tears. She tries to speak, her lips working. Nothing comes out but a sob: a horrible, rasping noise. Beth can't help herself. Her own eyes welling, she moves closer, her arms out.

Sofia bends her head onto Beth's shoulder and weeps as if she'll never stop.

CHAPTER FORTY-EIGHT

Beth

Sandy leaves the room, returning a few minutes later with tissues and water. They wait patiently for the sobs to subside.

Sofia sips with shaking hands.

"Feeling a little better?" Beth says gently, when the girl has blown her nose and wiped the tears from her face. Her breathing settles — she seems calmer now.

"Are you ready to answer a few questions?" Sandy asks.

Sofia nods, but continues to wipe her eyes, one hand in Beth's. It's so small and thin, all knuckle and bone. Her wrist looks as if it would break with the smallest knock, though her grip on Beth's hand is strong. Their legs and shoulders touch, as if the girl is gathering strength from their closeness.

All Beth wants to do is take her home and look after her.

"Will you need an interpreter?" she asks Sandy.

"She says not," Sandy says. "But we have one here in the station just in case. We want to be sure she understands what we're saying to her, and it's as well to have someone ready to help. Perhaps you could explain to Sofia why you can't stay for the interview?"

Beth says, turning to face Sofia, "I'm going to leave the room while you talk to Sandy. I'll be close by, in the next room, but I'm not allowed to stay while you answer Sandy's questions."

Sofia shakes her head, her eyes filling with tears again, her grip tightening on Beth's hand.

"It's okay, Sofia, it really is. I promise you. I will wait for you. Sandy will look after you." Sandy nods and smiles at the girl. Sofia lets Beth slide her hand from beneath her own.

As she stands to leave the room, Sandy says, "Are you able to stay a while?"

"Yes, I'll wait. I can stay as long as necessary. I'll call my children later. I will see you soon, Sofia."

* * *

Three hours later, Sandy puts her head round the door of the room where Beth sits reading a book on her mobile. Her interview with DI Thomson was over in half an hour, and she's been drinking their terrible coffee and waiting ever since.

"Thank you so much for waiting, I'm sorry it's been so long," Sandy says. "You can come in now. She's done really well."

"Good. Is it finished, the interview?"

"We need to do a little more tomorrow, but it's time to stop now. She's worn out."

When Beth enters the room, Sofia is slumped on the sofa, her eyes closed.

"Hi, Sofia," Beth says, sitting next to her. "Are you okay? Sandy says you did very well."

The girl nods. She looks close to exhaustion, her skin grey, blue shadows around her eyes.

"Let's take a break for the day. Do you need the bathroom?" Sandy asks.

"Yes, thank you." Sofia stands, stretching her back slowly, and steps towards the door.

"I'll take you." They leave the room for a few moments, Sandy taking her notebook with her. A few moments later she returns without the notebook, standing in the doorway to wait for Sofia.

"What will happen to her now?" Beth says. "Where will she go?"

"We'll take her to a safe house. Tomorrow, we'll finish the interview process, hopefully. She'll get all the support she needs, things like legal advice, counselling if she needs it. And we'll help her get home, of course. I'll be in close contact with her, don't worry, I'll look after her."

"Can I stay with her now, until she leaves?"

"Of course."

"I've brought some food for her. DI Thomson said not to, but I couldn't leave the house without bringing something. Is it okay to give it to her now?"

Sandy smiles. "Of course. She should eat. Then we'll see if we can contact her parents. She wants to speak to them."

When Sofia returns, smelling of soap, she accepts the sandwich, taking delicate mouthfuls, picking the crumbs from her lap when they fall. She indicates the apple, a question in her eyes. "Take it," Beth says. "It's all for you."

"Thank you," Sofia says. "Thank you for . . . everything." Her eyes fill with tears again and Beth looks away. She can hardly bear to think of what the girl has suffered, only a few feet away from her own house.

CHAPTER FORTY-NINE

Sofia

All I want to do is go home. No, that is not quite right. I want to go home very much. But first I want to be sure Sir and Madam are caught. Especially *her*.

So I go with them to the police station. I am very frightened. I am scared they will lock me up, send me to prison like she said. Then I remember how she lied to me.

I do not trust the police. I ask if the woman next door can come. She is the only person I trust. I don't know her, but I know she has helped me. I say I will not talk until she comes.

Her name is Beth. It is a nice name. When she comes, she smiles and is kind. I can't help it but because she is kind to me I cry and she holds me until I stop. Nobody has held me for three years. I feel like a child again in her arms.

I know Beth will help me through this. But they won't let her stay for the interview. I plead with them, but Beth explains that it is the law. To protect me, in case she is also bad, one of them.

The interview woman, Sandy, lets me talk. She asks questions if she doesn't understand, or if she wants more. I haven't spoken this much for a very long time. My mouth gets dry, my throat sore. It is hard to talk in English for so long, but I tell her I don't want an interpreter. They might twist what I say.

I tell the woman everything. How I saw the advertisement, how they said I would earn good money. How excited I was to get a job in England and see my cousin Elena. The bus journey, the other girls, the drugged drink. I describe the place I woke up in, the man who took me, how I felt, all alone in a strange country.

I describe Sir and Madam, how they make me work, lock me in. The beatings, the threats. How Sir disappears for weeks. The boat, the horses, the cars. I say they never paid me, not once, for all the long hours I work every single day. I tell them how I eat scraps and leftovers to stay alive, how I tried to escape and how she beat me, about the fire I tried to start, about the window in my room and trying to break it. The list of girls on Sir's desk. Sandy is interested in that, and I am glad she believes me.

There are some things I don't tell her — there is no need — but I make sure she knows that my employers are very bad people. Sandy writes it all down.

My journal is still hidden under my top. I will give it to Beth, and she can give it to the police. She will be a witness for me. I know it will be important to them. Everything is there, written carefully with my pencil stubs.

My story takes a very long time. I am tired but I want them to know how bad it was. Then suddenly, after hours of talking, I am too tired to speak. All I want is to lie on the sofa with my head in Beth's lap and sleep.

* * *

They say my parents and aunt and uncle reported me as a missing person three years ago. They have their phone numbers. When they say I can talk to my parents, right now, here, I jump up from my chair, I am so excited.

Sandy passes me a telephone. She gives me the number of my parents, with the code, on a piece of paper, and leaves the room. My fingers tremble so badly I have to redial two times before I get it right. It rings twice, three times, and I start to worry, and then . . . I hear my dear Mama's voice. I whisper, tears falling down my face onto my lap, "Mama."

A gasp at the other end, then a clattering sound, then she says, "Sofia, is it you? Is it really you?" Her dear voice breaks and she weeps and sobs and calls to my father to come to the phone.

I laugh and cry at the same time, my words falling over each other in my excitement. I tell them I am well, I am coming home, I have been rescued. I can't wait to see them. My father cries too, he can barely speak. I can hear them passing the handset between them, desperate to hear my voice. Then I hear my sister, screaming in the background, shouting, "Hello, Sofia, I love you!" Such a noise all at once, everybody talking, asking questions, weeping and shouting. I say I will tell them everything, I can't explain it all now, I am at the police station, but I will call them again when I know what is happening. When I know for certain the day I will be home.

My mama keeps saying, "I can't believe it. Is it true? I can't believe it!" And in the end I have to leave them to calm down. They don't want to let me go and they make me promise a hundred times to call them again tomorrow. I promise. I tell them I love them and I can't wait to see them. Then I say goodbye and put the phone down. I thought I would never see them again, but I have spoken to them. I am alive and I am free.

I feel like the luckiest person in the world.

* * *

After the call the tiredness returns, and I am glad when Beth comes back. She and Sandy go outside the door again and talk in soft voices. Then Sandy leaves and doesn't come back for a long time.

Beth says, "Do you want to lie down?"

I nod, and lie down next to her. She gently places the cream coat over me. She must know I have stolen it from Oksana, it is far too beautiful to be mine. I snuggle into its softness and reach out for Beth. She lets me put my head on her lap, like I used to do with Mama. She puts her hand gently on my shoulder and soon I am drifting into sleep, a different kind of sleep, like a lullaby my mama used to sing.

I am safe, at last.

I wake to the sound of whispering. Sandy is back with another woman. Beth talks to them at the door, glancing back at me from time to time. I sit up slowly, pushing my hair from my eyes, clutching the coat around me. A cup of water stands on the table in front of me and I take a sip. The lights in the room are on, too bright for my sleepy eyes.

It is getting dark outside. I know they are talking about where I will go, and I feel a shiver of fear at the thought. I don't want to stay in a police cell on my own — that would feel like punishment on top of punishment for me, but I don't want to go to a stranger's house either.

Beth smiles at me and I feel better.

"This is Jane, she's also from the Salvation Army," Sandy says. "We work together on cases like yours." The other woman nods and smiles at me. "Jane will take you to a safe place to stay for tonight, away from the people who took you. You will be comfortable there. Jane will look after you, and I will see you again tomorrow. Are you okay with that?"

The panic rises and I start to tremble again. I don't want to go with more strangers to another place. I want to stay with Beth.

I shake my head, but she goes on: "Over the next few days and weeks, Jane will help you to get identity papers, to go back to your family, or to stay here and find work and a place to live, if that's what you want."

I grab Beth's hand. "I want to go with Beth."

"Are you sure?" Sandy says. "Beth lives right next door to the house you were kept in. You'll be in the street where you were held prisoner. The house is right next to Beth's home."

I hesitate. "Will they be there?"

"Mr and Mrs Rayne—" she sees the confusion on my face — "Your captors will not be there," she says firmly. "Mr Rayne — Keith — is out of the country and will be arrested soon. Mrs Rayne, Oksana, has been taken into custody, but—"

I say, stumbling a little over the word, "Custody?"

"The police have her."

I recoil, I can't help it. I feel my eyes widen with fear. "Here?" I point to the floor.

"No, don't worry, she's not here."

It is what I was hoping.

"It's up to you, Sofia, you can choose. You can decide. The safe house with Jane, away from the place you were kept prisoner, or Beth's house."

"I want to go with Beth," I say again.

Sandy and Beth nod at each other.

"I understand," Sandy says. "You are an adult, so it is your decision. If Beth agrees, and I think she does—" Beth nods again — "you can stay with her and we'll finish doing the interviews tomorrow."

I breathe a sigh of relief. "Thank you, thank you, Beth," I say.

CHAPTER FIFTY

Sofia

I turn my head away when we reach the house, so I don't have to look at my prison next door. Beth, watching me, gives my leg a squeeze. Sandy is with us too. She wants to see where I will be staying, to make sure it is safe and suitable, she says. I know it will be.

The front door opens when we get out of the car, and a man comes forward. I stand back, but Beth puts her arm around me, and we walk together towards the house.

"This is Adam, my husband," Beth says. "Don't be frightened. Adam, this is Sofia, who I told you about, and this is Sandy, from the Salvation Army. She's here to help Sofia settle in."

"You are very welcome," Adam says, taking my hand in a warm grasp. He has a nice smile and shakes Sandy's hand too.

"Thank you. I am sorry," I whisper.

"No need to be sorry. We're very happy you're safe and we can help you," Adam says, leading us into the hallway. "Come in, come in. Here are the children. Tom, Abigail, this is Sofia. Oh, and this is Ruff." The little black dog I saw in the garden runs up to me and puts his paws on my leg, his tail wagging. I reach down to pet him and he kisses my face. It makes me smile.

"Sorry, Sofia, he's only being friendly," Beth says. She picks him up, holding him easily under one arm.

The boy I saw in the garden comes first down the stairs. He looks a little younger than me, though he is tall. He holds out a hand and I shake it, uncertain what to say.

"Hi," he says. "I saw you in the window."

"Yes," I say. "Thank you."

The girl comes straight to me and puts her arms around me. I pull away in surprise, though straight away I am sorry, I know she is only being kind. Beth says, "Abigail, don't overwhelm the poor girl! Give her a chance to get in before you smother her."

Abigail smiles and takes my hand. I squeeze it so she understands I am not scared of her. "Sorry, Sofia."

"It's okay," I say, feeling a little shaky, as if my legs will not hold me up too much longer.

"Come on, let's go to the kitchen and get Sofia something to drink and eat. Let me take your coat," Adam says, and I wriggle out of the cream coat, watching as he hangs it on a hook by the door. Everyone follows me into a warm, comfortable kitchen.

Beth indicates a sofa, inviting me to sit. But I feel suddenly very shy and tired. "Beth?" I say. She comes close, and I whisper, "I just . . . I would like to go to bed now . . ."

* * *

I wake to an unfamiliar feeling. I am warm and comfortable. My body feels heavy, relaxed. A gentle light sifts through thick, blue-striped curtains. It woke me up — I am used to waking in the dark, not seeing the light before I start work.

Realisation floods over me. Today I don't have to work. No need to be frightened. I am free, they are gone.

At last I can allow my mind to think of the future, my family, my home. Tears come quickly to my eyes, but I wipe them away and snuggle down into the warmth. I listen to the sounds of the house, so different from that place next door. From below comes the faint hum of voices, the radio, I think, and every now and then the thump of a cupboard door or a chair scraping on the floor. It must be late, and I wonder if the children are here or have gone to school. I can't remember what day of the week it is. But it could be Wednesday or Sunday, I don't care. All I know is I am here and I am safe. Everything is going to be okay.

I drift for a while longer until I need the bathroom. When I get out of bed I notice with surprise I am wearing strange pyjamas — a loose T-shirt and shorts, which I think must be Abigail's because they are small and pink. I don't remember putting them on last night — everything about yesterday seems like a dream now. I pad across the soft carpet to the bathroom.

When I return, I part the curtains a little, my heart pounding. But this room faces the garden, I can't see the house next door. Relieved, I look around. A neat pile of clothes waits for me on a chair. My old things are nowhere to be seen, and for a moment I panic. Where is my journal? Then I remember: I put it in a drawer next to the bed, the last thing I did before I fell asleep. It is still there.

I pick the clothes up, breathing in the clean smell of washing powder. There is a blue jumper, some denim jeans, and even some pretty underwear. Socks and shoes that look as if they will fit.

I laugh, for the first time for so long it sounds strange, even to me. Gathering up the clothes, I head for the bathroom, and my first shower for years.

CHAPTER FIFTY-ONE

Beth

When Beth hears the shower start, she smiles. She hopes Sofia takes all the time she needs. The next few days will be difficult, but she's on the way now.

It's a good feeling to have done the right thing this time. The relief is almost tangible after last time, when her life fell apart around her in a matter of days.

Today Sandy will continue the questioning. Beth hopes it won't take too long. She's curious about Oksana and Keith — and Julia too. Matt must have owned up by now, surely, to being there for a reason other than the love of gardening.

There's a lot to get through. She's glad that Sofia has had a good sleep and time to rest before the next stage.

She looks a different girl when she appears in the kitchen. Her eyes are bright and there's colour in her cheeks. Though Abigail's cast-off clothes hang from her bony frame, her newly washed hair is shiny and soft.

In her hand she clutches a sheaf of paper, a strange assemblage of separate sheets, some with folds flattened out, some small slips of what look like receipts. Writing covers every inch. She must have had it in her coat or folded it into a pocket yesterday, because it's the first time Beth has seen it.

Sofia holds the bundle out to Beth. "This is my journal," she says, taking care not to let any of the pages fall. "I stole pens and pencils, envelopes, small bits of paper. I write . . . wrote this to tell what happened to me. It is in Bulgarian. Everything is there. Dates and times. All details."

"Thank you," Beth says, placing the sheaf of papers on the coffee table carefully. "I think Sandy needs to read this. Can I give it to her?"

Sofia nods. "Yes. And to the police, please."

When Beth hands the journal to Sandy, her eyes widen.

"Thank you, Sofia," she says. "It will be very useful. We will look after it. Do you want it back afterwards?"

Sofia turns to Beth, a question in her eyes.

"Do you want to keep it, Sofia, after they have read it?" Beth says.

"No, no." Sofia shakes her head vehemently. "I don't want."

Sandy inserts the bundle carefully into her briefcase. "Thank you, Sofia. Now there are a few more questions before we let you go today. And Jane would like to explain to you what will happen next — how we will arrange to get you a passport, any other support you need, and get you home. Is that okay with you?"

* * *

Sandy has just left after an hour or so with Sofia when the doorbell rings. Ruff runs to the front door with a warning bark.

Tom jumps up from the kitchen table. "I'll get it," he says.

Sofia, standing with Beth, backs away, a look of alarm on her face.

"It's okay, Sofia," Beth says. "You don't need to be afraid — it's probably just a delivery. Tom orders a lot of things on the internet."

But when Tom comes back into the kitchen, Matt is with him. Sofia steps behind Beth.

"Sorry to disturb you," Matt says, standing awkwardly in the doorway.

Beth turns to put an arm around the girl's shoulders, feeling the tension in her fragile frame. "It's okay, Sofia, Matt's a friend. He helped us. He's not here to hurt you."

"I am a friend," Matt says, concern showing on his face. "I'm sorry, Sofia."

"Come and sit down, Matt," Beth says. "I'll put the kettle on. Why don't you tell Sofia your story — why you were working next door?"

Sofia hesitates still, reluctant to move from Beth's side.

"Come and sit with me and Mum," Tom says, pulling out a chair for the girl. He settles next to her, facing Matt.

Matt speaks slowly. "I'm not really a gardener, Sofia. I'm trying to find my sister. Her name is Julia and she was married to Keith, before Oksana. She disappeared and we don't know what happened to her."

Sofia gazes at him, unmoving. Beth says, gently, "Do you understand, Sofia?"

"Yes. I understand he didn't help me."

"I know, and I'm sorry," Matt says. "At first, I didn't know, and then I was so focused on finding Julia. It was wrong — I should have helped you before."

Sofia stares at her hands, her mouth a thin line. There's an awkward silence.

Beth turns to Matt. "Did the police interview you yesterday?"

"They did — and you?"

"I couldn't tell them much. Is there any news on the body in the building?"

He shakes his head. "Nothing yet, as far as I know."

"But they are going to do something now, to find Julia?"

"Thankfully, yes. They weren't terribly happy with me doing their job for them, but maybe now they'll take it seriously and look for her properly."

"Did they tell you about the messages that Sofia found?"

"What messages?" Matt says, leaning forward.

Beth looks at Sofia. "Shall I tell him?" she says.

Sofia nods and looks away.

"Sofia found some messages scratched in her room. The first said, 'JULIA HELP'."

Matt stares from Beth to Sofia, startled. "Julia?"

"Yes, and the word 'Help'."

"She was in that room?" Matt's eyes light up. "And she scratched a message? So we have proof!"

"Well it's proof she was in trouble, at least," Beth says. "She could have been locked in there, like Sofia."

"You said 'messages'. Was there another one?"

"Yes, a strange one. It said something like BOSEIO or ROSEIO." Beth spells out the letters. "You're not sure, are you Sofia, if it was a B or an R. And the Os and the Is and the Ss could be numbers. Then RHS or BHS or RH5 or BH5. We've tried, but we just can't work it out."

"A code — exciting!" Tom says. Beth frowns at him. He mouths "sorry" and subsides into silence.

"Do the police have any idea what it means?" Matt says.

"Not as far as we know. They didn't say so, anyway. Perhaps there was another girl, called Rose . . ."

Matt looks thoughtful. "I haven't heard anything about someone called Rose. It's a strange message. Can I write it down?" He pulls his mobile from his pocket. Tom does the same, tapping deftly. Beth spells the message out, checking with Sofia that she's got it right.

"I'm going to try to crack it for you," Tom says. "I love stuff like this!" He jumps up from the table and leaves the room, mouthing to himself.

"Ignore him. Though you never know, it might take a teenager to solve it," Beth says. "Matt, what's happening with Oksana and Keith — did the police tell you anything?"

At the mention of their names, Sofia shifts in her seat and gazes at Matt, her eyes enormous.

"Absolutely nothing," Matt says. "The house is cordoned off with police tape, including the garden. Uniforms everywhere. I'm not allowed near it. I was at the police station for a long time, but they didn't tell me anything."

"Do you think they'll let us know?" Beth asks.

"I really don't know what the protocol is. While they're still investigating, I doubt we'll hear anything."

"What will you do now, Matt?"

"I'm going to hang around, see what happens. If the police find anything on Julia, I want to be here."

* * *

Once Matt has gone, Sofia goes to her room without a word. Beth lets her go, mindful of the advice she's been given. The girl will need help, probably for some time, before she feels ready to face the world. She needs to rest, to be quiet and on her own when she needs it, for as long as it takes. Beth has explained this to her children, asked them to give the girl some peace, not to bombard her with questions or make loud noises while she's here.

How long Sofia will stay with Beth and Adam is uncertain. She seems unconcerned about being so close to Oksana's house, and Beth can't blame her for not wanting to go to a safe house. Though Sofia would be properly looked after and have the security she needs, she'd be meeting more strangers, sleeping in an unfamiliar room, learning to communicate all over again. That would be hard for any young person, let alone a girl who has met more people in the last three days than she has in three years.

As far as Beth's concerned, she can stay as long as she likes — until she can get home to Bulgaria, if necessary. She'll be safe and looked after here.

Beth is in the bathroom when there's a thundering of feet on the stairs, the dog's paws pattering, feet thumping after him.

"Ruff! Come here! No, no, no, come here . . . Ruff!"

"Tom?" she says, opening the door. There's no reply, the rumble of footsteps disappearing downwards. They've left clues behind them, though. Muddy paw prints and flecks of autumn leaves litter the carpet on the landing and the stairs. She sighs. She told them not to let him out without a lead. With all that's happened in the last few days and the empty house next door, the broken fence is still flat on the ground where it first fell.

In the kitchen, Tom is rubbing the wriggling dog with a towel. "Sorry, Mum, I forgot about the fence. I let him out and when he came back he was filthy. He must have been digging. He was so excited, he ran all over the place and I couldn't catch him. There's a bit of a mess. I mopped in here but I didn't know what to do about the carpet."

She smiles. How many boys his age would worry about the state of the carpet, especially if they'd let the dog out against instructions? "Okay, I'll sort it out later." She looks down at Ruff, who's sitting waiting for attention. His eyes are pools of hopeful brown. "As for you, I'm not sure you deserve any breakfast."

But she relents and gives him a scratch under the chin. "Hard to understand when you're a dog, isn't it?" she says. "Gosh, I hope he hasn't dug up any more plants next door. He's obsessed with that flowerbed. Still, I don't suppose it matters now, though the police might not be too impressed."

She gazes from the back door across the broken fence to the opposite side of Oksana's garden. It's too far to see if there's any further damage, but in their own garden, the lawn is strewn with sticks and twigs, and some empty flower pots have blown onto the grass. There's something that looks suspiciously like an uprooted bush, and beyond, more dark shapes she can't identify.

CHAPTER FIFTY-TWO

Sofia

I am happy in my lovely room, here. I know I am safe in this house, away from those horrible people.

I lie on the bed and gaze around. Everything is so beautiful. Warm and comfortable, not like next door, full of hard edges and gloss. Here are family photos on the walls, in frames on shelves, on the fridge door in the kitchen. Childish paintings on display, boots and shoes piled up in the hallway. Rugs and carpets soften the floor, and I can walk around in bare feet without my toes feeling cold. Here family is celebrated, welcomed. This house is full of love.

They thought I would be frightened, sleeping so close to next door. But I know there is nobody there. If Sir is back in the country, he will be arrested by the police. If not, they will wait for him. If he escapes, he will not return to the house.

I hope she is in a small, cold room, with bars on the window and a heavy lock on the door. I hope they give her only a thin mattress, one small basin to wash in, like I had. Nobody to wash her clothes, iron her blouses, pick up her precious shoes. Polish her toilet. I hope she eats dry crusts and stale biscuits for breakfast.

It is strange about Matt and the other woman, Julia. Perhaps he is kinder than I thought and he truly didn't know I was a prisoner. I don't know. But I hope they find Julia because that will be bad for Madam. And there might even be a third girl, Rose. I wonder what happened to her, if they will ever find her.

Later I will talk to my family again. Soon I will be able to tell them when I will come home, when everything has been arranged. I have to finish my story, answer many questions. I hope it does not take too long.

I will get a new passport, new clothes, a ticket home. I hope I can fly back. Though I have never been on an airplane, so when Sandy suggested it, I was scared. But she says someone will come with me until I am with my parents again, and it will all be paid for by the government. I can hardly believe it — at last I have some luck.

They want me to see a therapist. At first I didn't understand what they meant, but they explained that it can take a long time for people to get better when they have been kidnapped and locked away and beaten. Beth says it helps to talk to somebody who understands, who will help you get your confidence back. I told them I would see somebody, but only in the time it takes before I can go home. Going home will be the best thing for my health, I know it. Beth says I can stay as long as I like, but I want to go. I don't want to be in this country anymore. Perhaps Beth will come and visit me one day — and my dear Elena too.

Tom and Abigail are very kind to me and friendly. I like talking to them, but in the daytime they are at school and when they get back they have homework. I help Beth when I can, but she doesn't want me to feel like I'm working for her. Yesterday we walked the dog together in the park. It was strange and I felt nervous — I wanted to get back to the house.

I will never forget Beth and her family, but I think I will not return to England. What happened to me here is too painful. I need to forget. I want to go back to college in

Bulgaria and finish my education. Until then I will help my parents on the farm.

In the pocket of the cream coat, I have Madam's precious rings. I know I am a thief. But she stole three precious years of my life — of my childhood. The rings are worth money, but no money will buy me back those years. I am glad I stole from her, she deserved it. I hope she loses everything now, more than just her beautiful house, her clothes, her car.

I hope she went back into the house, just one more time, before they came for her . . .

CHAPTER FIFTY-THREE

Beth

"Tom," Beth calls. He's at the kitchen table with his laptop, earphones on. "Tom!"

He looks up, freeing one ear. "Can you hang on to Ruff for a minute, please? I'm going to check the damage in the garden and I don't want him making any more mess."

Tom jumps up. "I'm coming with you," he says, pushing his feet into a pair of trainers.

Leaving the dog in the kitchen, they slip through the back door into the garden. Ruff's barking follows them down the path.

They collect the empty flowerpots strewn around the lawn and pile them on the path at the side of the house, dropping stones in the top one to keep them from scattering again. Tom wanders down the wet grass, picking his way past clumps of compost, an uprooted rose bush, sticks and twigs scattered around.

"Oh dear," Beth says, when she sees the rose bush. "That's one of next door's. He's dug the whole thing up and carried it through."

"Nobody's going to care about that now," Tom says.

A half-chewed stick lies in the middle of the lawn, pieces of bark strewn all around it. Further down, the grass is spotted with lumps of earth and compost. She'll just have to leave it all until it dries out. One small dog seems to have made a huge mess in a short space of time. It's no wonder his paws were muddy.

She's about to go back to the house when Tom points to a clump of mud. "Look, Mum! He's unearthed something."

A plastic bag, ragged and torn, is tangled into one of the clumps of brown. But there's more to the lump than mud. Half in, half out of the bag is a notebook, so dirty you'd hardly recognise it. Tom extracts it gingerly with his thumb and index finger and holds it up. The cover is leather, one corner badly chewed, canine teeth marks in the rough edges. Ruff must have ripped off the plastic to get at the leather inside.

Tom wipes the worst of the dirt from the cover with his fingers and hands it to Beth. She opens it, careful not to rip the damp paper. Inside, the pages are covered with neat handwriting, a few of them water-stained — but otherwise the book seems more or less intact.

Inside the front cover are the words *Julia's Journal*.

She can hardly believe it. This could be the evidence Matt is waiting for. Why would a woman bury her journal in the garden, if she wasn't trapped and terrified? It must reveal what went on in the house — it could even lead them to Julia herself. The answer to many questions is right here, in this damp, muddy book. It has to be solid evidence, surely.

"Let's have a look, Mum," Tom says, reaching for it. She holds it away from his grasping fingers.

"Just wait, Tom. This could be really important. Let's dry it out a bit first," she says. "We don't want to damage it before we've even looked at it. In fact, we should probably give it straight to the police."

"Let's have a little look first — go on, Mum."

"I'm going to get some more of this mud off and put it in the airing cupboard for a bit," she says, though she too would love to read it now. "I'll take Ruff for his walk. We'll look when I get back — in the meantime, don't touch it, okay?"

Raindrops catch in her lashes as she walks, her mind on the journal. If Julia left of her own accord, wouldn't she have taken it with her? And how did she expect it to be found? It was pure chance that the fence came down and Ruff uncovered it. There must have been nowhere else to hide it. Maybe she guessed that a gardener would dig it up one day. Or she hoped that if Keith moved on, the new owners would find it and read it. She must have been desperate.

They should give it to the police, that's for sure. And they will. But not before Beth has had the first look.

* * *

Beth and Tom hunch together over the journal. Neat handwriting covers every page, the entries varying from one short paragraph to two or three pages. The first says:

I've decided to write a journal. It will help to pass the time. Here, living like a queen in this beautiful, glamorous house, I have everything I could ever want, and everything is done for me. I don't want to seem ungrateful — Keith is more than generous with his money — but he's away so much and I don't know anybody here. I'm so lonely! I've decided to keep myself busy with writing and books. Perhaps I'll learn something new, as well. With all this time to myself it seems wrong not to.

I suppose this is why women have children. With all the gadgets and home helps and technology, there's nothing to do but have children and look after them. I would like to have children, but it isn't happening. I hope there's nothing wrong. Thankfully I'm still young, so there's time.

I think I'm relying on Keith a bit too much now. I used to like playing tennis and going to the cinema, having coffee with friends. But he doesn't like me to see other people without him, and I don't want to upset him, so I've lost my friends. Dawn, Frankie, Kathy — I miss them. They did try for a while, but I said no too many times and they've stopped asking me now. Even the Christmas cards have dwindled away.

I would love a job, but I've never had one, so I can't imagine who would have me! If I ever got as far as an interview, I would be terrified.

Keith is in Russia right now, for three weeks, and I am on my own in the house. It is lovely, with five bedrooms, all with en-suite bathrooms, a beautiful modern kitchen, huge sitting room and all the latest gadgets. Keith is so kind — he knows it's what I've dreamed of! But it's very big for two people, let alone one person on their own all the time.

Keith has hired a girl to clean for us a few hours a week. She's Romanian, but her English isn't good and she's not much company for me.

I wander round the rooms, touching all the beautiful furniture, wondering why I feel so empty when I'm so lucky.

Perhaps in the summer we'll go to his boat. Last time, I enjoyed that, though his friends didn't speak much English. I read a lot of books and slept in the sun. Keith bought me beautiful clothes and took me to expensive restaurants. I'll ask if we can do that again. That will give me something to look forward to.

Keith calls me every day. I have to make up things I've been doing, because usually I've been doing nothing. He hates me going out without telling him where I am. But it's nice that he worries about me.

I so miss Mum and Dad. I love my husband, but I wish he'd let me see them.

They flick through the pages. The journal covers about a year, but the entries are sporadic. Sometimes there are gaps of a few weeks. Some of the entries show Julia excited that Keith is due home, cooking delicious meals for him. In some she seems anxious, especially when he expects her to entertain. She mentions her loneliness and her longing to see her family many times. Her feelings of helplessness and isolation appear on almost every page.

Towards the end of the journal the entries become shorter, more enervated. She seems very low. One simply says: *There's nothing I can do to stop this. I'm being side-lined.*

"What's happening to her?" Tom says.

Beth turns to the next entry.

This is terrible, my heart is breaking. But I can't stop this happening.

I'm such a fool. I really thought K was being kind, getting a full-time housekeeper for me. How naive could I be? I knew the minute I saw her. This girl is Russian, she's stunningly beautiful and there's clearly something going on between them. No wonder he didn't want to give her the attic room. I offered to redecorate it and furnish it nicely, but there was no discussion. Only the best guest room for her. He must have been seeing her before he got her over here — it's obvious now. A girl like that would never need to keep house for someone. He set me up. I waited, longed for him to come home and all the time he was with her. How could he?

She treats me as if I don't exist. She does nothing around the house, and I'm getting blamed when things aren't done. What's going to happen to me? Does he expect me just to cave in, to agree to having her here? K refuses to talk about it, he just waves a hand at me, dismissing me like a servant.

Then, a couple of days later, another entry blows a chill into Beth's heart.

Things are worse, much worse.

Now he's moved her into our bedroom, without a word. I am ousted. I've moved my things into another room, not the main guest room, where she's left all her stuff strewn around. I'm scared of what will happen to me. I have no money, none — no bank account or savings of my own. He has all the power, he can do what he wants. I begged him to let me go back to Mum and Dad, if they'll have me, but he was adamant. He doesn't want me, but he won't let me go. I don't understand what's going on.

Today I couldn't find my house keys — I think he's taken them. I'm more and more a prisoner here. What is he planning? What's going to happen to me?

A few pages later:

I'm really frightened now. Last night, I told him I wanted a divorce and he hit me, hard, right in the face. He's never done that before. I was so shocked I lost my balance and fell over. Luckily I wasn't badly hurt, but I have a horrible black eye.

He won't listen. He knows if we divorce I'll get a good deal, probably half his money, and all this will come out. And details of how he makes all his money. THAT's why he's not letting me go.

I don't even care about the money, I just want to get out of here. But I don't have a choice. O has poisoned him against me.

The last entry says:

O is telling me to move upstairs, to the attic room. She says K wants me to move up there before he gets home. I pleaded with her to let me leave, but she shook her head, pushed me into my room and told me to collect my things. She is utterly ruthless — a cold, grasping bitch.

Today she's wearing a huge diamond engagement ring. She's after his money, and she's not going to let me get in her way. I'm writing this quickly, while I can, and I'm going to bury the journal in the garden, in case something bad happens to me. Maybe one day someone will find it. I hope so, and K and O get caught for what they've done. If they don't there's something badly wrong with the world. That's it for this journal, I have to get outside while she's in the shower.

If you find this, please tell my family I love them.

CHAPTER FIFTY-FOUR

Beth

The buzzing fills the air, like the sound of an angry wasp. Beth extracts her head from the tumble dryer, where she's searching for lone socks, and reaches for her mobile.

"Hello?"

"It's Matt." There's a rumble of buses and taxis in the background.

"Matt — how are you? Any news on Julia?"

"Are you busy? Can I come over?"

"Of course—"

"I'll be right there."

Before she can say more, he cuts the call. She looks at the screen in surprise. There must be something important, or he would have told her on the phone. Have they found Keith — or even Julia?

When she opens the door, he says nothing, pushing past her with his head down. In the kitchen, he doesn't wait to sit down.

"I've just come from the police station," he says. "The body in the derelict building — they think it could be her."

Beth's hand flies to her mouth. "Really? Oh, Matt. Come and sit down, tell me everything."

He removes his jacket, throwing it onto a chair. His clothes are dishevelled, his face pale. He takes a deep, shaky breath.

"The journal has changed everything — it's really got them going."

"That's good — at last. But the body?"

"It might not be her, but the timing's right. It's a woman about her age, who died — or rather, was murdered — at about the time Julia disappeared."

Beth gasps. "Murdered?" Even though the thought had occurred to her, she'd dismissed it as melodramatic. The idea that people living so close to her family could be capable of murder sends a shock wave through her.

"She was strangled — garrotted, in fact, with wire. It was still around her neck."

"Oh, how horrible!" She can't imagine how awful that must have been for Matt, to hear that his sister could have been murdered in such a gruesome way, in a deserted building on the other side of town.

"Yes." He runs his hand through his hair, his head down. "Could I possibly have a drink of water, please?"

Beth jumps up. "I'm so sorry, of course." She hands him a glass. The skin on his hand is gnarled, like the bark on an ancient tree. It shakes slightly as he drinks.

"They're still doing tests — but they took DNA from me, so they can match it with hers."

"When will you get the results?

"I don't know, a few days perhaps. They're still processing the scene — there may be other DNA evidence there. They're also trying to find out who owns the building — apparently it's not as easy as it sounds. There's a complicated network of companies involved, some of them based abroad. DI Thomson's going to let me know as soon as they have anything."

Beth exhales. "I'm so sorry, Matt. This is hard for you, after you've looked for such a long time."

Matt nods, but she can see he's close to tears. He draws his hand across his eyes, and for the first time she notices how tired he looks. Without asking, she gets bread and cheese and puts them on the table. "Help yourself, you look as if you need it."

He gives her a crooked smile. "Thanks. Actually . . . do you have any brandy? I think I might be in shock."

"I wouldn't be surprised," she says, rising from the table. "Do you know what? I think I might join you."

She pours him a large shot and he gulps it down. "Another?"

"Yes, please. I'll be too drunk to cycle, but I can walk home."

Her own shot is smaller, and she sips it, feeling the warmth travel down through her chest. It has an instant effect, calming her, and she notices that Matt has more colour in his face already.

"That's better," he says. "Nothing like a large brandy to sort you out. Thank you."

Beth glances towards the stairs. Sofia is still upstairs sleeping, as far as she knows, but she closes the door anyway. They're careful not to talk about what happened in front of her.

"Did the police have anything else on Keith and Oksana?"

"Not much," he says. "They told you what happened to Oksana, right?"

"No, they didn't tell me anything."

"On the day we rescued Sofia, you know Oksana was out? The police waited for her to get back. That evening, they picked her up in the driveway. She wanted to get her coat, so they went with her to the bedroom. But when she opened the wardrobe, it fell on her."

Beth gasps. "Was she hurt?"

"Quite badly — it was a big old wardrobe, apparently. A lot of broken bones, and her face is quite bad. They had to call an ambulance. She's under police guard in hospital. They think she'll be there for some time."

"How awful."

For a moment, Beth feels sorry for Oksana. What a terrible accident — her beautiful face damaged, possibly scarred. But Beth's sympathy doesn't last long. The woman is a monster. What she has inflicted on Sofia is not only criminal, it's cruel.

There's no doubt in Beth's mind that Oksana will be charged and sentenced for kidnapping and domestic slavery, and will almost certainly serve a long sentence. But this seems like the best kind of retribution.

* * *

"Yes, I can confirm that. We didn't want to tell you quite yet, or Sofia. Not until we had Mr Rayne in custody." DI Johnson sounds tired at the other end of the line, his voice gruff.

"You have him now?" Beth says.

"He's been picked up in Paris, en route to Russia. He'll be brought back and arrested as soon as the formalities are done."

"Brilliant — that's good news. Should we tell Sofia?"

"I suggest you ask the Salvation Army for their advice on that. Is she still seeing them?"

"She is, on a regular basis. She goes home next week."

"They'll be able to advise. I imagine she won't be unhappy to hear the news, but you never know how traumatised people will react. Be careful."

"We will. Thank you."

As she cuts the call, the doorbell rings. She's surprised to see Karen on the doorstep, in her familiar workout clothes.

"Sorry, am I disturbing you? Were you expecting someone else? You look shocked to see me . . ."

Beth shakes her head. The events of the past few days have been all-consuming — she'd almost forgotten about Karen. "Oh Karen! No, you're not disturbing me. I'm a bit dazed, to be honest. So much has happened since I last saw you! Come in, come in."

"Sounds fascinating — I hope you can tell me about it," Karen says as they make their way to the kitchen, where Abigail is laying the table for the evening meal, placing knives and forks around laptops and newspapers without moving them. Beth resists the instinct to point this out — her daughter is helping, that's what matters.

"Karen, come and sit over here," Beth says, indicating the sofa. "Supper will be a while yet. I'll fill you in on what's happened, but we need to keep our voices down. Sofia — the girl from next door — she's here, talking to the woman from the Salvation Army in the living room."

Karen's eyes widen. "We knew something big had happened when we saw the police cars. How did you manage it?"

"Long story, but I'll give you the gist," Beth says. "Abigail, could you get Karen a drink please?"

Karen listens agog to Beth's story, only interrupting her once. But when she gets to the part about Oksana and the accident, Karen nods her head.

"I heard," she says.

"How on earth —?"

"Oh, news gets about at the club, as you know. Someone there has a husband who works at the hospital, and he was talking about this Russian woman who'd been crushed by a massive wardrobe. We put two and two together . . ."

"Well, you were right."

"She had it coming," Karen says. "Horrible woman. But did you hear what happened to her face?"

"What do you mean?"

Karen leans forward, conspiratorially. "It seems stilettos are dangerous in more ways than one. One of her precious Manolos, or probably those red Louboutins she was wearing at your drinks . . . anyway, one of her heels went right through her cheek, narrowly missed her eye, apparently. She's going to be scarred for life."

* * *

Once Karen has gone, Beth tells her family the full story.

"The wardrobe fell on her?" Adam raises his eyebrows. "How did that happen?"

"I don't know. Probably too full of expensive handbags. It doesn't matter, anyway, she's been caught. I'm sure Sofia will be delighted to hear it."

"She doesn't know yet?"

"Sandy is telling her now — they've been talking for quite a while. She's joining us for supper when they've finished."

"Oksana deserves everything she gets now," Abigail says. "She's evil, that woman."

"And Keith will be behind bars, hopefully for a very long time. They both will be."

"Mum!" The back door opens with a crash, startling Beth and Adam. Tom comes running in, followed by Ruff, who runs to his water bowl, leaving a trail of drops around him.

"What? What's happened?"

"I've worked out what the code means! ROSEIO, RHS. Rose ten, right-hand side. It's the tenth rose bush on the right-hand side of the garden if you look from their house — I counted. Ruff dug the bush up, didn't he? It was a code for finding the journal, and our clever boy found it." He crouches down and gives the dog a back scratch.

"Well done, Tom! I knew it would take a teenager to crack it," Beth says. "Who would have thought? Well that clears another thing up. I'll tell DI Thomson tomorrow."

At that moment, the living room door opens and Sofia appears in the hallway, followed by Sandy. They're both smiling.

"Everything okay, Sofia?"

Sandy nods at Beth, giving her a thumbs-up behind Sofia's back.

Sofia walks straight to Beth and gives her a hug. "I am very okay, thank you. I am happy at the news."

"She can't hurt you again," Beth says. "And neither can he."

At supper they sit, Sofia and Abigail on one side, Tom and Adam on the other, Beth at the head of the table serving the food. Already Sofia feels like part of the family. They will miss her when she leaves.

"I'd like to propose a toast," Adam says, lifting his water glass. "To Sofia, and to freedom." Solemnly, they raise their water glasses and sip, as if they're sipping champagne from the finest crystal flutes.

Later, when Sofia has left the room and Beth is flicking through the TV channels, Tom says, "I don't get it, Mum. How does a wardrobe suddenly fall over?"

"These things happen all the time, Tom," Beth replies. "You'd be surprised. It must have been a big wardrobe, though, to cause that kind of damage."

"Yeah, well, it figures she had a huge wardrobe, when you think about it."

"Indeed." She looks up at a small sound in the kitchen to see Sofia, a glass of water in her hand, her lips curling into a soft smile.

"Good night, everyone," she says.

CHAPTER FIFTY-FIVE

Beth

It's strange how things turn out. Beth never expected to get involved in such a huge drama — in fact, when she left London, drama was the last thing she wanted. Leaving Kingston had been a wrench. Arriving somewhere new without a job, knowing nobody, had been hard. Having lost all her friends, she'd vowed never to get involved in people's lives again.

But this time, if she had turned away, Sofia might never have escaped and Matt might never have found Julia.

The DNA test proved that the body in the disused building was Julia, and at last Matt was able to find some kind of closure. Though the outcome of his search was terribly sad, it was some comfort for him to be able to bury his sister in her home town with her parents.

It will be a long time before Keith and Oksana are tried and sentenced, but the evidence against them is overwhelming. Sofia won't be called back to testify, thankfully, though she may need to appear by video link. She's keen to give her side of the story as long as she doesn't have to return to the UK.

Once Oksana has recovered from her injuries, she will be held on remand without bail. She will serve a long sentence for kidnap and domestic slavery, and possibly more, depending on whether she's found to have been involved in Keith's criminal activity. It's likely she was.

It's unlikely her face will ever heal properly.

This Beth discovers in a call from DI Thomson.

"I wanted to update you, and to say thank you," he says. "You've helped us to nail down a criminal ring, operating right across Europe, kidnapping and trafficking vulnerable people, making huge amounts of money. Hopefully we've saved many people from a similar fate to Sofia's."

"I really hope so," she says. "So Keith was part of it?"

"Indeed he was, deeply involved. We've identified him as the owner of the building where his ex-wife's body was found. It's a key piece of evidence linking him with her murder. But even if we can't prove that one, he'll go down for a long time."

A second call, a few days later, was from Sandy.

"Delivered safely," she says. "Her family met us at the airport. It was a wonderful moment."

"I'm so glad," Beth says. "I hope she'll be able to rebuild her life."

"I'm sure she will. She's tougher than she looks. Did you know she'd stolen some of Oksana's jewellery?"

"No, really? How did you find out?"

"She confessed — she took it, and Oksana's coat, when she left the house. I think she was worried it would get her into trouble. I told her to keep it quiet, I don't want to know. After all she's been through, I felt we could overlook that. Anyway, where Oksana's going, she won't need flash jewellery."

"Well, I for one hope Sofia got the best bits. Good for her."

The third phone call is a surprise, almost a shock. For a moment, Beth can't place the voice, though she has an overwhelming feeling of familiarity.

"Hello, Beth." A woman's voice, melodious, warm. "How are you?"

"I'm sorry, who am I speaking to?"

"It's Annie."

Annie. Annie — the friend from her old life, the person she'd wronged so badly. Why would Annie be ringing her?

"Annie, how lovely to hear from you," she says, cautiously. "How are you?"

"I'm well — we're all really well, thank you," Annie says. "How's everything going? Are you enjoying the big house away from the smoke?"

"It — it's really good. I miss Kingston and my friends, of course . . ." Suddenly she doesn't know what more to say.

"We miss you too, Beth. Actually, that's one of the reasons I'm calling. It's Jack's big birthday soon and we're organising a 'do' for him at the church hall this Saturday evening. Nothing formal, just a bit of a party for friends and family. We — I — would really like it if you could come . . ."

There's a sudden lump in Beth's throat and she struggles to answer. "I — that's so kind, Annie. Thank you. I really appreciate it. Let me have a quick look at the diary."

She holds the handset away from her, rustling through a pile of papers on the worktop.

"Annie? I'm so sorry, looks like we're busy on Saturday. Perhaps another time?"

A few moments later she cuts the call. She pauses for a moment, then dials. "Hi, Karen, it's me, Beth. We were wondering — are you free for supper on Saturday? Nothing special, just us four and the kids, if they'd like to come . . ."

THE END

ACKNOWLEDGEMENTS

The idea for this story came from the notion that we never really know what's going on in other people's lives, even if they are close to us.

My sincere thanks go to the Salvation Army for their help, advice and early reading of this book. Their work helping victims of modern slavery out of danger and supporting them as they build new lives is invaluable, and I am grateful to them for confirming the authenticity of my story. For more information go to: salvationarmy.org.uk/modern-slavery. And you can find out more about how to support survivors here: salvationarmy.org.uk/modern-slavery/survivors-support-fund.

My thanks also to Boris Belchev, my Bulgarian friend and expert birdwatcher, who helped me with my research into rural life in Bulgaria. Sadly Covid regulations precluded a visit there this time, but I have promised myself that one day I will visit Sofia's beautiful home country.

As always I'm grateful to my early readers. Special mention goes to Judy Jones, who seems to have a gift for the role. Also to the marvellous Scribblers, who plough through multiple drafts of all my books. Particular thanks go to Lisa McDonald for the title.

Many thanks to everyone at Joffe Books — you are lovely to work with — and especially to Emma Grundy Haigh, my editor at Joffe Books, for her enthusiasm and support for my books.

And to all my lovely readers, thank you for reading!

ALSO BY SUSANNA BEARD

THE PERFECT LIFE
THE LOST BROTHER
THE GIRL ON THE BEACH
WHAT HAPPENED THAT NIGHT
THE PERFECT NEIGHBOUR

Thank you for reading this book.

If you enjoyed it please leave feedback on Amazon or Goodreads, and if there is anything we missed or you have a question about, then please get in touch. We appreciate you choosing our book.

Founded in 2014 in Shoreditch, London, we at Joffe Books pride ourselves on our history of innovative publishing. We were thrilled to be shortlisted for Independent Publisher of the Year at the British Book Awards.

www.joffebooks.com

We're very grateful to eagle-eyed readers who take the time to contact us. Please send any errors you find to corrections@joffebooks.com. We'll get them fixed ASAP.